Ann Barker was born and brought up in Bedfordshire, and currently lives in Norfolk with her husband who is a clergyman. She enjoys spending time with her children, Sally and Ralph, and her pet dog.

For more information about Ann Barker and her books visit www.annbarker.com

THE ADVENTURESS

Florence Browne lives in poverty with her miserly father, but seeking adventure, she goes to Bath under the assumed name Lady Firenza Le Grey. But there, she meets a man calling himself Sir Vittorio Le Grey, who accuses her of being an adventuress. When her previous suitor, Gilbert Stapleton, visits Bath, Florence is plagued by doubts. Is Sir Vittorio the wicked Italian he appears to be? Are Mr Stapleton's professions of love sincere? And how can she accept an offer of marriage from anyone while she is still living a lie?

Books by Ann Barker
Published by The House of Ulverscroft:

HIS LORDSHIP'S GARDENER
THE GRAND TOUR
DERBYSHIRE DECEPTION
THE SQUIRE AND
THE SCHOOLMISTRESS

ANN BARKER

◆

THE ADVENTURESS

Complete and Unabridged

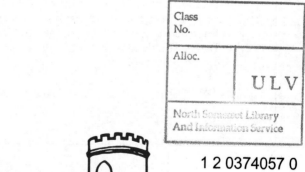

ULVERSCROFT
Leicester

First published in Great Britain in 2005 by
Robert Hale Limited
London

First Large Print Edition
published 2006
by arrangement with
Robert Hale Limited
London

British Library CIP Data

Barker, Ann
    The adventuress.—Large print ed.—
    Ulverscroft large print series: historical fiction
    1. Imposters and imposture—England—Bath—Fiction
    2. Bath—(England)—Fiction
    3. Large type books
    I. Title
    823.9'14 [F]

    ISBN 1–84617–360–4

Published by
F. A. Thorpe (Publishing)
Anstey, Leicestershire
Set by Words & Graphics Ltd.
Anstey, Leicestershire
Printed and bound in Great Britain by
T. J. International Ltd., Padstow, Cornwall

This book is printed on acid-free paper

*For my God-daughter and for Elizabeth,
her wonderful mother*

1

'Where are you going? Florence, where are you going?'

Florence Browne permitted herself a small sigh. 'Only to church, Father,' she said patiently, as she drew on her gloves. 'It is Sunday, after all.'

'I don't know why you have to go,' muttered the thin, elderly man from the depths of his armchair in front of the sparse fire. It was the only fire that was permitted in the house, apart from that which was kindled in Mr Browne's bedchamber when he had recourse to it, and the one which had to be lit in the kitchen for cooking purposes. The Browne family could not afford more. 'I should have thought that it was your God-given duty to stay here and look after me,' he went on querulously. 'I might be taken ill whilst you are away.'

'I am sure you will not, Father,' Florence replied in the tones of one to whom this argument was a familiar one. 'In any case, Stevens is on hand.'

'Huh! Stevens! What could he do?' Cuthbert Browne pulled the rug more securely about his knees.

'A good deal more than I could,' said Florence. 'He could run more quickly to the doctor's, I'm sure.'

'Doctors,' said her father scornfully. 'Scoundrels! Take all your money and make you worse instead of better. Dare say that doctor'll be at church anyway, wasting his time when he ought to be attending to the sick.'

'I will see you later, Father,' his daughter answered, before walking to the door. They did not kiss or embrace. Such intimacy played no part in their relationship, and never had. She had ceased calling him 'Papa' years ago.

'Don't put too much in the collection,' was her father's parting shot. 'I'm not made of money.'

Florence closed the door and crossed the hall. As she did so, straightening her gloves, she caught sight of her reflection in the mirror above the empty fireplace. She was a slender woman of medium height. Some would have said that she was thin, but with the meagre fare provided at her father's table, there was very little opportunity to be anything else. A drab brown bonnet, at least four seasons behind the times, was placed upon her dark-brown hair. It framed a face which might have been beautiful, her dark eyes which matched her hair in colour being a striking feature, had it not been for the perpetually resigned and faintly depressed expression that it always wore. Unfortunately, no one had ever told her so, and she remained unaware of the fact.

Because it was a raw January day, she was wearing her only winter cloak, which was brown, beneath which she was clad in a dull brown gown. Money being so short in the household, everything she wore ended up being dyed brown, to make it easier for one thing to be patched with another. A pair of brown boots peeped from beneath the hem of her gown. Out of everything that she had on, they were the only things that were new, bought with money salvaged from the housekeeping. Her old ones, which had even been patched on the patches, could not have survived another winter. The new ones had been chosen because they were stout, serviceable, and would last a good long time; Florence hated them.

If ever I become rich, she said to herself, not for the first time, I shall never, never, ever wear brown again. The walk to church was a familiar one. It took her out of the front door of The Laurels, where she had lived all her life, right at the gate, then along the main street of the village of Howton, and past the

3

haberdasher's, outside whose window she rarely lingered, knowing that she would never have enough money to buy anything there. From thence, she followed the road as it curved round to the right, and the parish church of St Philip stood before her, a rather squat Norman church with a square tower. She bumped into the vicar's wife beneath the lych gate.

'Good morning, Miss Browne.'

'Good morning, Mrs Bailey.'

'Such a fine morning, though cold,' went on the vicar's wife. Her boots, Florence noted, were shiny, black and stylish. 'How is your father? Such a pity he cannot join us for divine service.'

'Yes, he is always sorry to miss it,' answered Florence automatically. 'Perhaps he will come when the weather improves.' I've been saying the same thing over and over for the last eight years, she thought to herself. The same thing, and it's a barefaced lie. He's not a bit sorry to miss it and he'll never come here again until he's in his box. Anyway, I don't want him to come because this is one of the few chances I get to escape his mean spirit, his unkind criticisms and his demanding voice.

She glanced around guiltily as she entered the church porch. Oh dear, she reflected. I'm being very uncharitable thinking about that pathetic old man in that way. After all, he is my father. But I don't love him and I never have loved him. Perhaps I shall burn in Hell for having such thoughts. Well, she decided as she sat down, at least it will be warm.

Of course the church was cold, but no colder than her bedchamber. If I ever become rich, she said to herself, and again this was not for the first time, I shall have fires in every room and I shall never be cold again, if I can help it.

Meanwhile, at least coming to church meant a change of scene and some other faces to look at. She exchanged smiles with Mrs Bridge, the governess who looked after Mr and Mrs Chancery's two children at Tall Chimneys. When Father died, no doubt that would be the kind of thing that she would find herself doing.

The service was well attended. The pew belonging to the Le Grey family was unoccupied, but now it always would be, for Miss Agatha Le Grey was old, infirm and the last of her line. Florence looked up at the plaque on the wall above the empty pew. It was dedicated to the memory of Sir Victor Le Grey and his wife Dulcima, who had died within a few days of each other in the early years of the previous century.

If only I were called Dulcima Le Grey,

Florence sighed to herself, I'm sure I would not have had such a dull life as I have led being Florence Browne. I dare say it will go on being dull until the end of my days. They will find me dead, probably of boredom, and I expect I shall predecease my father because he will go on living for ever and ever. He will have me buried in these very clothes so as to avoid buying a shroud, and I shall be enclosed in the cheapest possible coffin. The funeral will be short, without any hymns so as to save time and avoid having to pay the choir and musicians. I shall have a small plain headstone which will say 'Florence Browne', with my date of death and nothing else, so as to avoid extra costs from the stone-mason. But what it will not say will be 'Here is Florence Browne, buried in dull brown; and she was.'

Luckily, since these thoughts made her want to choke back a rather hysterical laugh, a psalm was announced and she stood up to sing with everyone else. Stop being such a misery, she told herself fiercely whilst at the same time she intoned the words 'How long, O Lord, How long?' After all, Sunday was one of the few days when she was actually able to mingle with other people. Of course, those who made up the congregation tended to linger less about the church door on cold

6

days like today; but she always made certain of exchanging a few words with Margaret Bridge, who was the closest thing that she had to being a best friend.

'How is your father today?' Margaret asked her.

'Much the same as usual,' replied Florence. 'Miserable as sin and not letting anyone else forget it.'

'I don't suppose the cold weather suits him,' murmured Margaret sympathetically.

'I don't think any sort of weather does,' answered Florence dispassionately. 'Will you have a half-day off this week?'

'Yes, on Wednesday. Mrs Chancery is taking her children into town to buy new shoes, and I am not needed. Would you like to come round for a cup of tea?'

'I'll do my best,' said Florence, thinking longingly of the cosy schoolroom at Tall Chimneys, where the fire was always lit in cold weather. Half-a-dozen sentences exchanged and a cup of tea with Margaret once a week, Florence thought to herself. Other people's lives must surely be more exciting than that. On her way from the church door to the gate, three other people enquired after her father's health. If it were not for Father, would anyone find anything to say to me at all? she wondered. It was such a lowering reflection, that she decided to walk back home the long way round, encompassing the whole of the village green, and passing the bottom of the over-grown drive which led to Greystone Park, the old house in which Miss Le Grey lived. As she did so, she chided herself for feeling so melancholy. After all, at least she had her health and strength, unlike Miss Le Grey who was getting more and more frail with every passing day. Perhaps, she decided, she would pop in and see the old lady on her way back from visiting Margaret on Wednesday. Florence was one of the few people whom Miss Le Grey was prepared to see these days.

As she opened the front door, she suddenly thought about her mother. Towards the end of her life, she had suffered greatly, but even then her father had been self-obsessed. However great his wife's sufferings, he had never considered them to be half as painful as his own condition. It had been all that Florence could do to persuade him to allow her mother to have a fire burning constantly in her room, and summoning the doctor in time of need had been an almost unheard of luxury. The best thing would have been for Mama to spend the winter somewhere milder, but that had always been out of the question. There had been no money for it, Father had said. Well, that was not unusual, thought Florence to herself. There was never any money for anything.

'There you are at last,' he grumbled as soon as she came in. 'So long you have left me. Selfish! Selfish!'

'I am here now, Father,' Florence answered. 'I will just put my cloak and bonnet away, then I will come and read to you.' She did not particularly want to sit with the old man, but there was no other room in the house with a fire burning at this time, apart from the kitchen.

'Hurry up then,' he muttered testily. 'It is your duty, after all.'

Florence went upstairs with her cloak over her arm. It was just a normal Sunday.

2

When the doctor's wife popped in the following day with a few eggs that her hens had laid, Florence asked her if she would mind sitting with Mr Browne on Wednesday afternoon. 'Margaret Bridge has invited me to take tea with her on her half-day off,' She explained. 'I should feel much happier if someone would sit with him.'

'You mean the old skinflint might not let you go if he was going to be left alone,' said the doctor's wife. She was a stout, handsome, fair-haired woman, a farmer's daughter, whose home and family were organized on practical lines.

'Shh,' exclaimed Florence, glancing towards the drawing-room door. 'I wouldn't have put it quite like that.'

'Well, I would,' said the other bluntly. 'It's my belief there's nothing the matter with him that a good shaking wouldn't cure.'

'I think he's a little too old to shake,' answered Florence ruefully. 'Can you help me on Wednesday?'

Mrs Surrey shook her head regretfully. 'I'm very sorry, my dear,' she answered, 'but I have already agreed to meet my sister in town; and since she is to go away for a few weeks very soon, it will be my last chance to see her for a while.'

'I see,' murmured Florence regretfully.

'But don't you let that stop you going,' said Mrs Surrey firmly. 'There's no reason on earth why he shouldn't be left for an afternoon. The servants will be here after all.'

Florence nodded. 'I sometimes think he likes the servants better than he does me,' she said dispassionately. But the day after next, when she was due to meet Margaret Bridge, her father was far from well.

'Oh dear, I do feel dreadful,' he moaned, his voice a thread. 'Florence, do not go far away today, my dear. I need you within reach.'

Florence drew close to him. He was still in his bed, the covers drawn up to his chin, his night cap pulled well down. He certainly had a very poor colour. 'Where does it hurt, Father?' she asked him. 'Shall I send for the doctor?'

'No,' he answered, his voice a little stronger. 'No doctor; charge you the earth and do you no good. I think if you were to stay here and read to me, it might settle me down, perhaps.' He clutched his chest. 'Oh dear, my heart, my poor heart,' he moaned. 'I doubt if I will last out the day.'

So, abandoning her own plans as she had done so often before, Florence fetched the book and dutifully sat in the place to which he pointed, round the corner of the bed from where the fire was, so that she felt no benefit from it. By the end of the afternoon, she was perishing with cold. At last, her father declared that he was ready for a nap. 'Go away now,' he said testily. 'I've had quite enough of the sound of your voice for one day.'

Florence got up and walked to the door, but before she reached it, she was arrested by the sound of her father's voice calling her name. 'What a blessing you had no plans for today,' he said.

She looked at him and in his eyes there was such an expression of malevolent glee that she hurried out and closed the door. For a split second, she had almost felt the temptation to put a pillow over his face.

Horrified by her own thoughts, she hurried to her own room, but, as she opened the door, the cold inside came to meet her like a bucket of icy water. Suddenly, after the day's disappointment, it was not to be endured. She picked up her cloak and bonnet and went downstairs again.

'I am going out for a short time, Stevens,'

she told the butler. 'I'll be back for dinner.'

Although it was dark outside and bitterly cold, away from the house she immediately felt better. Somehow, her father's ill humour cast a constant gloom over the place that was almost stifling in its intensity. Hesitating briefly outside the gate, she looked up and the evening sky, lit up by the red and gold of the setting sun, lifted her spirits. At once, she made a sudden decision, and stepped out towards Greystone Park. If she were well enough, Miss Le Grey would be very glad to see her. If not, well, the walk would have done her good.

Agatha Le Grey lived alone with a very few servants to look after her. As far as Florence could tell, she was as purse-pinched as the Brownes, but far more cheerful about it. She was the last surviving child of Sir Victor and Lady Le Grey, who had had five children of whom Agatha had been the eldest. Of the other four, the two girls had both died in childbirth, and their babies had not survived. One of the two boys had been killed in a riding accident, and the other had died abroad.

Like Florence, Miss Le Grey had remained at home to care for her parents, but unlike Florence, all her memories of her departed relatives seemed to be happy ones. Her family was long gone, however, and Florence, at thirty, could not remember a time when Miss Le Grey had not lived in the old house alone.

Rapid, the ancient butler, answered the door, and declared that Miss Le Grey would be delighted to see Miss Browne. 'We've been very dull today, miss,' he said. 'She'll be pleased to see you.'

As always, Florence felt a great desire to giggle as she followed Rapid in his very slow progress through the hall. His name now seemed ludicrously inappropriate, although the reflection that in his youth he had by all accounts lived up to it prevented her from giving voice to the laughter that might have hurt him had she ever allowed it to come out. He conducted her to a door which, when opened, revealed a cosy book-room, with a good fire burning in the grate.

Florence loved this room. It was in such contrast to that in which her father sat for the whole of nearly every day. His room was plain, dark, and quite bare, with just one small rug on the floor, a few books on a table at his elbow, the drab, worn, brown curtains drawn most of the time, and a small fire that looked as if it was struggling against the cold with little hope of success. This room was about the same size, but always seemed to Florence to be filled with colour and interest.

The deep-red curtains, shutting out the cold, made the room look warm and inviting, as did the thick red carpet, patterned with blue and cream. The bookcases were filled with volumes of different sizes, mostly to do with travel. The pictures on the walls depicted scenes from exotic places, and the various artefacts to be found on the mantelpiece or on other surfaces were similarly unusual and intriguing.

Florence could never see Miss Le Grey as frequently as she would have liked, for the older lady's health was uncertain. Florence was permitted to call whenever she pleased, but she knew that Miss Le Grey would always deny herself if she was not well enough. In this way, both of them knew that when they did meet, they would be able to enjoy one another's company without reserve.

When Florence was admitted on this occasion, it was to see Miss Le Grey poring over a large volume of bird illustrations. 'Come and see this, my dear,' she said, in a quavery voice. 'This one, I believe, is only to be found in Africa. Look at the gold on those wings!'

Florence drew near and dutifully admired the print. 'It's lovely,' she said. Then she added wistfully, 'I don't suppose I'll ever be able to see such things in real life.'

'Nonsense,' replied the other. 'You are still young. You never know what might be around the corner. But tell me what you are doing here at this time. Is it not rather late for you to be out? Can you stay for dinner?'

Florence shook her head regretfully. 'I'm afraid not,' she answered. 'I told Stevens that I should be home. And besides, Father — '

'Yes, of course, I had forgotten your father,' said Miss Le Grey, in tones of long suffering.

'I'm afraid I never have that luxury,' sighed Florence.

'Well, never mind, I shall enjoy you for as long as I can,' said the other briskly. 'Rapid will bring us some tea, then we can talk. Bring your chair near to the fire.'

Florence did not need to be told twice. It was the first time that she had been warm since she had got out of bed that morning. Moments later, Rapid, who had clearly used his own initiative with regard to tea, came in with the tray, and Miss Le Grey asked Florence to pour. Then once they both had their tea, the older lady said, 'Now tell me what happy chance brings you here at this hour. How did you guess I was hoping for company?'

Florence stared at her for a moment then suddenly smiled. 'Today has been dreadful so far, but this part has redeemed it all,' she said. Miss Le Grey waited patiently, and eventually Florence went on, 'I am never quite prepared for how much he dislikes me. I keep hoping that deep down inside, he has some love for me, but today I saw it in his face. He really hates me, and he would be delighted to think that he could ensure that I would never have another moment's happiness.'

Miss Le Grey knew Florence far too well to utter well-meaning platitudes. 'If that is how he feels, it is his loss, my dear,' she said firmly.

Florence smiled and told her about the events of the day, and about how she had been denied the chance of seeing Margaret. 'It's only a little thing,' she acknowledged. 'I am foolish to let it matter so much to me. It's hardly as though it's the first time he has taken pleasure in spoiling things for me, after all.'

'No, but forgive me, you have very few pleasures to look forward to in your life. How I wish I were not such a pathetic old thing, unable to give you the support and friendship that you deserve.'

'Nonsense,' replied Florence, a note of decision in her voice. 'Just to know that you are here makes so much difference to me. But I cannot stay long, so do not let us depress ourselves with my troubles any longer. Tell me more about the book you are looking at.'

She stayed with Miss Le Grey for a little over half an hour, by which time her spirits had lifted considerably. She would have loved to go more often, but the older lady's health was too fragile for her to cope with frequent visits. Florence was also aware that Miss Le Grey would not object if she came to the manor house simply to warm up, but her pride was too great for her to take that step.

Her evening meal, taken in solitude in a cold dining-room, was boiled mutton, followed by half cold semolina. Her father had decided to take his meal in his room. If ever I become rich, she told herself, I shall have good wine with every meal, and I shall never have boiled mutton again as long as I live. *And*, she added as she got up from the table, I shall have a dog, and a string of handsome suitors, and fires in every room. Then, although it was only seven o'clock but because it was by far the warmest place to be, she went up to her room and got into bed.

At least, she mused, there were plenty of blankets, and with the bed warmed by the hot brick that she had ordered, and with the upper part of her body wrapped in any warm garment she could get her hands on, she picked up her notebook and in it, she proceeded to write down the events of the day. After a few moments' application, she paused in her work and smiled wryly. What London lady would even think of recording such trivial events when her life would no doubt be packed with incident? With a sigh, she put down her pencil and lying back against the pillows, allowed herself to think about Gilbert Stapleton for the first time in years.

Gilbert had come to stay at Tall Chimneys eight years ago, when Florence's mother had still been alive. He was some kind of connection of hers, but Florence had never known the exact nature of the relationship. She had gone to dine with the family one evening, in a gown that was very much behind the times, although nothing like as drab and unfashionable as the ones that she was obliged to wear now. At twenty-two, she had not quite been on the shelf, and still retained a tiny hope that there might be another life for her. It was at that family dinner that she had met Gilbert.

There had been a few other young ladies there, all dressed very stylishly, and she had felt like a wren set amongst a group of tropical birds. She had been aware of some wry amusement on the part of these ladies at her outmoded appearance, and she might have elected to disappear there and then, pleading ill-health or anxiety about her mother, had not Mrs Chancery brought Gilbert over to her side and introduced him as a distant relative.

He was quietly and appropriately dressed for the evening. He was a handsome man, having a pleasing, open countenance, with brown eyes, light-brown wavy hair, and a kindly, open smile, and he was tall and well built. Florence did not often have the opportunity of conversing with young gentlemen, and at first she was tongue-tied, but his conversation was so sensible and free from flirtatious innuendo, that she soon lost her fears, and found herself talking to him about the local scene and about the books she had read. There were a number of other young gentlemen present, all more extravagant in their dress and manner, and they became the target for all the other young ladies; Florence though was quite content to be in Gilbert's company and, by the end of the evening, she felt that he must have been as pleased with her as she had been with him, otherwise, why had he remained at her side?

That week, she received several more invitations to join the party and, encouraged by her mother, and emboldened by her growing interest in Gilbert, she had accepted them all. Gilbert continued to be as interested in her at every event, and by the end of the week, she was allowing herself to hope that she might soon be in receipt of a declaration. Then Mama became ill, and she was obliged to drive the gig into the nearest town in order to procure some medicine for her. It meant that she had to miss an event which Mrs Chancery had arranged and to which she had been invited, but she did not complain. Mama never did, no matter how great might be the pain from which she suffered. Why should her daughter do so at the loss of just one outing of pleasure?

The rest of the day was spent in caring for Mama; the following day was Sunday; Mama recovered, but there were no more invitations from Tall Chimneys. Far too shy to go to their house herself to try to find out what was happening, Florence could only wait at home to see whether any news might be forthcoming. The next Sunday, Florence learned that all the visitors had left.

She tried never to allow her feelings to show on her face in front of her father, for fear that he would use them to hurt her. On this occasion, however, she could not have concealed them as well as she might, for one day, as they passed in the hall, he said to her, 'No need to tell me why you're mooning around with a long face. It's because that good-for-nothing fellow who's been staying at Tall Chimneys has come to his senses, and cleared off back whence he came,' he remarked.

It was the first time he had given any indication that he had taken any interest in her affairs. She looked at him in surprise, her expression quite unguarded.

'Ha!' he exclaimed, with unconcealed satisfaction. 'I thought so. Tell me, whatever made you think any man would take an interest in an old maid like you with nothing to recommend her?' She continued to stare at him as he went on, 'Came to see me; don't suppose you knew that, did you?'

'He came here?' she exclaimed.

'When you were in town getting that medicine,' he explained. 'All interest, he was, until I told him you'd nothing to come when I'm gone, then he was off faster than a fox with a pack of hounds at his heels.' He bent his head and peered more closely at her, his eyes sparkling with spite. 'How does it feel, to know your only attraction for a man is the rumour that your father may have money to leave you?'

She had turned and hurried away not trusting herself to speak, the sound of her father's laughter echoing in her ears. Now, she sighed, turning her head on her pillow. Where was Gilbert now, she wondered? He had never returned to Tall Chimneys and she had never felt bold enough to ask about him. Then Mama had died, and after her death, Father had declared that with all the money that had been spent on doctors and medicines, there was nothing left. The gig had been sold, all evidence of comfort in the house had disappeared, and she had not had a new gown from that day to this. At the time, she had taken her father's word for it. Now, she wondered whether most of their money had come from an annuity which had ceased with Mama's death. If that were so, then it might provide some explanation as to why Father was so bitter.

Whatever might be the reason for their lack of money, in one respect her father had been right, she decided as she blew out her candle. No other man had ever come a-courting. She was thirty years of age and now, doubtless, no other man ever would.

3

The following day, Thursday, Florence set about her usual weekly task of sweeping and dusting the hall and the stairs. There had never been enough money to employ anyone to do this, but Florence did not mind, especially in winter, since to be physically busy at least kept her warm. Her father knew that these chores fell to her lot, but his only comment about this was to complain that she was not sitting with him. She smiled wryly as she polished one of the windows. Little did he guess how gladly she would perform the most menial of chores in preference to having to endure his company.

She was just finishing her work when there was a knock at the front door. She looked up in surprise, for callers were very few and far between. The doctor occasionally looked in on his way back from another call, but he had put his head round the door only a few days ago. The vicar had long stopped coming since Mr Browne had accused him of only calling in order to obtain extra contributions for the collection plate.

She waited for a moment, expecting

Stevens to appear from the back of the house, but then she remembered that he was replacing a rotten panel in the cellar door, and might not have heard that anyone had come. The knocker sounded again and, after another glance towards the back of the house, she put down her duster, took off her apron and went to answer the door. Whoever it was from amongst their small community, she decided, would hardly be surprised to discover that she cleaned the house. When she opened the door, however, she found herself looking at a complete stranger.

The woman standing on the doorstep was a little taller than herself, with fair hair, and brown eyes. She was warmly and fashionably dressed, her figure was full and her round face wore a courteous expression. 'Good day,' she said in a light, pleasant voice. 'Is your master within?'

It took Florence a moment or two to realize that she had mistaken her for a servant. Given her own shabby clothing, and the fact that she had opened the door, it was an understandable mistake, but it still took her aback. 'This is the home of Mr Cuthbert Browne, is it not?' the visitor asked.

'Yes indeed, but — '

'And is he within?'

'Well yes, ma'am, but — '

'Then please be so good as to inform him that his niece is here. Here is my card.'

Florence took the card and looked at it. *Mrs Anne Waring* it read, in flowing script. The name was followed by an address in London. Before she could speak, the door to the servants' quarters opened, and Stevens emerged, still struggling into his coat. 'I beg pardon, Miss Florence,' he said. 'I was busy and didn't hear the bell. Let me take that for you, ma'am,' he went on, holding out a silver tray that he had picked up in order to receive Mrs Waring's card.

'Thank you, Stevens,' said Florence in her soft voice.

Mrs Waring's face took on an expression of ludicrous dismay. 'Oh, good heavens! You must be Miss Browne — my cousin!' she exclaimed, holding out her hand. 'What a shocking mistake to have made! Can you forgive me?'

Florence laughed. 'By all means,' she answered. 'I have been doing some house-keeping, which accounts for my attire. But tell me, how does it come about that we are related?'

'My maiden name was Taunton,' Mrs Waring explained.

'I'm afraid I still do not follow you,' said Florence cautiously.

'Perhaps it will help if I tell you that my mother's maiden name was Browne,' replied the other.

'Then you must be . . . '

'The daughter of your father's sister.'

'Oh,' answered Florence a little blankly. Then she pulled herself together. 'Excuse me. I had thought that Father and I were alone in the world. How splendid to discover a relation! But I must warn you that he may not receive you. He does not enjoy good health, and is not at all sociable in his habits, I'm afraid. In fact, it might be as well if I take the card rather than Stevens, and see what he says.'

So saying, she left the hall and entered the saloon where her father sat if he felt well enough to get up. As usual, his chair was drawn close to the fire, a rug over his bony knees. 'Well, who is it?' he snapped. 'Another do-gooder come to plague us? Someone wanting money? Tell them to be gone.'

'It is neither, Father,' said Florence patiently. 'It is a lady called Anne Waring. Here is her card.'

'Waring? Never heard of her,' he muttered.

'It is her married name,' Florence answered. 'Her maiden name was Taunton.'

'Taunton,' he murmured.

27

'She says that she is your niece. Would you like to see her?'

'See her? Humph! Why should I? No kin of mine. All she wants is money.'

'Then — '

'Send her packing! Go on! And close the door behind you. I'd be a lot better if I was treated with a modicum of consideration.'

Florence left the room without another word to her father. 'I'm sorry,' she said when she reached the hall. 'I'm afraid he refuses even to see you. I told you that he wasn't very sociable.'

The young woman had been studying a rather second-rate picture of flowers and fruit which hung over the empty fireplace. She turned and at Florence's words her expression took on a rueful look. 'I had suspected as much,' she said. 'My father warned me years ago, before he died. But I am staying in Gloucester for a few days and I will try again.'

Florence rang the bell for Stevens, who soon came to open the door. 'I cannot promise you any better success, however many times you may try,' she said to the visitor. 'You may find that you have wasted your journey.'

'Not at all,' replied Mrs Waring. 'I am travelling from Bristol to London, having visited friends, and Howton is nearly on my way.' Then, with nothing more being said beyond the polite words of greeting on both sides she was gone.

'Did you know that I had a cousin, Stevens?' she asked the butler.

'I believe I did hear that Miss Lydia had a daughter, miss, but I never saw her before today.'

'Is she genuine, do you think?'

Stevens nodded. 'Oh yes, miss. Had a great look of your grandmother. If you look at the portrait in the passage upstairs, you'll see what I mean.'

'Thank you, Stevens.' Florence went upstairs to look for the picture of her grandmother. It was in a dark corner and in poor condition and, if she was honest with herself, she had long since ceased to notice it. But when she peered closely at it, the likeness between Old Mrs Browne and the young woman who had just left was most marked.

Florence thought about her with some regret. She must have been about her own age, perhaps a little younger, and she was married, which meant that she might have children. The thought pleased her. For so long, she had thought of herself as being alone in the world save for her father. Now, she had found that she had a cousin, and a perfectly amiable one at that. If she had a husband and children, that would be even better. Why, she herself would be an aunt! Well, almost.

Smiling, she went downstairs. The advent of this heretofore unknown relation had provided a bright spot in an otherwise tedious day, though whether Mrs Waring would come again as she had promised, or not, it was too soon to tell. One thing was certain, however. If she had come looking for money, she would by now be sadly disappointed. The merest idiot would surely be able to see that there was none to be had in this house.

★　★　★

Rather to Florence's surprise, Mrs Waring did call again the day after next. Her arrival met with the same rebuff from Mr Browne, but instead of leaving at once, she suggested that Florence might like to join her in a walk round the village. 'You could point out the sights of interest,' she suggested.

'That will soon be done,' Florence replied. But she did put on her bonnet, cloak and gloves, and soon they were outside in the bright November sunshine. As they walked, Florence could sense Mrs Waring eyeing her mended clothing. Even more than before, she would now be convinced that they had no money.

'I suppose you have lived here all your life,' remarked her cousin, as they walked towards the church.

'All my life,' agreed Florence, thinking to herself, all my long, long, tedious life. 'And what of you, Mrs Waring? Where were you brought up?' Seeing her companion's look of surprise, she said by way of explanation, 'My father, as you have seen, is a recluse. He interests himself in very little beyond his own health, and has never told me very much about my family.'

'My father was a cavalry officer,' Mrs Waring explained. 'Mama married him very much against her family's wishes and followed the drum, as did I until I was old enough to attend school. Then she stayed in England whilst I was educated. Father was killed in action about ten years ago. My mother died eight years later.'

'And have you no brothers or sisters?' Florence asked.

She shook her head. 'That is why I decided to seek out my uncle. He is my nearest relative. To meet my cousin, too, has made me feel very fortunate.'

'I feel the same,' Florence confessed, as they walked up the path to the church. 'May I

31

ask, Mrs Waring — I don't mean to be intrusive — but do you and Mr Waring have any children?'

Mrs Waring hesitated, before saying, 'We have not been blessed as yet, Cousin. I beg your pardon, may I call you Cousin?'

'Yes, please do so,' replied Florence. Judging that the subject of the Warings' childlessness might be a cause of private grief, she said no more on the matter, and the next time they spoke, it was about the architecture of the church.

By the end of the following week, Mrs Waring had called several times, but on each occasion Mr Browne had refused to see her. On the Friday, she said, as she was leaving, 'I shall have to return to London today. I have engagements there next week, and besides, poor Waring will think I have been stolen away! Do you still have my card?' Florence nodded. 'Pray write to me if you have any real anxiety about my uncle,' she said. 'I am very conscious that you are all alone should an emergency occur. There is nothing like having a relative on hand.'

Florence watched her go with a very real feeling of regret. She had enjoyed having the company of another woman, and Mrs Waring's presence had provided a touch of interest to what was a very dull round.

'Mrs Waring has gone back to London, Father,' she said that evening, as they played chess. She was, as always, very careful to let him win, otherwise he would be quite unbearable afterwards.

'Good,' replied her father. 'She won't be round any more, making a nuisance of herself.' He looked at her, a crafty expression on his face. 'You weren't thinking she might take a fancy to you and carry you off to London, I hope? No one would want a plain old maid like you around — especially without money to sweeten the pill.'

'No, Father,' Florence said colourlessly. She had long since learned that to rise to his baiting only encouraged more of the same.

'Mind you,' he went on, 'there's no saying I might not change my will in her favour anyway. After all, she's married, and there's no denying that money is handled best by a man.'

'You must do as you think best, Father,' Florence answered. She had already resigned herself to the fact that when her father died, she would probably have to become a governess or a companion. The notion was appealing rather than otherwise.

'Oh, go to bed,' he snapped, his face changing. 'I don't know why I have put up with you all these years.'

'No, Father, neither do I,' she sighed, as she mounted the stairs.

On Sunday morning, it was clear from the interested looks cast in Florence's direction that more than one person had seen her in company with an unknown lady. It was with Margaret Bridge that she shared a little of what had happened. 'Was it a complete surprise to discover that you had a cousin?' the governess asked.

'Oh yes; Father never talks about his sister, or about any of his relations; but if she married against the wishes of her family, then that would be easily explained. I had quite thought that he and I were alone in the world.'

'It must have been a delightful surprise to find that you had a relative — and such an agreeable one.'

'Yes, it was pleasant,' Florence agreed. 'But Father would not see her and now she has gone away. I doubt if we shall see her again in these parts. Do you have a half-day again this week?'

Margaret nodded. 'On Wednesday. Come and see me, and tell me all about it.'

Florence readily agreed, but upon her arrival home, she found that a new situation had arisen which suddenly altered all her plans. Stevens was looking out for her, and hurried to meet her as she reached the front gate. 'Oh Miss Florence, Miss Florence! The master has been taken sick, and I made so bold as to send for the doctor. He came straight away, and is still with him now.'

'My father is ill?' exclaimed Florence. She had been so accustomed to think of her father as a semi-invalid, prey to complaints which were largely of his own imagination, that to discover that he actually was ill came as something of a shock. She hurried into the hall, pulling off her gloves and unfastening her bonnet as she did so. 'What happened, Stevens? Is he in bed?'

'Mr Cummings went to help him up as usual, miss, but he couldn't stand, and his speech was slurred.'

'It sounds as if he has had a stroke,' said Florence, hurrying up the stairs. Knocking softly on her father's door before going in, she found the doctor inside pouring out some medicine, whilst Cummings hovered by his master's bedside.

As she approached, her father opened his eyes and fixed them on her with an unmistakable expression of hostility. 'There you are at last,' he said in faint but malevolent tones. 'Where were you when you were needed, eh?'

'I was at church, Father,' she replied.

'Church! Pah! Your duty lies here with me, d'you hear? Can't wait to get out of the house fast enough, can you?'

'Now, now, my dear sir, calm yourself,' said the doctor. He was a big, handsome, hearty man, with a great booming voice outside the sickroom, but mellow tones in it and surprisingly gentle hands. 'Your daughter's presence would not have prevented this, you know. What you need now is peace and quiet. Come, drink this medicine.'

'Will it make me live another day?' asked Browne.

'I can't answer for the consequences if you don't take it,' replied the doctor.

'Give it here, then,' said the old man. 'I want to see my solicitor in the morning.'

'Mr Renfrew, Father?' asked Florence.

'Of course Mr Renfrew, you fool. What other solicitor do I have? Got a job for him.'

'Think about it in the morning,' said the doctor. 'What you need is a good night's sleep.'

'Go away all of you, then,' said the old man. 'But mind, girl, I want to see Renfrew tomorrow, first thing.' He stared at her for a moment, his eyes filled with hate. 'Send for that young woman that was here — Mrs Waring; and her husband. I've a mind to see them after all.'

'Very well, Father,' agreed Florence.

'I'll call again in the morning,' said the doctor, as Florence said goodbye to him in the hall. 'In the meantime, you get a good night's sleep as well. Leave sending for Renfrew until I've been. People who have had strokes sometimes get these strange fancies, and the idea may pass.'

'I'll do as you say, Doctor,' replied Florence. 'But I will send for Mrs Waring. She did say that she would come if Father's condition gave cause for concern.'

Mr Browne awoke the following morning, feeling tired but still insisting that Mr Renfrew should be sent for. 'Have you written to that young woman?' he asked his daughter.

'Yes, Father,' replied Florence obediently. 'Stevens has taken it so that it may be sent to London.'

'Humph!' Browne looked at his daughter slyly. 'More attentive than you've ever been, I'll say that for her. Attentive young woman like that deserves some reward, wouldn't you say so, Surrey?'

'I think you could not have a more attentive daughter than Miss Florence,' replied the doctor.

'Why wasn't she here yesterday when I needed her, then?' the old man demanded, his voice rising. 'Send for Renfrew at once! I want to see him. I want . . . '

As they watched, a change came over the old man. His eyes seemed to roll back, his breathing became distorted and the movements of his hands were arrested.

'Another stroke, I fear,' said the doctor. 'Cummings, support your master.'

'Shall I fetch him a drink?' asked Florence. 'Brandy, or . . . '

The doctor shook his head. 'I fear that nothing will help now. As I said, Mr Browne has suffered another, much more severe stroke, and all that we can do is make him comfortable.'

'Should I send for Mr Renfrew?' asked Florence.

'If you wish, but I doubt whether there is much point in it, save to ease your mind.'

Mr Renfrew came an hour later, but by that time, Mr Browne had lapsed into a deep sleep, breathing stertorously. He died ten minutes after the solicitor had arrived.

'Do you have any idea why he wanted to see me?' asked Mr Renfrew as he was leaving. He only stayed long enough to offer Florence his condolences.

'My cousin, his sister's daughter, came to see him about a week ago, but my father refused to meet her,' Florence replied. 'I think that perhaps he may have decided to make some provision for her, but what it might have been I cannot think. You can see how we live.'

'Yes Miss Browne, I can see,' replied the solicitor rather grimly.

4

Had Florence been asked beforehand, she would have stoutly refuted the idea that she would find it in the least bit difficult to sleep in the house with her father's corpse laid out upon the bed in his room. As might have been expected, however, the real situation was very different from her imaginings, and so she was very glad when Mrs Chancery insisted that Margaret Bridge should come and stay until after the funeral. Out of courtesy, she had sent a messenger to inform the inhabitants of Tall Chimneys of her father's death as soon as she had leisure to do so. Mrs Chancery came round immediately, bringing Margaret with her, and she embraced Florence more warmly than she had ever done before.

'My dear, this is a shock to you, but I am not going to pretend that his passing can be anything other than a relief,' she said. 'I would suggest that you should come to stay, but my sister is with us at the moment, the house is full to overflowing, and things may be rather more hectic than you would care for. So with her agreement, I am offering

Margaret to you, to stay for as long as you need her. Would you like that?'

'More than anything,' Florence confessed.

'Then let it be so,' declared Mrs Chancery waving her arms rather in the manner of a fairy godmother. 'I shall have Margaret's things sent over when I return.'

That evening, Florence and Margaret sat in the small saloon after dinner. It was a room which had not been used very much since Mrs Browne's death, but somehow Florence did not want to occupy the room in which her father had always sat. She had gone in there earlier to collect something, and had been startled because she had almost imagined her father staring at her from the depths of his chair in his sly, malevolent way. As soon as she could decently do so, she resolved, she would have that chair burned.

Because the house had been all at sixes and sevens that day, dinner consisted merely of baked potatoes, cheese, ham, pickles and an apricot tart. 'Really, I think that Mrs West manages better when she doesn't try so hard,' said Florence, as they finished their meal. She had given Stevens no orders concerning wine, but was intrigued by the fact that that which was poured into her glass was far more palatable than what was usually served at table. After one mouthful, she looked up at

41

Stevens, a startled expression on her face.

Stevens inclined his head. 'Out of respect for the master, miss,' he said solemnly.

'Just so,' replied Florence after a pregnant pause. 'Stevens, would you care to join us in a glass?'

'Thank you, miss,' said Stevens. 'I should be honoured.'

After a toast had been drunk, ostensibly to Mr Browne's memory, Florence said, 'Stevens, we are going to sit in the small saloon after dinner. Will you see that the fire is lit?'

'Yes, miss,' answered Stevens. 'I will attend to the matter immediately.'

'Stevens.' The butler paused at the door. 'A *good* fire.'

'Very well, miss. Would you like fires kindled in the bedrooms, as well?'

'Yes, certainly,' said Florence.

Later, when they were sitting by the fire in the small saloon, Margaret said, 'What will you do now?'

'I had intended to ask your advice,' Florence confessed. 'I have long since resigned myself to the fact that I should need to find employment after my father died. He had a small income, but that will have died with him, and I cannot afford to keep this house on and employ servants to care for it and me as well.'

'Will you sell the house, then?' Margaret asked her.

Florence shook her head. 'Provided that father has left no debts, and I do not see how he can have done, I shall ask Mr Renfrew to arrange for it to be let. If it can earn money for itself, then I can afford to keep it and it may build up a little nest-egg for me. But tell me, Margaret, what kind of occupation would suit me? Shall I be a governess or a companion?'

Margaret looked at her very directly. 'Florence, do you really have the smallest desire to be a companion to an elderly person?'

Florence recalled her father and blenched visibly. 'No, I don't think I do,' she said, barely repressing a shudder. 'I'd better be a governess. You like the work, don't you?'

'I am very fortunate,' Margaret replied. 'Mr and Mrs Chancery are kind and the children are obedient and responsive. But not every position is like that.'

'Perhaps not,' agreed Florence. 'But what else can I do?'

Margaret looked thoughtful. 'You could take a smaller house with the proceeds of letting this one, and you would be at nobody's beck and call.'

'No, but I should still be alone,' Florence

43

protested. 'I have been isolated here all my life. I would like to live amongst more people. And besides, Margaret, although I am talking blithely about what I will do with the house, I cannot be sure that Father will have left it to me.'

Margaret looked shocked. 'Surely he must have done,' she exclaimed. 'If he has not, well, it would be so unjust after all you have done for him and all that you have given up.'

Florence was silent for a long time. 'I sometimes think that he hated me,' she said eventually. 'I don't know why.'

'No, surely not,' protested her friend, still in shocked tones. 'I know that with age, he became difficult and cantankerous, but — '

Florence shook her head. 'He was always like it,' she replied. 'Now that I think back and remember my childhood, any affection came from Mama, or from my governess, never from him. I cannot even remember any acknowledgement from him that I had done something well or done right in any way. Then when Mama died . . . ' She was silent for a time, then eventually she said, 'Margaret, I will tell you, but I probably won't tell anyone else, that nothing I ever did for him was done out of affection. The world will say that I did my duty, and that's about the best that can be said. If I'm really honest

44

with myself, I stayed with him because I was too afraid to do anything else. I was never brave enough to take any risks, you see.'

Florence spent quite a lot of time before the funeral thinking about the past. She had always been an only child, never living anywhere other than in this quiet village where she had been born. The only excitement she knew, she experienced vicariously through the books that still remained in the library, and these she devoured voraciously, whenever she got the chance. She had not seen a great deal of her father during her childhood. He was either away or, if he was at home, he avoided being with his family, joining them only for meal times. Any peace or joy she experienced as a child had been in the company of her gentle mother. Not for the first time she wondered why her mother had ever married her father. Now they had both gone to the grave, there was no one left to ask.

The night before the funeral, Florence lay in bed thinking about Gilbert Stapleton, wondering what had become of him. Had he married and produced a fine family, or had he remained single for her sake? She smiled cynically in the darkness. What could be more unlikely?

Despite the letter which Florence had

written, Mrs Waring did not appear for the funeral, nor did she communicate at all. Either she had not received it — although Florence had written the address very carefully — or in view of the very chilly welcome that she had received, she had decided not to bother to come. She could not have been blamed after her very unfriendly reception, but Florence felt that it would have been agreeable to have had the support of a relative under these circumstances.

Since she had no male relative to represent her, Florence took the somewhat unusual step of attending the ceremony in person. She was conscious of very little that took place, except that every few minutes, she kept thinking that she could hear her father saying 'Don't know why you bothered with that. What on earth did *that* cost? Waste of money!'

Mr Chancery attended the service with her, standing with her at the graveside, and offering her his arm to and from the church. She reflected that this was uncommonly kind of him, especially considering the fact that her father had never had a good word to say for him and had even, on one occasion, implied that he might have pocketed some of the silver.

After the ceremony, Mr Renfrew waited

upon her at the house. Mr Chancery asked her if she would like him to remain with her and she accepted gratefully. 'My wife's family have returned to their own home today, and Clarice has asked me to say that you are very welcome to stay with us. Naturally, you may keep Margaret for as long as you need her, but — '

'But of course the children's lessons must be resumed,' Florence concluded for him. 'You are very kind, but may I tell you my decision later? I cannot think of anything until Mr Renfrew has gone.' They were silent for a few moments, until a sudden impulse made her say, 'Do you ever hear anything of Mr Gilbert Stapleton?' She could have bitten her tongue afterwards. She could not even have explained why she had asked the question at that moment.

Mr Chancery glanced at her sharply. 'Young Gil? Fancy your asking about him! We haven't heard from him in years. I've a feeling he married and settled in the north of England.'

The will was read in the book-room, and only Mr Renfrew, Mr Chancery and Florence herself were present. Margaret tactfully absented herself, remaining in the small saloon with a book. 'I know that you have attempted to communicate with your cousin,

Miss Browne,' said Mr Renfrew as they sat down, 'but she has not contacted me, and as there is no bequest for her, I did not feel it necessary to make more strenuous efforts to seek her out.' He was sitting behind the heavy oak desk at which Florence could just remember her father sitting in times gone by when he had summoned her to upbraid her for some fault. She tried to recall what some of those misdemeanours had been, but she could not do so. She had long ago stopped thinking that she might please him. Even before that, she had stopped hoping that he might love her. Had there been something wrong with her, she wondered? Could she have tried harder?

'Miss Browne, this is most unexpected.' Mr Chancery's shocked voice aroused her from her thoughts.

'Unexpected,' she murmured. Then, pulling herself together she said in brisker tones, 'I beg your pardon, I am not taking things in very well at the moment. You were telling me about the house,' she hazarded.

'Indeed, indeed,' said the solicitor shaking his head gravely. 'It is most unfortunate, but quite within the character of the late Mr Browne, I am sorry to say. You have six weeks in which to assemble your own possessions and find alternative accommodation. Given the contents of the rest of the will, that will easily be found but even so, the callousness . . . but I must not say more.'

'Upon my soul, I never heard anything so wicked,' declared Mr Chancery, his normally pale complexion turning quite red. 'To repay all your hard work and duty in such a manner!'

'To whom did you say he has left the house, Mr Renfrew?' Florence asked. She was quite amazed at how calm she felt.

'It is to be sold, and the money given to the nearest poor house.'

'And when did my father decide to do this?' she asked.

Renfrew cleared his throat. 'He made this will a week after Mrs Browne's death,' he said, shuffling his papers.

Florence recalled the number of times that he had mentioned his will in the past, often trying to use it as a means to manipulate her. All the time, it seemed, he had never had any intention of changing it in any way. She smiled slightly. 'So that's that,' she said. It would be a relief, in a way, never to have to see this house again.

'Not quite, Miss Browne,' said the solicitor. 'I must be honest with you and tell you that you are more fortunate than I believe your father ever intended. When your parents married, your mother brought with her an income of her own which, as you know, ceased upon her death. But she also had a sum of money which I believe could be described as respectable. It passed into your father's hands and he took complete control of it, investing it in speculations of his own choosing, which in the short term proved to be unwise. Henceforth, he told me that he wished to hear no more about them.' He was silent for a few moments, and to Florence's surprise, he coloured in a most uncharacteristic way. 'Forgive me for saying this, Miss Browne, but I suspect that you have very few illusions with regard to your father.'

'Very few, if any,' replied Florence. 'I am not surprised that he has left me nothing. I am quite reconciled to the fact that I shall need to find work as a governess.'

'Needless to say, my dear, you may come to us until you have found something suitable,' said Mr Chancery firmly.

'It seems quite clear, that Mr Browne intended to leave you with nothing,' said Mr Renfrew carefully. 'When he discovered that his speculation had been unwise, he left the worthless shares and any proceeds from them to you in his will.'

'I see,' she said levelly.

'I do not think you do. You see, a short time

ago, another attempt was made by the company to work the mine in which your father's shares were invested. This time, the owners met with better success. In short, ma'am, they struck gold.'

'Gold?' Florence breathed.

'Yes indeed.' Mr Renfrew shuffled his papers again. 'At the latest computation, I should say that your shares are worth something in the region of fifty thousand pounds.'

For the first time that day, Florence looked really shocked. 'Fifty thousand . . . ?' she faltered.

'Pounds, yes,' Mr Renfrew completed.

'And my father knew nothing about this?'

'Nothing at all.' He smiled a little self-consciously. 'Naturally, had he ever asked me about them, I would have been bound to tell him, but he never did so. He had been so insistent, you see, that he wanted to hear no more about them, that I held my tongue. Why Miss Browne, whatever is the matter?'

A small choking sound proceeded from Florence's direction and then, to both men's consternation, she burst out laughing.

'Oh, poor Father,' she declared as soon as she was able. 'Poor, poor Father!'

'My dear Miss Browne, you are over-wrought,' said Renfrew concernedly. 'Pray,

51

allow me to send for some wine.'

'I'll ring the bell,' said Mr Chancery getting to his feet. 'But this is capital, capital! Poor old Browne! I don't know when I've been more pleased. And as for you, Renfrew!' He laughed. 'My word, I've a good mind to put some business your way. There's guile for you!'

Suddenly the solicitor's face took on an expression of great consternation. 'Oh hush, Mr Chancery, pray do not say so!' he exclaimed. 'All I did was carry out my client's wishes to the letter; to the letter, sir!'

'Why, so you did,' replied Mr Chancery clapping him on the shoulder.

After the wine had arrived and everyone had been given a glass, Florence said, 'Please tell me, Mr Renfrew, what would you advise me to do about these shares? Shall I sell them all, for I have not a penny in the world, you know.'

Renfrew shook his head. 'I would certainly not advise you to sell them all,' he replied. 'They are doing well, and there is no sign of a collapse at present. I would sell one fifth immediately, then when you are settled some-where, invest in a reliable bank, and we can make enquiries as to what to do with the rest.'

Mr Chancery renewed his offer of some-where to stay before he left and, remembering how that offer had first been made when he believed her to be penniless, she thanked him gratefully. 'It may well be that I shall have to accept your kind offer, at least until I decide where I am to go. All this is so very new to me.'

'It has just occurred to me that you are now in a position to buy this house for yourself,' he told her. 'That might be a possible solution to your dilemma.'

Florence barely repressed a shudder. 'No, thank you,' she replied.

5

The day after the funeral, Margaret told Florence, rather self-consciously, that she thought that it was time that she returned to Mrs Chancery. 'She has been very good, but I feel that I cannot neglect her and the children, and after all, she does pay my wages.'

'Pray do not worry about me,' Florence replied. 'There is plenty for me to do here, if this house is to be prepared to be sold. No doubt I shall come and stay at Tall Chimneys for a short time, since the Chancerys have so kindly invited me.'

'Will you be all right sleeping here alone now?' Margaret asked, looking around.

Florence laughed. 'Yes, I shall be quite all right,' she replied. 'Are you thinking that I might imagine ghosts around every corner? I shan't, you know! And at the advanced age of thirty, I am quite capable of looking after myself.'

In truth, it was a strange thing, Florence thought to herself after Margaret had gone, but the death of her father had proved to be such a liberation that it almost seemed as if his memory had been completely erased. Instead, she found herself thinking about her mother, and recalling the happy relationship that they had enjoyed. Keeping her promise to herself, she had given orders that fires were to be lit in every room which she might chance to use. She had also instructed that better provisions should be purchased so that meals would be more appetizing.

One other change she had also made. It so happened that she heard that the doctor's black Labrador bitch had given birth to puppies and, on impulse, she went round to enquire about one. For as long as she could remember, she had wanted a dog, but her father had always set his face against such an idea. 'Waste of time and money,' he had declared. 'Eat you out of house and home and take up space in front of the fire.'

Mrs Surrey welcomed her warmly and ushered her into the parlour. Like all the rooms in the doctor's house, it was cheerful and welcoming. 'Oh, that's old news,' said Mrs Surrey, on learning the reason for Florence's visit. 'They've been ready to leave their mother for a long time now.'

Florence's face fell. 'Oh dear, I am too late,' she said.

'Well not quite,' said Mrs Surrey. 'We've just got one left. He's not promised to anyone, so you can have him if you like. Excuse me for a moment and I'll go and see about some tea.'

When she came back in, a beautiful, glossy black puppy was bouncing at her heels. Florence fell to her knees with a cry of delight and called him over. 'Is this the one?' she asked, her eyes shining.

Mrs Surrey laughed. 'He certainly is,' she said, as Florence allowed the dog to lick her hand. 'It looks to me as if you've chosen each other already!' The doctor's wife would not allow her to pay for the puppy. 'It's payment enough for me to know that he will have a good home; and from what I can see, you're going to spoil him to death.'

Florence took the dog back with her, and he soon became an accepted member of the household. 'Brings a bit of life to the place,' Stevens said to Mrs West in the kitchen one day as the cook was feeding the dog with scraps of fat from the meat. Stevens and Mrs West were now the only full-time servants left. Florence had settled a generous sum of money on her father's valet, and he had gone to live with his sister in Sussex. In preparation for selling the house, she had employed two girls from the village on a daily basis to come in and clean. It was lovely to enjoy the luxury of not having to do everything herself, and she made sure that she always thanked them properly for what they had done. She had lived for too long without thanks of any kind for her to ever take that kind of courtesy for granted.

Shortly after Margaret's departure, Florence set out for Greystone Park, taking the dog on a lead. It had taken her a little time to decide what to call him. She had been debating various ideas with herself one evening, and he had sat looking at her with one ear cocked. 'How intelligent you look; how wise,' she had remarked. Then, 'I know! I'll call you after one of the wise men. Casper, that's what you'll be!' And Casper had wagged his tail as if in acknowledgement that his mistress, all unbeknownst to herself, had hit upon exactly the right name.

On her arrival at the house, Rapid declared that his mistress was feeling well and would be delighted to see her, and her new companion.

The old lady embraced Florence warmly, and was delighted to bend and stroke the little dog when he danced around her skirts in order to investigate her thoroughly. 'My dear, I am so sorry that I have not been able to come out and visit you, but you know the state of my health, especially in the winter.'

'But you wrote me such a comforting

letter,' Florence replied. 'I have read it several times and always with great pleasure.'

'I have wondered so much about how you would manage after your father's death,' Miss Le Grey went on. 'The fact that you have acquired a dog tells me that you expect to be able to keep your home, and that is a great comfort to me.'

'I will be able to do rather more than merely that,' Florence replied, and she told the older lady about her good fortune.

'It is no more than justice,' Miss Le Grey replied. 'But what will you do? You will hardly remain here.'

'No,' answered Florence. 'I have lived in this one place all my life and have never travelled anywhere else. I am going away, and I am going to have adventures.'

'What kind of adventures?' asked Miss Le Grey curiously.

'Oh, I don't know,' replied Florence. 'When you live the kind of life that I have lived, then anything is an adventure.' She paused. 'Where do you think I should go? I want to go somewhere where there is some life.'

'I think you would be wise to go to Bath,' suggested Miss Le Grey, after some thought. 'I would not advise London. London is a dangerous place for those who do not know society's rules. Bath is smaller, and so less daunting.'

'Then Bath it shall be,' declared Florence. 'But *not* dressed like this.'

Miss Le Grey looked at her young friend's black gown, suitable for mourning, no doubt, but by no means new, for she had had it when her mother had died eight years before. 'No, certainly not. For how long did you say you are permitted to remain in the house?'

'Less than six weeks,' replied Florence. 'But Mr and Mrs Chancery have invited me to stay with them after that, until I am settled.'

'Then may I suggest that you ask Mrs Chancery to advise you as to materials and designs? I believe she knows a very capable woman who should be able to make them for you.'

'I expect Mr Chancery might help me find somewhere to live in Bath,' mused Florence. Miss Browne of Bath. But after she had left the old lady, she thought, I shall be plain Miss Browne, who never married. How dull that sounds!

*   *   *

For the next few days, her mood fluctuated between elation at the thought of escape, and the fear that she would somehow never overcome the stigma of being poor, plain Miss Browne. Even though she reminded herself that she now had a fortune at her disposal, plain rich Miss Browne did not sound much better. Oh if only, she sighed to herself as she sat in her usual pew on Sunday, if only I could be Lady Dulcima Le Grey! I'm sure people would look at me very differently then.

'I have made a decision,' she told Miss Le Grey the next time she visited her. 'I am going to be a widow.'

Miss Le Grey looked rather startled. 'Is this not a little premature?' she asked. 'After all, you are not yet married, and your future husband — whoever he might be — might be in very good health.'

Florence laughed. 'No, no, you do not understand, ma'am,' she declared. 'I meant that I would *pretend* to be a widow.'

'Why?' asked Miss Le Grey after a pause. She sounded frankly puzzled.

'To give myself a past,' replied Florence enthusiastically. 'To give myself more freedom. A widow does have more freedom of movement than a single woman. All I need to do, now, is to invent a married name for myself.'

'Why not simply be Mrs Browne?' asked the older lady.

'Because Mrs Browne sounds as dull to me as Miss Browne,' replied Florence. 'I want a complete change. In any case, if I take on another name, I need not lose my past completely. I can still have been Miss Browne from this village before I married. If I do that, then I will not have so many new facts to remember.'

Miss Le Grey was silent for a few minutes. 'I still cannot really understand why you need this new identity,' she said.

Florence sighed and also sat in silence for a while before saying, 'I have lived all my life in this village. I have been dressed in drab styles and colours for I do not know how many years. My life has been dull and dutiful. While I thought I would never escape, I disciplined myself to put up with it, escaping only in my mind, and in my visits here. Now I have the chance to get away, I want some colour in my life! Something other than brown!'

There was another silence, until suddenly the elderly lady said, 'How about grey?'

'Grey?' asked Florence uncomprehendingly.

'You could be Mrs Le Grey; or better still, Lady Le Grey! Would that be exotic enough for you?'

Florence clasped her hands together. 'If you only knew!' she breathed. 'I sat in church on Sunday and longed to be Lady Dulcima Le Grey! But are you sure that you do not mind if I borrow your name?'

'Not at all. I am the last of my name, so there is no one to object. Besides, there is another advantage. If anyone should make any enquiries of me, I can say that you are indeed a connection of mine — a rather mysterious and exotic connection!'

'I still do not sound very exotic with a name like Florence,' Florence replied. 'And I do not think that Dulcima suits me, really.'

It was Margaret Bridge who provided Florence with a suitably exotic Christian name. The governess had been a little shocked at first at Florence's expressed intention of reinventing herself; but since she knew as well as anyone how dreary her friend's existence had been in the past, she made no real objection, although she did counsel caution. Rather to Florence's surprise, she approved of the suggestion that Miss Le Grey's name should be adopted.

'If you are to adopt an assumed name at all, it might as well be one that is familiar to you, and at least you have the owner's permission,' she observed later that week when they were both visiting Miss Le Grey.

'But what of my Christian name?' Florence asked.

'The same thing applies,' answered Margaret calmly. She took out a book which she had brought with her. 'This is a book about travel in Italy, but it has been written by an Italian. See here.' She showed them a page with a map printed on it. It seemed to Florence that only someone with quite remarkable sight would be able to read it with any ease. 'Remember that when we refer to places in other countries, we use an English pronunciation. An Italian would not say 'Rome', or 'Naples' or 'Florence'.'

Florence's eyes shone. 'Margaret, what is the Italian for Florence?'

'Firenze,' replied Margaret. 'But I suggest that you substitute 'a' for the final 'e' and call yourself Firenza.'

'Excellent,' declared Miss Le Grey. 'A charming, exotic form of your own name, which you should easily remember.'

'And,' continued Margaret, 'it would not be hard to make a perfectly legitimate case for using it. It could even be the pet name used for you by the late Sir Victor, and you have continued to use it in his honour.'

'The late Sir Victor?' said Florence blankly.

'Why certainly. You are in mourning, are you not? People will obviously assume that it is for your late husband.'

'Obviously,' agreed Florence, lifting her

handkerchief to her eyes. 'Poor Victor!' But when she took the handkerchief away from her eyes, she was laughing.

★ ★ ★

In the end, the hardest part of the whole business was persuading Mrs Chancery that there was no need for Florence to have someone to live with her in Bath. 'My dear Florence,' she said firmly, 'you may think that you will be perfectly all right on your own in Bath, but I must tell you that it will not do. A single woman, even one of comparatively mature years, will always attract criticism and unwelcome attention if she lives alone. Edmund will serve you by procuring a house for you; indeed, he has been there these last few days on that very errand. Allow me to help you in my way by finding you a companion.'

Florence smiled. She knew that she must be very tactful, for the Chancerys had been all kindness, but this was exactly what she had dreaded. 'Yes, I do understand,' she said. 'It is so good of Mr Chancery to go himself, and just as good of you to spare him, but I must tell you that I would very much like to take up residence in Bath and settle down there first before engaging a companion.'

Mrs Chancery shook her head. 'That will not do at all,' she declared. 'The Masters of Ceremony will know as soon as you arrive that you are alone, and then the damage will be done.'

Suddenly Florence thought of a bright idea. 'Exactly,' she said, 'which is why I am daring to ask of you an even greater favour than you have already offered to perform for me.'

'And what might that be?' asked Mrs Chancery.

'Would you be so very kind as to allow me to take Margaret with me?' Florence ventured. 'It will only be until I settle in. Furthermore,' she added craftily, 'she will be able to help me interview prospective companions, then she can tell you all about the person I engage when she returns.'

Mrs Chancery thought hard. 'Very well,' she said at last, her brow clearing. 'I can supervise Rebecca's music practice, sewing and drawing. I daresay Stephanie will not mind missing Geography and Mathematics.' (A sentiment with which Miss Stephanie, when she heard the news, concurred with great enthusiasm.)

On the day when Florence shut up The Laurels for the very last time, she did so without a twinge of regret. Mr Renfrew met her at the front door and took possession of the keys. 'Would you like to know who buys the property, or how much money it raises?' he asked her.

Florence shook her head. 'No, thank you,' she said. 'I want to shake the dust of this place off my feet.' In some ways, she felt as if part of herself had already gone. Any personal possessions had already been taken to the house that Mr Chancery had rented for her in Bath. In truth, there were very few of them, and mostly they were items that had some association with her mother. Of her father she desired no remembrances at all.

Even her clothes were different. Mrs Chancery's dressmaker had been delighted to oblige the young friend of one of her best customers. Mrs Chancery had deplored the fact that Florence was obliged to wear mourning, but Florence had not minded. Black was not brown, after all, and there was something about the colour, together with the fact that her garments, made just for her, actually fitted her properly, that made her look not too thin, but almost heart-breakingly fragile. Her new hair-style made a difference too, revealing as it did the length of her neck and the rather elfin shape of her chin. It occurred to Mr Renfrew that she would probably be pursued for quite other attributes than her considerable fortune.

'Very well, Miss Browne,' he said. 'Is there any other way in which I may serve you?'

'Only by sending on any items of post that may come for me,' replied Florence, 'although I doubt if there will be anything, unless Mrs Waring belatedly decides to get in touch with me. Stevens and Mrs West have gone to the house in Bath to make preparations for my arrival, and Margaret goes with me. If I need any other advice, I shall write to you.'

Renfrew took a card from inside his coat. 'A college friend of mine is practising in Bath, and he may prove helpful to you. May I write and ask him to give you every assistance?'

'Please do,' replied Florence, taking the card and putting it away. She had had more kind words from this country lawyer, she reflected, than she had had from her father all through her life. For a moment, she contemplated sharing her plans with him, then bit her lip. Knowing how averse he was to telling any kind of untruth, it would be very unfair to involve him in any kind of deception.

Her only regret was having to leave Miss Le Grey. 'Perhaps in the summer, I shall come and drink the waters,' the old lady said. 'But until that time, I shall expect long, interesting letters from you. I want to know all about your adventures.'

'In that case,' replied Florence, her eyes sparkling, 'I shall have to make sure that there are some!'

6

'Now,' said Florence in a business-like tone as soon as their journey had begun, 'there are things to be sorted out and there is no time like the present.' She took a small notebook and a pencil out of her reticule. 'Let us set down the chief facts concerning Lady Firenza Le Grey.'

'Lady Fi — ' began Margaret in consternation. 'But I thought you were joking. Surely you did not really intend to do such a thing?'

'I most certainly did,' retorted Florence, 'and I thought that you had understood. I am going to reinvent myself.'

'But why?' asked Margaret.

'I've already told you why,' said Florence impatiently. 'Now are you going to help me, or are you not?'

'Oh all right,' Margaret said eventually, in long-suffering tones. 'But don't expect me to tell lies for you.'

'I'm not telling lies,' answered Florence. 'I'm just . . . adding a bit. Now, Lady Firenza Le Grey. And my husband, Victor. I like that. It's the same name as on the plaque in church so I shan't forget. For how long do you think we were married?'

'Not long,' replied Margaret, beginning to enter into the spirit of it. 'In fact, the less time the better, really. Then anyone who only knew you as Florence Browne will not find it odd that you have been married and they didn't know about it.'

'Struck by falling masonry as we left the church after the wedding, perhaps,' murmured Florence thoughtfully.

'No, too bizarre. But killed only a few days afterwards; drowned, possibly, whilst on your honeymoon; that would sound reasonable.'

Florence jotted it down in her book. 'Does any of my money come from him or is it all my own?'

'Does it matter? Will anyone ask?'

'I suppose not.' Florence looked down at the bald facts recorded in her notebook. 'It still looks rather pathetic,' she said. 'Do you think that I might perhaps have been married more than once?'

'No!' exclaimed Margaret in horror. 'It would make you sound like . . . like . . . '

'Well?'

'Like an adventuress,' Margaret concluded.

'So it would,' murmured Florence, smiling secretly.

Mr Chancery had lent them his carriage for the journey, which was accomplished in one day, with a long stop for lunch, and to rest the horses, and a shorter one in the afternoon. They entered Bath late that afternoon, and Florence, accustomed to the dark brick in which her home had been built, was entranced by the golden stone from which everything in Bath seemed to be constructed, and which caught the late sun in such a pleasing way. 'Oh Margaret,' she exclaimed. 'We are going to be so happy here!'

They were welcomed by Stevens at the door of the hired house in Laura Place, and Florence thanked Mr Chancery's servants with a generous sum of money. 'Now, Stevens, please conduct us round our new home,' she said.

'Very good, miss,' replied the butler.

Florence glanced swiftly at Margaret. 'Stevens, for how many years have I known you?'

He thought for a moment. A slim, spare man, only a little taller than herself, he had always appeared to Florence to look perpetually old, depressed and weary. Today, he seemed younger as well as much more upright and alert. It occurred to her that he had suffered just as much under her father's regime as had she. 'Twenty years, I think, miss, give or take one or two.'

'You know why I have come here.'

'For a change I expect, miss.'

'Then perhaps you will understand my longing to reinvent myself.' She took a deep breath. 'Stevens, I am very tired of the name Browne; so tired that I will expire if I do not change it immediately. So as a harmless pretence, I have decided to say instead that I am Lady Firenza Le Grey, widow of Sir Victor Le Grey, who tragically died when we had been married only a matter of days. If anyone hears that Miss Browne lives here, we will say that I travelled under that name in order to ensure privacy for myself. I have Miss Le Grey's permission to use her name, so you need have no scruples.'

Stevens permitted himself a small smile. 'Very good, *my lady*,' he said. 'Is it permitted to ask how poor Sir Victor met his death?'

'He was drowned, Stevens. Drowned whilst fishing in a lake at a country house we were visiting.'

'Tragic, tragic,' answered Stevens shaking his head. 'And he such a fine swimmer, too. I will make sure that any staff we employ are informed of your tragic situation, my lady. And now, may I show you around the house?'

'By all means,' replied Florence. 'Stevens, you're wonderful.'

'Just enjoying the change as much as

yourself, miss ... I beg your pardon, my lady.'

Over the next few days, Florence established her new identity. The story that they gave out was that after the death of Sir Victor, she had found herself a little unwell, so she had come to Bath for her health, accompanied by her dear friend Mrs Bridge. Those whom she met soon discovered that the loss of her husband was something about which she did not care to talk.

Her servants had grasped quickly an important requirement of their mistress, namely, that above anything else, she liked to be warm.

'Oh, Margaret!' Florence exclaimed, as they sat in their pleasant drawing-room after their arrival. 'I don't think I shall ever again take the pleasure of being warm for granted!'

Margaret, remembering the biting chill that had always been characteristic of the rooms at The Laurels, could well understand her feelings, and Casper, who had travelled with his mistress from Howton, also showed his appreciation of a good fire by stretching in front of it with a deep sigh.

Soon after their arrival, they were honoured with a visit from the Master of Ceremonies from one assembly room, and not long afterwards, the other called as well. Both were delighted to express a willingness to be of service to such a charmingly fragile widow and her attractive companion, and although they understood that dancing was at present out of the question, they explained that many other entertainments were available, such as the concerts, particularly those featuring sacred music.

To one who had lived a lively social life, this recipe might have seemed to be somewhat bland. To someone like Florence, however, whose social life had been non-existent, this was heady stuff. Strolling on the lawns in front of the Royal Crescent with the fashionable crowd was enjoyable; the occasional walk up to Beechen Cliff prevented her from feeling constricted by town life. Even attending divine service at the abbey was touched with glamour, surrounded as they were by fashionably dressed people.

'I declare, I shall never tire of this,' said Florence to Margaret, as they walked to the Pump Room one morning. 'Why are you smiling? Have I said something foolish?'

'Not at all,' answered Margaret warmly. 'It's just that it is so lovely to see you looking happy. Do you remember how our friendship used to have to survive on about fifteen minutes a week?'

'Yes I do,' replied Florence fervently.

'Thank heaven those days are over.'

'You must know that I cannot trespass on Mrs Chancery's goodness for very much longer,' Margaret ventured. 'I shall have to return soon if I am not to lose my place.'

These words filled Florence with dread, but she was determined not to put pressure on her friend. 'I shall very much miss you, for I value your company, but my position in Bath is becoming established, and I shall soon be able to manage on my own,' she said with a determined smile.

'But what shall I tell Mrs Chancery? She will want to know who has been found to replace me.'

'Well you know, kind as she is, it really is not any of her business.'

'Yes perhaps,' agreed Margaret. 'But I cannot very well say that to her, can I?'

'Then tell her that I have found another lady to reside with me,' Florence suggested as they entered the Pump Room. 'Make something up.'

'I don't think I have your talent for fabrication,' Margaret responded, but with a smile.

The Pump Room had now become familiar territory to them, and it was there that they had made a number of agreeable acquaintances. Among them were the Earl of Braintree and his mother. Lady Braintree appeared to be something of an invalid and Lord Braintree, a devoted son, was accompanying his mother as she diligently tasted the waters and took the bath. Lord Braintree was a heavily built man of about forty, with tawny hair and rather thickset features, which were redeemed by a pair of kindly eyes. His very real concern for his mother's health had to command respect.

'My mother has never been robust, and two years ago, my father's death seemed to take away any strength that she had. They were a most devoted couple.'

'Such a loss is not easily recovered from,' Margaret replied sympathetically. 'I know, from my own experience.'

'Ah yes,' replied his lordship. 'And of course, Lady Le Grey as well.'

Florence, who had allowed her attention to wander a little, turned back looking blankly at them. 'I beg your pardon?' she said in puzzled tones.

'Your own marriage has ended prematurely,' remarked the earl sensitively.

'Has it? Oh, oh yes, of course,' corrected Florence blushing a little. 'Forgive me, but my mind was elsewhere. Are you an only child, my lord?'

He inclined his head. 'I'm afraid so,' he

said ruefully, 'so making all the arrangements for her care falls upon my shoulders. It is not that I resent it, you understand, but sometimes I wish that there was someone else to share the load.'

'He seems a most agreeable gentleman,' said Margaret later, glancing slyly at her friend.

'Yes, very pleasant,' Florence responded, not noticing the look that her friend had given her, but darting one of her own in turn. So each lady was able to muse privately on how nicely the earl would do for the other, without having any idea that her friend was having exactly the same thoughts.

Thereafter, his lordship often called in Laura Place, and entertained both the ladies with his sensible conversation, laced with wry wit.

Among their other acquaintances were Lady Trimm and her daughters, Dianne and Maria. Lady Trimm was a stout, good-humoured woman and a fond parent. She was particularly concerned for the health of Dianne, who had been severely weakened by a bout of pneumonia, and had been advised by her doctor to take the bath.

'She has always been delicate,' Lady Trimm confided, whilst her daughters were talking with some other acquaintances, 'so I am determined to spare no expense in promoting her recovery.'

Florence looked across at the two young women who were talking animatedly with a gentleman in military uniform. Both looked to be in good health, with charmingly pink complexions. 'You will be thinking that she looks very well, and supposing that I am just a fussy mama,' said Lady Trimm, reading her mind. 'But indeed, although she is feeling better, her strength is soon exhausted, and I want her to be well for the season.'

'That's quite understandable, ma'am,' Florence replied. Later, Lady Trimm introduced her daughters, and Florence, expecting two rather spoilt young women, was agreeably surprised to find them charming and unassuming. She looked at them with envy. They were to have opportunities that she had been denied.

These thoughts did not last long, however, for there were advantages to her circumstances, or at any rate to her imagined circumstances. She was a widow of independent means, and she was able to decide her future for herself. That, at any rate, was worth a lot.

One morning, as they were about to leave the Pump Room, Lady Trimm came hurrying up with an invitation. 'I am holding a small private party for Dianne and Maria in my house in Henrietta Street. Pray come,' she pleaded, guessing that Florence might use her mourning state as an excuse. 'It will be a private party, with just a little dancing for the young people; of course you need not dance you know.' Still seeing them hesitate, she went on, 'It is the right time for Dianne to do a little more and I feel that it is so important for girls of that age to have good examples to follow.'

'Then we accept with pleasure,' answered Florence.

'I am so pleased,' declared Lady Trimm. 'It is possible that Lord Trimm might be with us, as he has had business to do in Bristol. I will be so very happy for him to meet you.'

'I wonder whether she would consider us to be such good examples if she knew how many lies I have told recently,' Florence said gleefully after Lady Trimm had gone. 'She would probably think of me as a grim warning instead.'

'Don't,' begged Margaret. 'I feel as if I am sinking more deeply into infamy every day.'

'Well for my part, I am enjoying myself hugely, and don't tell me that you aren't feeling the same, for I shan't believe you.'

Margaret had to smile at that. It was the first time that she had taken such an active part in social occasions since coming out of mourning for Captain Bridge and she was surprised at how much she was looking forward to each event.

Henrietta Street was just around the corner from Laura Place, and the two ladies debated as to whether they should hire sedan chairs or walk. 'We ought to take chairs,' said Margaret. 'You are still establishing your consequence here, and ought to take no risks with your reputation.'

'Oh pooh,' declared Florence. 'Why send for two sedan chairs and chairmen for the sake of half-a-dozen steps? And besides, I have heard that it is possible for it to take so long for all the waiting carriages and chairs to draw up in turn outside the place where one is going, that it would have taken less time to walk there. In any case, who is to know?'

Before she put on her outdoor clothes that evening, Florence looked at herself in the full-length mirror in her bedroom. She was wearing her customary black, her gown dripping with rich lace, with a black head dress that was just the right side of frivolous. 'Plain Miss Browne?' she said. Then, with a smile, she snapped her fingers before allowing her maid to put on her cloak. Margaret was waiting in the hall, her blonde hair and dull yellow gown providing a pleasing contrast with Florence's complexion and attire. 'Why, we might appear as a tableau of 'Day and Night',' Florence remarked as they left.

If Lady Trimm's front door was not quite obscured by the number of carriages, there were certainly enough of them outside for Florence to be able to turn to Margaret with a smile of satisfaction. 'See what a tiresome wait I have saved us,' she said.

They had almost reached the entrance when a carriage opened immediately next to them and a tall gentleman leaped down without waiting for assistance. He turned hastily and bumped into Florence, causing her to bump Margaret in her turn.

'Sir!' Florence said indignantly.

'*Santa Maria*,' exclaimed the gentlemen in accented English. 'Your pardon, ladies.' He looked around. 'You are unescorted, I see.' His tone had subtly changed. 'Surely a little unwise, even in Bath. But a lucky chance for me. Your obedient servant.' So saying, he took Florence's hand, lifted it and, with great audacity, and before she could collect herself, turned it palm up, peeled back her glove and kissed her on the wrist, holding her eyes with his the whole time.

Florence was completely lost for words. It was Margaret who spoke, saying, 'Sir, you are insolent. Your accent proclaims that you are a stranger to these shores, so perhaps your over familiarity should be excused, but I must tell you that such behaviour is not welcomed here. And now, we must allow you to go on your way, for we have an engagement.' She took Florence's arm and pulled her gently towards Lady Trimm's front door.

'But so do I, *signore*, and to me it looks very much as if we have the same destination. Shall we go in?' He made a polite gesture as if to usher them forward, then strolled in casually behind them.

'Margaret, he is following us,' whispered Florence, as their cloaks were taken by a waiting servant.

'Perhaps that will teach you to ride next time,' Margaret whispered back. 'Come, let us go up the stairs quickly. I am sure he has only followed us into the hall out of devilment, and will soon be gone.'

They mounted the stairs and reached the top to be greeted by Lady Trimm, her husband and her two daughters. Although not as stout as his wife, Lord Trimm was a portly man, and he looked delighted to be there and share in the proceedings. Lady Trimm introduced him to Florence and Margaret, then said, 'I have a delightful surprise for you this evening; and here he is, just behind you.'

With a deep feeling of foreboding, Florence turned to see that the gentleman from outside was just behind them. He was tall and dark, with a swarthy complexion, jet-black hair and snapping black eyes, black brows, a straight nose and a rather thin-lipped mouth, and he looked to be in his mid-thirties. He was dressed elegantly, in a manner that proclaimed the dandy, with a blue coat of watered silk, and shirt and cravat heavily trimmed with fine lace.

'Allow me to introduce to you a gentleman who I am sure must be your kinsman,' went on Lady Trimm. 'My dear Lady Le Grey, this is Sir Vittorio Le Grey.'

Florence stared at him. For a split second, it seemed as though he was as astonished as was she. Then he smiled, showing all his teeth, and to her his expression looked wolfish in the extreme. 'Oh, good God,' she breathed, and having surreptitiously established that there was no obstacle behind her, she sank gracefully to the floor.

She hear Lady Trimm's agitated voice saying, 'Oh my goodness me, how dreadful! Oh, poor Lady Le Grey!'

Then Margaret said 'Fee! Oh, good heavens, what has happened?'

'She has only fainted, I believe,' said the voice of the swarthy gentleman. 'No doubt the surprise of finding a long lost kinsman was a great shock for her.'

Then to Florence's surprise, she found herself scooped up off the floor by a pair of masculine arms. She was conscious of the faintest scent of cologne.

'Pray bring her into the small saloon, Sir Vittorio,' said Lady Trimm. 'It is not being used this evening and it will be quiet, so that she can recover.'

Florence could feel herself being carried, clearly by this unusual stranger. The panic that had caused her to simulate a faint had subsided somewhat, but she still had no idea of what to say to this supposed new kinsman. From where had he sprung, and what relation was he supposed to be to her?

She felt herself being placed upon a sofa and then she heard Margaret say, 'Please go back to your guests, Lady Trimm. Lady Le Grey will soon recover if she is allowed to be quiet.'

'Yes, perhaps that would be wise,' replied Lady Trimm.

'Some smelling salts, also, would be a good idea,' said a masculine voice.

'Yes, I have some,' said Lady Trimm eagerly.

Florence heard the door close, and assuming that she had been left alone with

Margaret, opened her eyes at once, and swung her legs down off the sofa. 'Thank goodness for that,' she exclaimed.

'Ah, but how it rejoices my heart to see you so much recovered, *signora*.' She turned her head swiftly in astonishment. Sir Vittorio was standing with his shoulders against the door and they were quite alone in the room.

7

She stared at him for a moment, then, recollecting that she was supposed to have fainted very recently, she raised her hand to her brow. 'Oh dear,' she murmured in a tone which she flattered herself was convincingly weak and confused. 'Perhaps I should have not have moved so suddenly. Oh where am I, pray?'

'You are in a small saloon in the house of Lady Trimm; a fact of which I think you are very well aware, *signora*.' He moved away from the door, walked over to where she was sitting, and helped himself to snuff.

Deciding to ignore the rather cynical tone of his comments and instead take them at their face value, she said, 'No I did not know. I am not very well acquainted with Lady Trimm's house, you see. Did I faint? I have never done so before.'

'That I can well believe,' he replied, putting away his snuff box.

'It must have been the heat,' she remarked.

'Do you find it so very warm?' he asked her, shaking out his ruffles. 'It seems to me to be a little cold, if anything.'

'But then, you are from warmer climes than these, sir — or so I should surmise,' remarked Florence, seeing an opportunity to change the subject.

'You are correct, *signora*,' he agreed. 'I was, until lately, in Tuscany.' He paused, then without warning, he said, 'Tell me, who exactly are you?'

At that very moment, Margaret came hurrying back in with the smelling salts. 'Forgive me for leaving you! But you are better, I see!'

'You did not need to be concerned, *signora*,' said the gentleman soothingly. 'After all, it was clearly only a very mild disorder.'

'It's all right, Margaret, I do not need those now,' said Florence waving away the smelling salts that her friend was trying to hold under her nose. 'I am feeling very much better and shall rejoin the company.'

'But Fee, I thought that you would want to go home at once,' Margaret protested.

'Fee?' murmured Sir Vittorio, raising one brow.

'It is short for Firenza,' Florence explained, blushing to her great annoyance.

'Firenza!' exclaimed the gentleman. '*Parla l'Italiano*? Do you speak Italian, then?'

'I do not,' replied Florence. She looked at Margaret. After the turmoil of the last

87

half-hour or so, she would have been very glad to return home, but she hesitated. She was only just establishing herself in Bath, and yet here was a man from Italy, bearing her name, or so he claimed, and clearly already well on the way to making himself accepted here. Who was he? Was he an impostor? It certainly seemed likely, for Miss Le Grey had been quite clear that she was the last of her name. That being so, what was his purpose for being here? Did he intend to impose upon his new acquaintances in some way? She did not know how she could stop him, but she certainly would not be able to achieve this by going home meekly. Fixing a smile on her face, she looked up at the man who was claiming to be her kinsman. 'Nor do I wish to go home. In fact, I am very ready to rejoin the company if Sir Vittorio will give me his arm.'

The baronet bowed elaborately. 'I am, of course, at your service, *signora*,' he declared, extending one blue silk-clad arm so that she might lay her hand upon it. 'When you choose to return home, I shall take you home myself,' he told her as they walked. 'I should hate you to be the object of some' — he paused. 'Forgive me, the English words escape me for a moment.'

'Perhaps you wanted to say 'some insult','

suggested Florence sweetly, not believing his hesitancy for a moment.

'No, that was not the expression,' replied Vittorio. His tone suggested uncertainty, but his face betrayed that he had known precisely what words he had intended to choose. ''Some excessive gallantry' was, I think, what I meant to say. But here we are, back amongst the other guests. We must reassure Lady Trimm as to your good health. And then, Lady Le Grey, you and I will spend a little time establishing precisely how we happen to be related to one another.'

But this, Florence was quite determined not to do. She had no intention of saying anything more to him about her history until she had thought matters through, and at least discussed them with Margaret. She therefore spent the evening keeping well away from him, starting conversations with those who could be depended upon to keep her by their side, and moving to the other side of the room whenever Sir Vittorio came near so that the baronet, if that was what he really was, began to stare at her in a manner that showed signs of temper.

Eventually, she approached Margaret and said, 'I think it is about time that we were going. We have remained for long enough to establish that we are not ashamed of ourselves, but whatever happens, I do *not* want to occupy a carriage with that man!'

'Then what shall we do?' asked Margaret helplessly.

'Wait until he is dancing, then sneak off quickly,' replied Florence. 'He thinks himself too much the gentleman to leave his partner standing on the floor, I fancy. Come, let us approach Lady Trimm now, then we will be ready to go as soon as he is otherwise occupied.'

If Lady Trimm found their precipitate departure surprising, she did not comment upon it. She said merely, 'I am so glad that you were able to come tonight. And how delightful for you to have met a relative here.'

'Yes it was, wasn't it?' Florence answered, before hurrying with Margaret out of the door.

'If only we could be sure that he does not follow us,' muttered Margaret, glancing behind her nervously as they walked back to Laura Place as quickly as they could manage.

'And risk ruining those shoes?' Florence said wryly. 'Come along, let's get home, then we can put our feet up and decide what to do about this new problem.'

Sir Vittorio noticed their departure but, as they rightly surmised, was too aware of the niceties of social behaviour to leave Miss

Maria Trimm deserted on the floor. For her part, she was delighted to be partnered by a man of such grace and elegance, and if his compliments and sallies were uttered with a little less than his usual panache, no one unacquainted with him would have known.

When the dance was over, he escorted Miss Trimm off the floor, and wandered over thoughtfully to speak to Lord Braintree. The two men had already been introduced and they acknowledged one another politely. 'A charming evening,' remarked the baronet, as he offered the earl a pinch of snuff.

'Thank you. Yes indeed, charming as you say,' replied Braintree, as he helped himself from Sir Vittorio's box.

'I must count myself fortunate to have been given this invitation so soon during my stay in Bath.'

'Were you previously acquainted with Lord and Lady Trimm?' the earl asked him.

'I met Lord Trimm in Bristol. We travelled together and he urged me to come to this entertainment,' Vittorio explained. 'I have but recently arrived in England from Italy.'

'A beautiful country,' observed Braintree.

The other man bowed slightly at the compliment. 'But England has its beauties too, and I look forward to exploring them.'

'You speak as though you do not know

England at all, sir, yet you speak English fluently, and you have an English name.'

Le Grey eyed him suspiciously, but could see nothing but polite interest in the other man's gaze, so he relaxed a little. 'English mixed with French surely,' he replied. 'My mother was Italian and very attached to her homeland, and since my father was estranged from his family because of some youthful misdemeanour, he was happy to reside amongst his wife's people. It is only now that my parents are both gone that I feel able to come to England and visit my father's native land.'

'And you have a relative here too.'

'So it seems.'

'You are fortunate indeed, sir. It must be rare to find a hitherto unknown relation and discover her to be young and charming, as is Lady Le Grey.'

The baronet smiled briefly. 'You assume that I did not know about her before,' he murmured. A footman came past with a tray of wine, and each man took a glass.

'Was I wrong in my assumption? I do know that your existence was unknown to Lady Le Grey, for she has spoken about herself as being without any male relatives.'

'No, you are correct. I had never met Lady Le Grey before tonight. I must count upon those who know her to help me further my acquaintance with her.'

'She has not been in Bath for very long, so we are all still getting to know her.'

'I am sorry that she and her companion have left without my escort, for I had intended to take them home myself,' said the baronet casually.

'I dare say they have walked,' the earl suggested. 'They live only a short distance away in Laura Place.'

On hearing this, Sir Vittorio smiled faintly, and after chatting for a few minutes more, he left the earl's side, wandered over to Lady Trimm, and took his leave.

★　★　★

'Now, what are we going to do?' asked Florence, as soon as they were sitting in their own home once again. After taking off their outdoor things, they had ordered tea, and gone to sit down in the cosy sitting-room which they were accustomed to use more than any other. As soon as they arrived, Stevens made haste to have the fire lit.

'You had better tell me what he said to you while I was out of the room,' Margaret suggested. As far as she could remember, Florence recounted the conversation to her.

After she had finished, Margaret thought carefully for a few moments, whilst her friend looked at her anxiously. Eventually, she said, 'Are you sure that matters are really so desperate? You say that he seemed to doubt whether you had really fainted, and he was right to do so, you must admit. As for wanting to know exactly who you are, that is a perfectly reasonable desire, surely? After all, you want to know exactly who he is, don't you?'

'Yes, I do. But the difference is that I know that he is an impostor,' declared Florence.

'Forgive me, my love, but so are you,' ventured Margaret. 'Don't eat me, but it is so, is it not?'

'Certainly not,' retorted Florence, colouring a little. 'I have Miss Le Grey's leave to use her name. He cannot be entitled to it, for I know that Miss Le Grey has always said that she was the last of her line. Furthermore, I am not looking for any pecuniary advantage through the use of the name.'

'You do not know that he is either,' said Margaret reasonably.

Florence snorted. 'Of course he is,' she declared. 'You only have to look at his clothes. Did you ever see such a dandy? However much must it cost to dress him?' She paused briefly; then another thought came to her. 'Why did you go out of the room and leave me alone with him?' she asked.

It was Margaret's turn to colour. 'He suggested smelling salts, if you recall. Then Lady Trimm said that she had some and, well, he opened the door with such a flourish, that before I knew what had happened, I had gone out of it! But you need not worry about your reputation. Lady Trimm said something about your being safe with your cousin, so obviously the nature of your relationship has been assumed by Bath society already.'

'That's something, I suppose,' Florence conceded. 'I should hate anyone thinking that I was seeking for an opportunity to be alone with a strange man. The fact remains, though, that I have no idea what I am going to say to him when he comes to see me, for I have no doubt that he will do so.'

'You could deny yourself when he comes,' suggested Margaret.

'No,' said Florence decidedly. 'I have been hidden away for the last thirty years. I refuse to hide myself away now. But I must think what to say to him. Oh well, perhaps the night will bring counsel.'

When Florence came downstairs for breakfast, however, Margaret was waiting at the table with an anxious expression on her face. 'Fee, I have had a truly disturbing thought,' she said.

'May I eat my breakfast first?' asked Florence. 'If your thought is a really dreadful one, I might not be able to eat afterwards.'

Margaret waited with great impatience until Florence had consumed an egg with some toast and a cup of coffee, then gave voice to her fears. 'I have been remembering that when he met us outside the house, he showed a disposition to flirt with you.'

Florence did not need to ask to whom Margaret was referring. 'Yes he did, and very insolent I thought him. Go on.'

'Well, then he was the one who picked you up and put you on the sofa, *and* he made sure that he had got rid of everyone else.'

'Yes?'

'*And* he declared his intention of seeking you out and finding out more about you.'

Florence sighed. 'Margaret, you are only telling me things that I already know.' Suddenly, her face took on an arrested expression. 'Oh good God. You are going to say that you think he might want to pursue me, aren't you?'

'Yes; but it is worse than that,' said Margaret. 'You said that he knew that your faint was not a real one. What if he thinks that *you* were trying to encourage *him*?'

'Oh no,' Florence breathed, her hand going

to her mouth. 'Margaret, do you suppose that he thinks I am an adventuress?'

'Why not? After all, you think that he is an adventurer, don't you?'

'Yes, I do,' said Florence crossly. 'But that is quite a different thing. Come along, let's go to the Pump Room. It might take our minds off things.'

They went upstairs to put on their outdoor clothes, but when they came downstairs, Florence's face was wearing a thoughtful expression. 'Margaret, it has occurred to me that if he does have this false idea of me, then it may be to our advantage,' she mused. 'If he is really in pursuit of me, then if I flirt with him in turn, it might take his mind off enquiring as to my antecedents and origins.'

'You mean that you might in very truth become the adventuress that he is suspecting you to be,' breathed Margaret in shocked tones.

'Well, I did say that I wanted adventures,' replied Florence. 'Who better to have them than an adventuress?' Suddenly she tucked her hand in her friend's arm. 'Yes, I know you are shocked at my conversation and I am sorry. But isn't this better than being dull Miss Browne?'

Margaret refused to be pacified, and even started talking about the need to return to

Mrs Chancery quite soon, so Florence dedicated the rest of the journey to soothing her friend's fears.

'All this talk about his possible interest in me is pure speculation,' she insisted. 'To be absolutely truthful, I do not believe a word of it. Why, look at me, thirty years old, and only one suitor. I know that I look better than I did, but what man would pursue me when Dianne and Maria Trimm are in view? It's far more likely that he simply wants to find out if I really am who I say I am.'

'And you still have not decided what you are to say to him,' Margaret reminded her, as they reached the Pump Room.

'He has only just come from Italy. He will know nothing about possible family connections on this side of the Channel.'

'You don't know that for sure,' whispered Margaret urgently. 'That Italian accent and air may be assumed. He might be an urchin from the back slums near Covent Garden.'

At that very second they caught sight of Sir Vittorio Le Grey. His linen was sparkling white and liberally trimmed with lace, and his coat was of gold brocade. As on the previous night, he seemed to be just a little bit more of the dandy than any other man present; not a hair was out of place. Suddenly, the amusing contrast between his appearance and Margaret's suggestion about his origins struck Florence and she burst out laughing. It was at that moment that he turned and saw her. With a polite acknowledgement to those who were standing with him, he strolled across the room towards her and favoured her with a courtly bow. If he had been raised in a back slum, she decided, he had certainly come a long way; once more, she found herself wanting to giggle.

'Good morning, *signore*,' he said, acknowledging them both. 'You encourage me to think that I did not offend beyond forgiveness yesterday, for you greet me with a smile.'

'Ah, but that is because I am pleased to . . . ' Florence paused.

'To see me?' suggested the baronet audaciously, offering her his arm. Margaret excused herself in order to speak to an acquaintance.

'To be in the Pump Room,' Florence corrected, feeling annoyed that Margaret had deserted her so soon. 'Really, sir, you must not make so many assumptions, it is very rash of you.'

'It is a failing of which I have been accused in the past,' agreed her companion.

'By members of your family?' suggested Florence. She knew that the subject of their relationship could not be avoided for ever, and she had decided that to be the first to bring up the matter might give her an advantage.

'By my mother, certainly, and by other ladies, including one very formidable aunt.'

'And is your mother still alive?'

'Sadly, no, my mother died three years ago. My father died more recently.' He had led her to the side of the Pump Room and now invited her to be seated, before sitting down next to her. 'Signora Le Grey, I confess that you intrigue me. Last night perhaps I seemed discourteous, but that was because I was taken by surprise. Today, you find me more polite, I hope, but no less curious. Tell me, if you please, exactly who are you?'

She looked up at him. His expression was indeed perfectly courteous, but quite determined. She opened her mouth to speak, but then closed it again, suddenly realizing that she did not have the slightest idea of what she was going to say. To speak about Miss Le Grey, although tempting, might very well be unwise, when she knew so little about this man. Fortunately, before the silence became noticeable, Lady Trimm came hurrying over to them.

'My dear Lady Le Grey, I am so glad that you are fully recovered. I was hoping that you might be well enough to be here. Sir Vittorio, good morning. I trust that you are persuading your kinswoman to drink a glass of the famous water. It will be just the thing to ensure her continued good health.'

'Lady Trimm,' murmured the baronet, who had risen to his feet and bowed with impeccable courtesy. 'You remind me how remiss I have been. I shall procure one for her immediately.'

Florence breathed a sigh of relief. Again, she had been rescued from having to explain herself, but who knew for how long?

'He is very handsome, your kinsman, is he not?' murmured Lady Trimm.

'Yes, very handsome,' replied Florence, observing him with a critical eye. He walked with an easy pace, effortlessly negotiating his way through the crowd around the pump. 'He is something of a bird of paradise amongst the other gentlemen, is he not?'

'I believe that fashions in Italy tend to be more elaborate than in this country,' commented Lady Trimm. 'Of course, he is very Italian in appearance, but I have to confess that I am quite an admirer of dark good looks.' She lowered her tone a little. 'I must tell you, in confidence, that I am not the only one,' she added, indicating Miss Maria with a movement of her head. 'Tell me, my dear, what exactly do you know of him? In what way are the two of you related?'

At that very moment, Sir Vittorio returned with a glass in his hand. 'It is a very complex business, is it not?' said the baronet, in response to the tail end of the conversation. 'We have not yet succeeded in unravelling the matter.'

'But you are definitely related?' Lady Trimm pursued.

Florence, taking a sip of water, was conscious of her ladyship's eye upon her, and felt herself obliged to say 'so it would seem'.

Lady Trimm smiled. 'What an agreeable surprise for both of you,' she commented. 'Excuse me, I see Dianne waving to me.'

The relief that Florence felt at Lady Trimm's easy acceptance of her words evaporated as soon as she looked at Sir Vittorio's face. His expression was one of anger, mixed with contempt.

'So we are definitely related, are we, *signora*? And when exactly did you decide that? No doubt it would suit you very well if I were to ask no more questions. But logic tells me that if you were really who you pretend to be, you would not accept that you were related to me quite so easily. So choose your words well next time we meet, for one way or another I *will* find out who you are.' So saying, he executed a flourishing bow, and left the Pump Room without stopping to speak to anyone else.

The instant he had gone, Margaret came over to her side. 'My dear, you look a little agitated,' she said. 'Did that man say anything to distress you?'

'Oh, nothing more or less than he has said before,' replied Florence wretchedly. 'Why upon earth has he chosen to come here at such a time, and to pick that name? He says that he is determined to find out who I really am, Margaret. Then no doubt he will broadcast it to the world and everyone will pity me as a poor mad spinster who has to invent new names for herself, just to make her life more exciting. Oh, how I wish he would go away.'

The following day, it seemed as if she was to have her wish. Perhaps because the thought of meeting the Italian was preying on her mind, Florence awoke with a bad headache and declared that she would not go to the Pump Room that day. After offering to bathe her temples with Hungary water, Margaret declared that she would not go either.

'No, please go,' said Florence weakly. 'I want you to see if he is there, and find out if anyone knows anything more about him, or if he has said anything about me.'

Margaret looked at her friend uncertainly. She did indeed look very pale, with dark circles under her eyes, and Mrs Bridge felt a surge of anger against the man who had managed to undo the good that the last few weeks had done to Florence's spirits. 'All right,' she said eventually. 'As long as you promise to try and sleep.'

After she had gone, Florence lay thinking about the dilemma in which she had found herself. If was the most unfair stroke of bad luck that had ordained that a man bearing, or pretending to bear the same name that she had chosen, should appear in Bath at exactly the same time as herself. She had only taken on a new identity in order to procure for herself the freedom that a married woman of her age would have as a matter of course, and also to have a little bit of fun. This adventure was proving to be altogether more exciting than she had bargained for. But despite everything, she felt a sudden lift of her spirits as she realized that even given her present problem, she would not willingly have changed back to her old situation for anything.

This was such a cheering notion, that she managed to fall asleep, and when she awoke an hour later, her headache had gone. She rang for water so that she could wash and dress, but no sooner had she done so than there was a scratching on the door, which opened to admit Margaret.

'He's gone!' she declared as soon as she had closed the door.

'What?' exclaimed Florence sitting up in bed.

'He's gone,' said Margaret again. 'Lord Braintree told me. He chanced to meet Sir Vittorio early this morning as he was going riding. He has some business to take care of which would not wait, and he has gone!'

'Oh, thank goodness,' sighed Florence. 'Do you suppose he has gone for good, or is he coming back again?'

'That was the first thing that occurred to me,' Margaret replied. 'But Lord Braintree does not know, for he asked me that himself.'

'I wonder where he was staying,' mused Florence. 'If he has left some belongings behind, then that would indicate that he is to return. But in the meantime, Margaret, at least we may enjoy ourselves again.'

'Perhaps your presence frightened him off?' Margaret suggested.

Florence brightened even more. 'If that is the case, then it would almost certainly prove that he is a fraud,' she replied. 'Perhaps we have nothing to worry about after all.'

As they went about the town, it became clear that Florence's supposed kinsman had made his mark. It seemed that she could not go anywhere without someone's asking about him, or commenting about how handsome he was, how gallant, how well-dressed. Although one or two older folk hovered on the edge of declaring him a popinjay, the impression, on the whole, seemed to be favourable.

She found herself saying as little about him as possible, confining her responses to other people's comments to the strictly neutral, and making the point wherever possible, that she hardly knew him as yet. Given that she did not know whether he would return or not, she could not think what else to say.

In the meantime, from being attentive to both the ladies in Laura Place, Lord Braintree had gradually begun to show a decided preference for Margaret Bridge. The earl often seemed to drift towards them whenever they were in a public place, and he was a frequent caller. Florence had expected Margaret to return to Mrs Chancery by now, but Mrs Chancery, surely the most easy-going of parents, had sent a message to say that the children were going on perfectly well without lessons, and Margaret might stay in Bath for as long as she liked. Florence was glad of it. With all the excitement that the arrival of the Italian had entailed, she felt that she needed someone with whom to confer.

If she was honest, however, she could not help feeling a little jealous. It was not that she herself had any designs on Lord Braintree. It was simply that it seemed so unfair that Margaret, who had already been married once, should be attracting the attention of another man, whereas she herself had never had any suitor to speak of. But Margaret was starting to look so happy when Lord Braintree's name was mentioned, that she did not have it in her to refuse to go with her anywhere where he might be found. It did not occur to her that the severe black of her widow's weeds was sufficient to put many gentlemen off.

It so happened that they had attended divine service in the abbey one day, and were stopped by Lord Braintree as they were leaving. 'I am planning a little excursion to Wells,' he said. 'The weather is not warm, but we may look around the cathedral and if it is fine, we can explore the town afterwards. The Crown has a good reputation, and I thought that we might eat there.'

'It sounds delightful,' said Florence. 'Do you have a date to suggest?'

'Perhaps next Thursday, if you are agreeable?' ventured the earl.

'We have no other plans for that day, I believe, so we shall be glad to accept your kind invitation, shall we not, Margaret?'

Margaret's happy smile confirmed the arrangement; if anything she looked even happier when the earl offered to walk home with them. Florence spoke to someone else to allow the two of them to walk ahead a little and exchange a few words; but before she could follow them, she heard a gentleman speak, 'Pardon me, ma'am, but I think I know you.'

She turned to look at the man who had addressed her. He was tall, with wavy, light-brown hair, brown eyes and a tanned complexion, and he was dressed fashionably, but with quiet restraint. 'Good heavens,' she murmured in astonishment. 'It is; it must be . . . Mr Stapleton?'

'I am honoured that you remember me, Miss Browne.'

Lady Trimm was standing quite near to them, and although she did not appear to be listening, Florence knew that she had to correct him. 'I am not Miss Browne now, Mr Stapleton.'

'You are married?' he exclaimed, looking a little vexed.

Flattered by his interest and evident chagrin, she said, 'Married, but widowed also, I fear.'

'Good heavens,' he declared, trying hard not to betray the delight that he was clearly feeling. 'How dreadful to be widowed so young! But pray tell me how I address you, for I do not have the slightest idea.'

'You may address me as Lady Le Grey,' replied Florence.

'And your husband . . . '

'Sir Victor died very suddenly. It is not something that I care to speak or even think about.'

He inclined his head in obedience to her wishes. 'You have my deepest sympathy,' he said. 'But tell me, are you now residing in Bath? Have you come for your father's health? Is he here with you?'

'I am residing in Bath, but my father is not here. Indeed, my father passed away just a few weeks ago.'

Mr Stapleton's face fell. 'Oh good God,' he exclaimed. 'Pray forgive me! I have distressed you again by my remarks, but that distress was quite unintended, I assure you.'

'Of course,' Florence said at once. 'How could you have known?'

'What a dreadful time you must have had!' he continued. 'I do not wonder at your desire to get away completely. But you are not living alone, surely.'

'No indeed, I have my very good friend

Mrs Bridge living with me; which reminds me that I have allowed her to walk on without me, and must catch her up without delay.'

'Then pray, allow me to escort you,' said Mr Stapleton, politely offering her his arm.

'You are very kind,' replied Florence, smiling as she took it. 'We are living in Laura Place.'

'Then you must show me the way,' said Mr Stapleton. 'This is my first visit to Bath.'

'Not for your health, I hope,' remarked Florence. She stole a sideways glance at his tall, athletic figure. He certainly did not look as if he needed to take the cure!

'By no means,' he smiled. 'I am on my way to Bristol from London for business purposes, and merely decided to break my journey in Bath. Naturally I could not travel further on a Sunday, so I made up my mind to attend the service in the famous abbey that everyone talks about. Who would have imagined that I would have been so fortunate as to encounter you again?' He paused. 'It has been a very long time, Lady Le Grey.'

She drew a deep breath. 'Yes, it has,' she replied. 'Oh look, we are nearly at the house and there is Margaret waiting for us with Lord Braintree.' Florence introduced Mr Stapleton then invited both the men inside, but they declined. Lord Braintree needed to make sure that his mother was getting the treatment that she needed, and Mr Stapleton agreed to walk back with him.

'I shall call upon you tomorrow, if I may,' he promised, touching his hat politely.

'I thought you were only passing through on your way to Bristol,' Florence objected.

'That was before I attended the service today,' he replied, with a twinkle in his eye.

'Now tell all,' Margaret said, after they had put off their outdoor things and sat down in the small saloon.

'There's very little to tell,' replied Florence. 'We met at Tall Chimneys several years before you were employed there. It was when Mama was still alive, and I received a number of invitations to join the party there. Mr Stapleton gave every indication of being interested in me, but one day he called at the house whilst I was out, and Father sent him away.'

'How did he manage that?' Margaret asked her curiously.

'He said that Mr Stapleton beat a hasty retreat when he discovered that I had no portion,' Florence said matter-of-factly. 'But I cannot help wondering whether Father just frightened him off.'

'Don't you think that it was rather poor spirited of him — of Mr Stapleton, I mean

— just to go off like that?' Margaret ventured.

Florence shrugged. 'He was very young, I suppose. And when all is said and done, it wasn't exactly a great romance between us.'

'He certainly seemed very pleased to see you again,' said Margaret.

'Yes he did, didn't he?' answered Florence with a smile.

★   ★   ★

Braintree and Stapleton walked for a short time in silence, which the earl broke by asking the other man where he was staying.

'At the White Hart,' replied Stapleton. 'It seems very tolerable.'

'It has a good name,' agreed Braintree. 'Was it a complete surprise to see Lady Le Grey?'

'Yes, and a very pleasant one; especially when I found out that she was still free.'

'It is perhaps a little too soon to be talking of her freedom when her widowhood is of so recent a date,' answered Braintree in disapproving tones.

'Yes indeed,' agreed Stapleton. 'But we knew one another many years ago, and I had hopes even then.' He paused briefly. 'She seems to be more prosperous than she was then. I am glad of it for her sake.'

'All her friends must be glad of her prosperity, I believe,' replied the earl in neutral tones. The next time they spoke, it was concerning the Bath scene.

8

The following day, it became clear that Mr Stapleton did not intend to let the grass grow under his feet. When they arrived at the Pump Room, he was already there, and came striding towards them, looking very handsome but, at the same time, very manly. In her mind Florence contrasted his restrained appearance favourably with her memories of the dandified Sir Vittorio. He had aged well. His shoulders had broadened, his face was a little more tanned than when she had first met him, and he had an air of easy assurance that was very attractive.

'Good morning, ladies,' he said, bowing with simple grace. 'I trust you are well today.'

'Very well, thank you,' replied Florence. 'I hope that you are too. Did you sleep well? Are your lodgings comfortable?'

'Yes, thank you. I am staying at the White Hart and am very pleased with it. Lord Braintree walked back with me. He seems a most amiable man.'

Margaret positively glowed. 'He has been all kindness to us,' she replied. 'It is very good of him to help us, especially when he has his elderly mother to think about.'

At that moment, Lord Braintree approached them with the happy tidings that his mother was feeling much better. 'I need have no qualms about leaving her when we go to Wells, if she continues to make such good progress,' he said.

After this, it seemed perfectly natural to ask Mr Stapleton if he would like to go with them to Wells on Thursday. He looked regretful. 'I am afraid that I cannot put off my business for so long,' he explained. 'But I will hope to return soon. Bath seems such a delightful place that I shall be very sorry not to get to know it better.' By the way that he smiled at Florence, she understood that he was not talking about bricks and mortar.

'Do you have a family requiring your attention, Mr Stapleton?' The ladies smiled discreetly at one another, for Lord Braintree had asked the very question that they had been too shy to put to him.

'No one who depends upon me,' answered Stapleton. 'I am a widower, and my parents are both dead. I'm rather alone in the world, I'm afraid.'

'Then you will be all the more pleased to rejoin conversable friends when business permits,' suggested the earl.

'Indeed I shall.'

Although the earlier part of the week was marred by rain, which made any but the briefest of expeditions impossible, Thursday morning dawned bright and clear for the visit to Wells. The party was to be just Florence, Margaret and Lord Braintree. His lordship was always very kindly and gentle in his manner towards Florence, and she could only suppose that his concern for her recently widowed state meant that he considered the invitation of an unknown gentleman might be distressing to her. Florence did not mind. Her only anxiety was lest she should prevent Lord Braintree and Margaret from furthering an acquaintance that was clearly so pleasant for both of them.

They put on warm outdoor clothing for the day, though fine, was cold. Lord Braintree had thoughtfully made sure that rugs were provided, so they were sure of a comfortable drive. They were just leaving the house when the earl said, 'By George, there's a lucky chance! I'll ask him to join us.'

Florence glanced along the street, her spirits rising at the thought that Stapleton must have returned unexpectedly, but to her dismay, the man whom Lord Braintree had spotted was a far more elaborately dressed gentleman, swathed in a swirling greatcoat of dashing cut and sporting an ebony cane. In short, it was the one man she had hoped never to see again — Sir Vittorio Le Grey.

It very much surprised her to hear the earl sound so enthusiastic and see him approach the other man so eagerly. Although she was hoping against hope that the offer would be refused, she was not really surprised when the two men drew near and the baronet said '*Bon giorno, signore*! How fortunate I am not to miss you! Braintree here has kindly invited me to join you; that is, if I am not in the way?'

Florence would have liked to have said yes you are, very much. Unfortunately, common courtesy made this impossible, so after glancing at Margaret, she said, 'You are very welcome, sir, but perhaps Lord Braintree has not made it plain that we are to be away for the whole day. You might possibly have made other arrangements.'

He smiled and spread his hands, which were encased in the finest of pale-grey kid gloves. 'I have no other plans. In fact, I was on my way to visit you, and can think of no better way to spend the day than sightseeing and conversing with my charming kins-woman.'

'Then the matter is settled,' said Braintree beaming. 'Let us be on our way. This is the first fine day we've had this week and we don't want to waste it.'

Florence glanced at her supposed kinsman, half expecting him to say something challenging about her identity or their relationship, but instead, he made a bland remark about the state of the London road. Lord Braintree then made a similarly neutral comment of his own, and they were soon conversing easily.

'Is this your first visit to England, sir?' asked the earl, as they travelled.

'My first as a man, but I spent a little time here when I was a boy,' the baronet replied.

'The chilly winds of England must have come as something of a shock,' Margaret observed.

'They are not as cold as the winds of Russia, I think,' responded Vittorio.

'You have been to Russia!' exclaimed Florence involuntarily.

He smiled at her as if they shared a secret. 'I have been to many places,' he answered. 'I suppose you could call me a . . . ' He furrowed his brow in thought, and Florence could remember him doing the same thing on another occasion. He's going to say something shocking, she decided. Vittorio's brow cleared. 'An adventurer!' he exclaimed. 'That is the word, is it not?'

The earl smiled and shook his head. 'It

118

sounds a fine word, but it carries a wrong impression,' he said. 'It implies someone who behaves in a way that is not always moral or creditable. To say that you were well-travelled would be better; or that you had travelled extensively, perhaps.'

'Thank you; that is helpful,' said the baronet with his charming smile. 'I should hate' — he glanced at Florence briefly — 'hate to say anything that might cause offence.' Florence decided privately that she would take that particular remark with a pinch of salt.

'Your English is very fluent, sir,' said the earl.

'Thank you. I had an excellent tutor. Forgive me, I hardly dare ask for fear of causing offence again, but would it be in order for me to invite you to call me Vittorio?'

'I should be honoured,' replied the earl, inclining his head. 'And you must call me George.'

'Have you, also, travelled extensively?' Vittorio asked.

'As a young man, I made the Grand Tour,' the earl admitted. 'But I have not travelled since. I have had my mother to think about. But we must be not talking about our travels. We will bore the ladies.'

'Not at all,' said Florence. 'I have led a very

dull life and would be glad to have my mind opened to a different world.'

'I cannot believe that it was as dull as you say,' said Le Grey, with a challenging expression in his eye.

'You would be surprised,' she answered, not allowing her gaze to drop from his. 'But tell us something about your own adventures. Have you visited Florence? Have you seen the Duomo, and the Battisterio?'

The baronet smiled. 'Yes, I have seen them. Also the Uffizi.'

'What an experience it must be to be able to wander round and look at all those wonderful pictures!' exclaimed Florence.

'It would be an especially piquant experience for you to go there, as you are named after the place,' remarked Lord Braintree.

'Of course,' murmured Sir Vittorio. 'Lady Firenza Le Grey.'

'Have you been to Rome, sir?' said Margaret quickly, seeing that her friend was blushing. 'My husband used to tell me that it was very fine.'

Sir Vittorio seemed quite happy to talk to them about his travels and, as Lord Braintree also had experiences to contribute, the journey passed very pleasantly. It went much against the grain, but Florence was forced to admit that she found the baronet's stories fascinating. She had always enjoyed looking at Miss Le Grey's books of fine plates, but it was not the same as hearing about such places from someone who had really been, especially when the stories were recounted with that accent which gave them more than a hint of the exotic.

Upon their arrival in Wells, Lord Braintree suggested that they might like to look around the cathedral first. 'You will be wanting to see the mechanical horsemen, I daresay.' The party all looked to him for enlightenment, but he smiled and shook his head. 'You will have to seek out that delight for yourself. But I will point out to you the man with toothache if you like.'

The ladies were quite relieved to discover that the latter was a piece of carving rather than a real sufferer of the earl's acquaintance, and after laughing at the trick that he had played upon them, they split into pairs, promising to meet up later.

If the urbane facade that Vittorio had worn during the journey had lulled Florence into thinking that he had decided to accept her at face value, she was soon to be rudely awakened. 'And now, *signora*,' he said menacingly, as soon as the others had gone, 'you have played me for a fool for quite long enough. You have avoided me, and when you could not do that you have turned the subject. Well, no more. You will tell me who you are, and you will tell me now.'

Deciding that attack was the best form of defence she tossed her head and said, 'I cannot think why you should suppose that you can demand explanations from me, *signor*.'

'You cannot? When I arrive in Bath and find that you are using my name?'

'I am using it with permission,' she said swiftly; then could have bitten her tongue out for being so indiscreet.

He pounced on her words. 'Aha!' he exclaimed.

'It is no good to cry *aha* like that as if you were performing on the stage,' Florence retorted, hurrying to retrieve her position. 'I mean that I have the permission that comes from having acquired it honourably. I doubt if the same can be said for you.' He opened his mouth in order to reply, but the appearance of an elderly clergyman halted their conversation for the moment.

'Come,' he said, catching hold of her by the arm, and escorting her up the worn steps into the chapter house. This portion of the cathedral had been completed in 1319, and was reputed to be one of the most beautiful chapter houses in England, with its stained glass windows, and magnificent central pillar. Regrettably, however, both occupants were too preoccupied to notice its beauties. There was no one else there, and suddenly Florence became conscious of her vulnerability. 'You speak of the stage,' he went on, 'and rightly so in my opinion, for you are undoubtedly putting on some kind of performance for those around you. It might fool them, but it does not fool me.'

'How dare you imply that I am some kind of actress?' Florence stormed, drawing herself up to her full height.

'I did not imply it, I stated it openly,' was his outrageous reply. 'You are wantonly deceiving those around you. I do not know why, but I shall find out. How did Braintree describe an adventurer? Someone behaving in an immoral and discreditable way, was it not? You, *signora*, are an adventuress.'

Florence took a deep breath. 'You have no justification in saying so,' she said indignantly, forgetting that just recently she had enjoyed thinking of herself as that very thing. 'I have come to Bath openly, accompanied by my companion, Mrs Bridge, a lady of unimpeachable respectability. You, on the other hand, have appeared from nowhere, your antecedents are doubtful, and you have no one to vouch for you. If anyone is an adventurer, it is you!' She made as if to leave the chapter house. 'I have it on the best authority that your name has died out, *signor* — if you are a *signor* at all. I suspect that that accent is assumed, and that you hail from some back slum in London and have learned to live by your wits. Threaten me again, and I shall denounce you as a liar and a fraud.'

He caught hold of her, pulled her back into the chapter house and pushed her against the wall. He looked down at her, his face a mask of fury, his eyes narrowed to slits. 'The best authority!' he snarled. 'Whose?' When she was silent, he shook her hard. 'Tell me, or by God you will find that no boy from the slums can be half so ruthless as I.'

Florence was very frightened, but she could not give him Miss Le Grey's name. He had proved during the past few moments that he had a violent streak. What if he should pursue the old lady with violence? Such treatment would mean the death of her. 'I will not say,' she panted. 'Believe me, *signor*, I can be every bit as determined as yourself. And by the way, I would be grateful if you would decide what it is you want.'

'What I want?'

'One moment you call yourself my kinsman; then the next time we meet, you upbraid me for confirming the relationship. Upon my soul, sir, I think you had better make up your mind.'

'Ah!' His expression relaxed, and a slow smile spread across his features, but his hold upon her did not slacken by so much as the tiniest fraction. 'Perhaps we are both adventurers.'

Florence thought about the tedium of her existence in Howton, the poverty, the cold and the hardship, and her longing for a different life. She thought about the plans that she had made to assume another identity, just for the sake of adventure. 'I suppose I am — in a way,' she conceded, in a small voice.

He released her then, but stood with his elbow resting against the wall, his head leaning casually against his hand. If she wanted to leave the chapter house, she would have to walk round him. 'Then I have a proposition for you,' he said. 'We, as fellow adventurers, will support one another's stories. I will vouch for you, if you will vouch for me. Then we may both be easy.'

'If I don't agree — ' Florence began.

'If you don't agree, I shall become very angry again, and I don't think you would like that, would you?' He was silent for a moment. Then he straightened, and took hold of her shoulders again. 'Think about it. I'll come and see you tomorrow for your decision. But I think you will agree. After all,' he went on, taking his left hand from her shoulder to encircle her waist, and lifting her chin with his right, 'we adventurers are essentially practical — as well as being discreditable and immoral.' Then he leaned closer, and for the very first time, Florence experienced the feel of a man's lips pressed to hers.

His kiss only lasted for a few seconds, but in that time, it became clear to Florence that he knew what he was doing. She might sometimes think of herself as an adventurer, but he was the real thing, and his experience far outstripped hers. Dangerous seducers must, she thought, be engaging, and here was the proof, for the feeling of his mouth moving against hers was entirely seductive. Much later, she was to ask herself impatiently why she had not struggled. Now, as it was happening, it did not occur to her to do so.

Eventually he drew back, looking down with an expression that was half satisfied, half puzzled. '*Bellissima*,' he sighed. '*Bellissima Firenza*.' He kissed her once more, briefly, before saying, 'Now come, my dear. We must not linger here any longer. Braintree will be asking us about this cathedral and its beauties and we will not be able to answer.'

Florence stared at him, infuriated that he should speak as if she was as much to blame for their remaining in the chapter house as was he. 'You speak as if *I* were responsible for our . . . our ─ '

'Dalliance?' suggested the baronet. 'You see, Cousin, it can sometimes be *I* who can find the right word for *you*.'

'You . . . you . . . ' she stuttered. Beyond speech, she pulled away from him and began to descend the stairs at speed. Unfortunately, however, their unevenness was almost her undoing, for in her haste, she lost her footing, and would have fallen, had not the baronet swiftly caught hold of her with one arm about her waist and held her firmly. She glanced up at him, a startled expression on her face, as it occurred to her that those elaborate, dandified coats actually concealed some rather powerful muscles.

'Calm yourself, *signora*,' he said, smiling down at her. 'I but sought to tease you a little. Come then; and take a little more care this time.' He held out his arm, and after a moment's hesitation, she took it.

'Thank you,' she said in subdued tones.

They found their fellow travellers standing and gazing up at the wall; as they approached, the hour struck, and the

127

mechanical clock whirred into life. Florence gazed entranced as the little horsemen galloped round. 'How charming!' she declared, when the display had finished.

Vittorio smiled down at her indulgently, his eyes glittering. 'One of these days, Cousin, I will take you travelling, and show you sights even more remarkable than that.' She looked up at him, startled. What could he mean? Then she realized that his gaze was fixed upon her mouth and suddenly she started to tremble.

'Have you had your fill of looking round in here?' asked Lord Braintree. 'I think we should adjourn to the Crown, now, and have luncheon. Then this afternoon we can explore a little more.'

Both ladies agreed that they had seen enough and were ready for refreshment. They began to depart, but before they left the cathedral, Vittorio, with a murmured word of apology, took a few steps up the nave, bent his knee to the ground and crossed himself.

As they walked the short distance to the Crown, Florence asked him, 'Are you a Roman Catholic?'

'No, but my mother was,' he replied. 'I like to show respect.'

Except to me, she added silently.

The luncheon at the Crown proved to be a

very satisfying one, and the prospect of an afternoon nap in preference to another walk seemed attractive to more than one of the party. But eventually they all set out again, this time looking around the ancient town, entering the cathedral precinct once more and hunting for the fresh-water spring after which the city was named. To Florence's relief, the party kept together. She thought that Margaret seemed rather quiet, but when she found the opportunity to ask her, in an undertone, if she was feeling all right, her companion quickly said yes. 'It is just that the cathedral was so very cold,' she whispered. 'I am not used to places being cold any more.' Florence smiled in sympathy, but reflected that the embarrassment of the encounter in the chaper house had resulted in her being uncomfortably hot, rather than anything else.

Margaret Bridge looked at Florence. She would very much have liked to confide in her, but felt reluctant to burden her with anything else. She had come to Bath largely out of loyalty to her friend, but partly from a desire to have a complete change of scene. She was very happy at Tall Chimneys, and from correspondence with two friends who were also governesses, she knew how fortunate she was to have found such a considerate employer. But she could not forget that for her, life had once been very different.

Born Margaret Hammond, the daughter of a gentleman farmer, she had met and fallen in love with Lieutenant Neil Bridge at a provincial assembly. Both families were happy with the match, and their engagement and marriage had duly followed. They were not blessed with children straight away, but Margaret had been thankful for that, since Neil was on active service, and it would have been hard for her to travel with him with a baby to consider. Babies could come later; but there never was a later for them, because Neil was killed in action soon after gaining his captaincy. The money that he left her was sufficient to form a small nest egg for emergencies, but was not enough to live on, and neither Margaret's family, nor Neil's family was sufficiently well-off to support the demands of another person. A recommendation at just the right time had brought her the post at Tall Chimneys, and careful saving from a generous salary meant that she had been able to add to her nest egg and provide for a comfortable old age.

But to one who had willingly followed the drum, life in the Chancery household was not very exciting, and she had seized the chance of coming to Bath with Florence. She had looked upon it as an interlude and she had not expected to fall in love again. Then she had met Lord Braintree, and all her expectations were suddenly different.

At first she had thought that the earl was interested in the fascinating 'Lady Le Grey'. Soon, however, it became clear that his lordship's interest lay in another direction, but Margaret was very careful not to allow her hopes to be awakened too soon. She had heard of too many governesses and companions who had become the target of bored noblemen. Lord Braintree, stranded in Bath with his elderly mother, could quite easily be one of those.

As time passed, however, this did not seem to be the case. Far from wanting to flirt with her, he seemed ready to converse on a number of subjects, and he listened to her views with genuine interest. In the cathedral, he had pointed out several features to her, including the famous scissor arches, and had spoken about the building with real understanding. She was horrified when she realized that his respect and intelligent conversation were beginning to irritate her, and made renewed efforts to listen to him, commenting herself on articles with military connections with particular enthusiasm. It was to no avail. She wanted some more positive demonstration of his interest in her as a woman, and when Florence had emerged from the chapter house with Sir Vittorio, looking very slightly rumpled, she could have screamed with vexation. Of course, she did not want Lord Braintree to manhandle her in some dark corner of Wells Cathedral, but it would have been flattering if she had felt that he had wanted to.

While they were strolling about the town in the afternoon, Margaret said to the earl, 'Have you ever brought your mother here?'

He shook his head. 'She has been, but some years ago, when my father was alive. I have hopes that she may be able to travel a little more in the spring.' He glanced sideways at her. 'She is thinking about engaging a companion,' he went on. 'I very much hope that she will be able to find someone congenial.'

'Yes indeed,' agreed Margaret, in a colourless tone. So that was the reason for all his interest in her! He had been making sure that she was a suitable person to be his mother's companion! She could have kicked herself for being such a fool. It was at that point that she decided she must return to the Chancerys as soon as Florence could spare her.

As they travelled back, Lord Braintree said

to all of them, but looking pointedly at Margaret, 'I trust that you have all had an agreeable day.'

Everyone remarked that they had, but Margaret could not help adding waspishly, 'You'll have to tell your mother all about it.'

The earl looked surprised, but said merely, 'You may be sure that I shall do so.'

On their arrival back in Laura Place, Florence invited both men inside, but Lord Braintree declined. 'I must make sure that my mother is well,' he said, colouring a little as he glanced at Margaret's face. After thanking him again for a pleasant day, the three remaining companions went inside, and Florence offered Vittorio a glass of wine.

'Thank you, that would be very pleasant,' he answered.

'And for you, Margaret?' asked Florence.

Margaret shook her head. 'I have a little headache, I think, from the motion of the carriage, so if you don't mind I shall go and lie down for a short time.'

Florence looked concerned. 'I didn't think you seemed your usual self,' she remarked. 'Shall I ask someone to bring you a cup of tea?'

'Thank you; perhaps in half an hour,' replied Margaret, leaving the room at the same time as Stevens entered it with the wine.

'You may leave it there. I will pour,' said Vittorio in what Florence felt was an irritatingly proprietorial manner. As soon as the door had closed behind the butler, Vittorio said, 'Well,' in a very drawn-out, deliberate way and strolled across the room towards her, grinning.

'You look like a cat,' she said, without thinking about what she was saying.

'Then you must be the mouse,' he replied, hooking his fingers into the bodice of her gown, and pulling her towards him. 'Well, *signora* adventuress, what are you going to do now?'

'Slap your face?' she suggested, preparing to suit her action to her words.

'I think not,' he replied, catching hold of her wrist with his left hand whilst keeping the fingers of his right hooked into her bodice.

'Your effrontery knows no bounds,' she declared, whilst trying without success to detach his fingers from her gown. 'Are you so conceited that you imagine yourself to be irresistible to all women?'

'Only to you, *cara*,' he breathed and, as he pulled her closer, she realized that once more he intended to kiss her.

'I shall scream,' she warned.

With a jerk he pulled her against him, his arms around her now, his eyes glittering. 'I shall stop your mouth,' he declared. But before he could do so, there was the sound of the door knob turning, and they sprang apart. Vittorio walked over to where the wine had been placed, and began to pour it out, whilst Florence sat down hurriedly on a nearby chair, telling herself crossly that of course she wasn't disappointed at the interruption.

Stevens entered the room and announced, 'Mr Stapleton is here, my lady.'

'Gilbert!' exclaimed Florence, getting up in relief, and giving her visitor both her hands. 'When did you return to Bath?'

He smiled and lifted first one then the other to his lips. 'Just this morning,' he replied. 'But had I known that I would receive such a kind welcome, doubtless I would have returned sooner.'

Florence smiled, but coloured. She was conscious that her relief at having that embarrassing scene with Vittorio interrupted had caused her to greet her visitor with rather more familiarity than their present relationship warranted. Thoughts about Vittorio reminded her of the necessary courtesies. 'You are very kind,' she said. 'But allow me to present you to my . . . my kinsman by

135

marriage.' She turned to Vittorio. 'This is Mr Gilbert Stapleton, an old acquaintance of mine. Mr Stapleton, this is Sir Vittorio Le Grey.'

The two men bowed, and once again, Florence could not help contrasting the manly courtesy of Mr Stapleton with the dandified grace of the baronet. 'Your servant, *signor*,' said Sir Vittorio. 'It is a pleasure to me to meet my cousin's acquaintances.'

'And for me, sir, it is a pleasure to meet her relative,' replied Mr Stapleton politely. 'Have you known one another for long, or did you meet for the first time in Bath?'

'We were delighted to meet here for the first time, were we not, my dear Firenza?' smiled Vittorio. 'Both of us believed ourselves to be almost alone in the world, but received a most happy surprise. May I offer you a glass of wine?'

Stapleton inclined his head. 'Thank you. Do you intend to make a long stay in Bath, sir?'

'My plans are uncertain. But tell me, Mr Stapleforth, for how long have you been acquainted with my cousin?'

'Stapleton,' corrected that gentleman, putting up his chin a little as if the very question were an impertinence. 'For some time, sir,' he said.

Florence decided that it was about time

that she played a part in this conversation. 'We have known one another for eight years,' she said. 'Mr Stapleton came to stay with Mr and Mrs Chancery, and we met at their house.'

'How charming and convenient,' remarked Vittorio.

'Convenient? For whom?' enquired Stapleton, in a tone that was just the right side of belligerent.

'Why, for everyone,' replied Vittorio, smiling warmly. 'You must forgive my seeming impertinence,' he went on. 'The role of elder male relative is strange to me, so you must not blame me for feeling protective.'

'Nonsense,' declared Florence. 'There is no need for you to feel any such thing. Mr Stapleton and I have known one another for a long time.'

'But you see, I never met him before today,' remarked Vittorio gently. Stapleton put down his glass with a snap, but before he could say anything, the baronet spoke again. 'Firenza, you must forgive me if I leave you now, but I have some important correspondence to deal with which will not wait.' He put down his glass, crossed to where Florence was standing, took her hand and kissed it, and then, more lingeringly, her cheek. 'Thank you for today,' he murmured. Unseen by Stapleton, once more the baronet's gaze rested on her mouth. 'The joys of family life are new to me, and I shall treasure the pleasant memories that your kindness has given me.' He bowed to Stapleton with a flourish. 'Your servant, sir,' he declared. 'Doubtless we shall meet again.'

Stapleton bowed in response, but after Vittorio had gone he said scornfully, 'What a mountebank! Forgive me, my lady, but I cannot think you fortunate in your new relation. Are you quite certain he is genuine?'

Florence stared at him. She could have replied that she was not at all sure how genuine the baronet might be, but then, she herself was masquerading as what she was not. There was only one way to stop Stapleton's questions. 'You forget yourself, sir,' she said with dignity. 'I appreciate your concern, but you take too much upon yourself.'

'I beg your pardon,' he said in mortified tones, colouring a little. 'I did not mean to offend you.' Striving for a lighter tone, he added, 'You must acknowledge that he is an original.'

Florence laughed briefly. 'Oh yes, he is that,' she agreed.

'How closely is he related to you?' he asked her.

She shrugged. 'As to that, we are still trying to establish it ourselves,' she said evasively.

'He called you cousin,' Mr Stapleton persisted. 'Would that be a cousin of your late husband?'

Florence put her hand to her head. 'Would you mind very much if we left this subject?' she said. 'It is rather painful to me, you understand.'

'Of course,' he assured her solicitously. 'You have only been widowed for a brief time.' He paused. 'May I ask why your cousin called you Firenza?'

'It is a form of my name in Italian,' Florence replied. 'My . . . my husband liked it, and I have adopted it in his memory. But tell me, Mr Stapleton, for how long do you intend to remain in Bath this time?'

He smiled down at her. 'Like those of your cousin, my plans are uncertain,' he replied. 'I have one ambition, however.'

'And what might that be, sir?' Florence asked him, enjoying this mild flirtation.

'I am hoping to remain at least until you consent to call me Gilbert once more,' he answered.

'I cannot say how long that may be,' she murmured.

'In that case, ma'am, you leave me with mixed feelings,' he replied. 'If I say that I hope that it may be soon, you will think that I want to leave you, and that, I can assure you, is very far from being the case.'

Florence lowered her eyes modestly, but before she could reply, the door opened and Margaret came in. 'I was feeling so much better that I decided to come downstairs. But I will leave if I am interrupting you.'

'Not at all,' replied Florence. 'Come and have a glass of wine, or ring for tea, if you would prefer it.'

'I think I would,' answered Margaret.

'Then allow me,' said Stapleton, walking over to the bell. 'But for now, I must take my leave. Are you intending to go to the concert at the Lower Rooms this evening? May I escort you, if so?'

Florence glanced at Margaret. 'We had not yet decided,' she replied. 'May I send a messenger to your hotel when we know what we are doing?'

He smiled. 'By all means,' he replied, taking up her hand and bowing over it. 'But whatever you decide, be sure that I will call again soon.' He bowed to Margaret, this time more formally, and left them, ushered out by Stevens who had just come to take the order for tea.

'What a day!' exclaimed Florence, sinking into a chair after he had gone. 'First, I am cornered in the chapter house by the wicked Italian and . . . well, never mind that,' she went on hastily. 'Now Gilbert Stapleton seems bent on attaching me.' She thought for a moment, then gave a gurgle of laughter. 'It's certainly one in the eye for Father. He never believed I could attach anyone at all.'

'Fee!' exclaimed Margaret. 'I know you did not get on well, but he is barely in his grave.'

'Yes, but you know what he was like,' Florence retorted. 'Whilst I was alive, I gave him all my duty, but I could not give more.'

'Exactly,' answered Margaret, as she sat down opposite her friend. 'Think how anyone else might feel who had heard you just then. You should hold his memory in respect, or at least give the appearance of it, for form's sake.'

Florence sighed. 'Yes, you are right,' she agreed. 'But privately, between the two of us, acknowledge that there is something in what I say.'

Margaret smiled, but her smile was rather forced, and she soon turned her head away.

'Margaret, what is it? Has something happened to distress you?' Florence asked quickly.

'Not to distress me precisely, but . . . ' She looked up from pleating her handkerchief on her knee. 'Fee, I think it is time I left you and went back to Tall Chimneys.'

9

'This is very sudden,' said Florence carefully. 'Was there a communication from Mrs Chancery when you came back?'

Margaret shook her head. 'No; but I have been thinking. Mrs Chancery has been very good to me, to both of us, and I must not trade upon her good nature. It would be quite unfair.'

At this moment, Stevens came in with tea, and the conversation could not resume until he had left. Whilst he was setting the tray down, Florence began to take in these unwelcome tidings. Of course, she had always known that Margaret's residence with her was only temporary, but during the time that they had spent together, she had lost sight of that fact. When she considered that their friendship had had its roots in little more than the few minutes that they had been able to converse together after church every week, it was remarkable that they had turned out to be so compatible when living together in the same house. Now, it was difficult to imagine what life would be like once Margaret had gone.

Furthermore, a closer acquaintance with Bath society had revealed to her that it would be considered rather fast of her to live alone, even as a widow. The obvious solution would be to find another companion, but where would she find anyone as congenial as Margaret?

She knew that she must not put any pressure upon her, however, so she merely said, 'I will miss you very much, of course, but I quite understand your feelings. When do you think you ought to go?'

'As soon as possible,' said Margaret in subdued tones.

'As soon as possible!' exclaimed Florence, in her surprise quite forgetting her resolution not to put any pressure upon her friend. 'Margaret, there is something else that you have not told me.' She narrowed her eyes suspiciously. 'Did Lord Braintree say anything to upset you today?'

'To upset me? Good heavens, no,' Margaret replied, her airy tone completely unconvincing. 'He is the most gentlemanlike of men. So considerate and thoughtful; so kind to his mother.'

'Yes, well — ' Florence began, but Margaret interrupted her.

'He wants a companion for his mother, Fee. A companion!'

'I see,' exclaimed Florence with sudden understanding. 'Did he say specifically that that was what he wanted you to do?'

'Not in so many words, but his meaning was quite plain. And I . . . ' Her voice trembled a little. 'I was hoping that . . . ' She dabbed her handkerchief to her eyes.

'Oh, Margaret!' murmured Florence, putting an arm around her friend's shoulders. 'So was I! But who knows?' she went on in a more cheerful tone. 'Perhaps if you do leave, Braintree will find that he misses you after all; for your own sake, not just for his mother.'

'Perhaps,' Margaret answered, not sounding very hopeful. 'But what about you, Fee? I hate to leave you in the lurch like this.'

'Don't worry about me,' Florence replied, more confidently than she was feeling. 'You have seen how our acquaintance in Bath has grown in a short time. One of our new friends — Lady Trimm, perhaps — might know of someone who will oblige me. And if not,' she went on, trying to think of something to divert Margaret's mind, 'I am sure that the wicked Italian would be very happy to persuade me into an illicit relationship.'

'Fee!' exclaimed Margaret. 'How could you!'

'It's true,' replied Florence. 'When we were in the chapter house, he said — and did

145

— some very wicked things.' And despite her rallying tone, she blushed at the memory of his mouth on hers.

'I'm surprised a thunderbolt did not fall upon his head, then,' answered Margaret virtuously. 'Fee, how can I be happy leaving you alone when you are being threatened by such a man?'

'Oh, don't worry,' replied Florence, feeling an absurd desire to defend the man whom she had just been vilifying. 'He doesn't frighten me; I'm sure that something will happen to help us.'

Neither of them felt like going to the concert, so they dined alone together, but although they both made an effort to converse politely, neither of them was concentrating fully on what was being said, which sometimes meant that they answered one another entirely at random. After this had happened for the fourth time, and Florence had suddenly realized that in answer to Margaret's question about whether the theatre had been open for very long, she had replied 'I expect so, as long as it remains fine', she sprang up from the table.

'This is absurd, Margaret,' she said decisively. 'Look at us! We are warm, comfortable, we have our good health and we have just been well fed. Why are we being so foolish?'

Margaret stared at her for a moment, then stood up as well. 'You are quite right,' she agreed. 'Let's find something with which to entertain ourselves.'

A pack of cards was found at the back of a drawer, and they sat down at the table in their cosy saloon to play for enormous but quite imaginary stakes. By the end of the evening they were feeling much more cheerful. 'Though why I should be when I owe you something in the region of fifty thousand pounds, I cannot imagine,' Margaret declared.

'You can pay it in easy instalments,' Florence conceded handsomely. 'Margaret, I have been thinking, would you consider leaving Mrs Chancery permanently, and coming to be my companion? We have proved to be very congenial, have we not, and I cannot imagine liking anyone better.' Seeing that Margaret was about to speak, Florence held up her hand and went on, 'I can understand that you might not want to live in Bath, and I'm not sure that I do, either, after all that has happened here. In the summer, I think I might go to the sea. Then, perhaps, I might look about me for a house to buy, for I don't want to live in rented accommodation all my life.'

'I'm very tempted by your offer,' said Margaret, smiling gratefully. 'But may I think about it for a little while, and see how I feel when I am back with Mrs Chancery? Besides, even if I do leave her, I ought to give her notice so that she will be able to find someone else. Not that I suppose she would worry too much,' she added. 'I don't think she's nearly so concerned about those girls' education as I am. Anyway,' she added, 'has it occurred to you that you might not need a companion at all? Before you ask, I *don't* mean any vulgar suggestions made by the wicked Italian. Mr Stapleton seems to me to be very interested in you, and I am sure that any offer that he might make would be an honourable one.'

'Perhaps,' agreed Florence. 'But I'm not counting on it.'

That night, Florence found it hard to get to sleep straight away. It would be a blow to lose Margaret, and not just because they were good friends. It would also be because Margaret had been in on the planning stage when she, Florence, had decided to assume a new identity. Would she be able to let another person in on the secret with confidence, or would she have to rely upon herself not to make a mistake, even within the confines of her own home? Alternatively, would she be obliged to leave Bath, and either return regretfully to being Miss Browne, spinster, or continue to be Lady Le Grey and rely on Sir Vittorio's lacking either the energy or the desire to pursue her? It was a problem that would need a good deal of thought before it could be resolved.

The following morning as they entered the Pump Room, Florence found herself looking at those around in a new way. Lord Braintree, who had previously seemed to be a considerate, thoughtful gentleman, and a loving son, now appeared to her to be tied to his mother's apron strings. Instead of looking upon Lady Trimm as simply a pleasant acquaintance, she started wondering whether that lady would know anyone who might make her a suitable companion after Margaret had gone. Margaret, she noticed, carefully avoided Lord Braintree, merely bowing politely when he came to speak to them, but soon making an excuse to go and converse with someone else. The earl looked a little taken aback, but he said nothing, and continued to speak with Florence about the pleasure that the previous day's outing had given him.

'No doubt your pleasure in such events would be all the greater if you could be sure that your mother was well cared for in your absence,' suggested Florence, hoping to find out more for Margaret's benefit.

'Indeed it would,' agreed the earl. 'In fact, I am hoping that I have found the very person. I was speaking to Mrs Bridge about it yesterday.'

'Yes, so she has told me,' Florence replied. Poor Margaret! So it was true; his only interest in her was as a potential companion for his mother.

'You will wonder why my mother is not provided for already in that respect,' the earl went on. 'But the fact of the matter is that my aunt, who has fulfilled that role until very recently, has married again, most unexpectedly, at the age of fifty-seven. Although all her friends and family must rejoice in her happiness, as indeed my mother does herself, it leaves us with something of a problem.'

'I can see that it does,' Florence answered, but in truth, her attention had been caught by the sight of two figures crossing the room and converging upon them from two different directions. One was Sir Vittorio, attired on this occasion in rich brown brocade, with a cream waistcoat, as usual looking as though he had stepped straight out of his dressing-room. The other, dressed stylishly in a walking dress of dark blue, was Florence's cousin — her *real* cousin — Mrs Waring.

'My dear cousin,' exclaimed Mrs Waring. 'What a pleasure it is to find you here! After hearing of your father's death, I went to seek you out, only to be told that you were here in Bath. But now I arrive, and learn that you have married and are Lady Le Grey.'

'Yes, that is correct,' Florence replied. 'Have you also been told that I am a widow?'

Mrs Waring's face took on a serious expression. 'I have. I am very sorry, my dear. Your marriage must have been tragically brief.'

'It was,' agreed Florence. 'So brief that I prefer not to speak of it. But now I must make you known to my cousin by marriage, Sir Vittorio Le Grey. Sir, this is my cousin, Mrs Waring.'

The two acknowledged one another politely but, it must be acknowledged, each had a measuring look in the eye.

'I count myself very fortunate, Firenza, for since you and I are related, it follows that I must also be related, albeit very distantly to Mrs Waring also,' smiled Vittorio. 'But for now, I will take myself off, for I can see that you will have much to discuss. Until later, Cousin.' So saying, he bowed with his usual grace and withdrew.

'My dear, what an original!' exclaimed Mrs

Waring. 'How well do you know him? Is he genuine?'

Remembering her conversation with Vittorio in Wells Cathedral, Florence said, 'Yes, quite genuine, as far as I know. But what brings you to Bath? Are you really here just to see me?'

'Just to see you,' Mrs Waring echoed, smiling at Florence, and Florence felt a warm glow as she thought about the concern shown by her new kinswoman. 'Shall we sit down, so that we may talk?'

They walked to the side of the room and sat down together. As soon as they were settled, Mrs Waring said, 'I gather that you must have written to inform me of your father's death, and also of your marriage?' Florence nodded, reflecting that she was answering truthfully to at least part of Mrs Waring's question. 'I received nothing from you,' Mrs Waring went on confidingly. 'I believe that some of these postmen are shockingly dishonest. But however it may be, I heard nothing until by chance I met an acquaintance in Town who had heard of your father's death. Then, of course, there was nothing for it but to hurry to Howton at once, to find out the truth of the matter. Your lawyer informed me that you had come to Bath and gave me the direction; so here I am, ready to give you what support I can.'

'That is very kind of you,' answered Florence, genuinely touched that this lady, whom she hardly knew, should have taken such trouble on her behalf. 'Has Mr Waring come with you?'

Mrs Waring looked regretful. 'No, he is not here,' she said. 'Business has taken him to the north of England. Oh, how I long to present the two of you to each other!'

Florence smiled sympathetically, but she could not in truth summon up a great deal of enthusiasm for meeting a gentleman to whom she was distantly related by marriage, and about whom she had heard very little.

At that point, she caught Margaret's eye and, beckoning her over, introduced the two women to one another. 'Have you left Mrs Chancery's employment permanently, or must you return?' Mrs Waring asked.

'I will be returning shortly,' Margaret replied.

'And you will be left alone?' enquired Mrs Waring of Florence.

'Only temporarily, I am sure,' Florence replied.

'Then, if I am not being presumptuous, may I suggest a solution?' said Mrs Waring diffidently. 'I have no commitments in Town at present, and am resolved to remain in Bath for a time. Would it be helpful to you if I were to come and reside with you? I have no wish to put myself forward, but it would seem to be an answer to your dilemma. If the idea does not appeal to you, of course, I can always remain in the hotel.'

'It is very kind of you to make such an offer,' answered Florence, feeling that no other response would really be polite. 'It sounds very well worth considering, but Mrs Bridge and I must discuss the matter between ourselves, as I am not sure what she has planned.'

'Of course,' answered Mrs Waring. Then, as if sensing that a change of subject was appropriate, she said, 'You must tell me all about what there is to see in Bath, for it is my first time of visiting the place, you know.' Florence was rather impressed than otherwise at Mrs Waring's manner of accepting the gentle rebuff offered to her, and so she readily gave a full description of all the entertainments that Bath had to offer.

'Of course, there are some entertainments which I cannot attend, because I am in mourning,' she concluded. 'But I still find plenty to do.' She paused briefly, then said, 'Pray come and dine with us this evening, and I will be able to tell you more.'

'Thank you,' replied Mrs Waring, smiling

warmly. 'I accept with pleasure.'

Soon after this, Margaret and Florence excused themselves, and returned to Laura Place. 'I am almost resolved to accept Mrs Waring's offer,' Florence told her companion as they walked. 'Do you think that I should?'

'It is hard for me to offer an unbiased opinion,' Margaret replied. 'After all, if you invite her to stay, then that will mean that I will be free to go back to Mrs Chancery straight away.'

'That is true,' Florence agreed. 'But try, if you can, to set that on one side and advise me as if your own wishes were not involved in the case.'

Margaret wrinkled her brow. 'That is difficult,' she said eventually, 'but I will try.' She was silent for a few moments, then said rather diffidently, 'I must confess that it concerns me a little that your cousin has only appeared after it has been revealed that you are a wealthy woman. And then, of course, she appeared at exactly the same time as the wicked Italian came into the Pump Room. Has it occurred to you that they might be in conspiracy together?'

'To what end?' Florence asked.

'Forgive me, but as I have said already, you are now a wealthy woman. It might be to their advantage to worm their way into your good graces.'

Florence thought for a moment or two. 'I cannot believe it,' she said eventually. 'The wicked Italian's behaviour has so far been designed to set me all on end if anything, not to find favour with me. And as for Mrs Waring, I cannot forget that she first offered friendship when I was living in my father's house and did not have a penny. No, their appearance in the Pump Room must have come about quite by accident.'

'There is one other thing that concerns me,' said Margaret carefully. 'Forgive me, but I understand that Mrs Waring sought out your lawyer. Why did she not speak to Mr Chancery? It argues an interest in your circumstances that I cannot like.'

By this time, they had reached the house in Laura Place and, as they entered the hall, Florence said, 'My mind is quite made up. I shall invite my cousin to come here for a short stay. I doubt whether I shall find her as congenial as you, but I can make it clear that it is only to be for a short time. I am not discounting all that you have said, but she can be as interested in my circumstances as she likes; it will not do her any good. She herself is married and will have her husband to tend to before long.' They entered the saloon, having surrendered their outdoor clothing to Stevens. 'Have you thought any further about coming to me eventually as my companion?' she asked, when they were settled by the fire. As always, the room was warm, by Florence's express orders.

'Yes I have, and I have almost decided to say yes,' answered Margaret. 'But I definitely do not want to live in Bath; at least, not permanently.'

'Agreed!' exclaimed Florence getting up to embrace her friend. 'So the sooner you go back to Mrs Chancery the better; for the sooner you go, the sooner you will return.'

That evening when Mrs Waring came for dinner, Florence told her of her decision. 'I am so pleased,' answered Mrs Waring, her faced wreathed in smiles. 'I have been accustomed for so long to thinking of myself as being without relations, that it will be very agreeable to get to know one another a little better.' These words so reminded Florence of all that she had been feeling that she was instantly conscious of a bond of sympathy between them.

That evening, the ladies chatted happily together. The only sour note struck was when Mrs Waring asked if Florence always kept the house so warm for she found it a little too hot, but when Florence assured her that warmth was very important to her, she uttered no further criticism. She did not even object when Casper sniffed around her ankles.

It was arranged that Margaret would leave the next day, and that Mrs Waring would move in later that afternoon.

It must be confessed that Florence and Margaret both shed tears as they parted. 'I have so much enjoyed our adventure,' Margaret said, as she got into the chaise which Florence had hired for her.

'But there will be more adventures to come,' Florence assured her. 'Give your notice to Mrs Chancery as soon as you arrive, then you will be able to come back as soon as may be.'

After she had waved Margaret off, Florence made her way back inside, feeling a very real sense of loss. Suddenly, the entrance hall seemed very lonely, so she was particularly glad when the next moment the doorbell rang, and Stevens opened it to reveal Mr Stapleton.

'You come in a very good hour,' Florence declared thankfully. 'I am feeling at a low ebb and badly need to be cheered up.'

'Then I am delighted that I have the privilege of being the one to do it,' he replied. 'Shall we go out for a walk around the shops, perhaps, and take in a different scene?'

'Gladly,' replied Florence. 'Give me but five minutes to put on some outdoor clothes.'

When she came back down the stairs, Stapleton was still in the hall, looking carefully at one of the pictures that was hanging there. He was dressed with neatness and propriety in leather breeches and top boots, with a warm-looking greatcoat over the top, and Florence felt that he cut a manly and imposing figure. He smiled warmly as he caught sight of her, and held out his arm as she reached the bottom of the steps. 'Shall we go?' he said. 'Every man will envy me today, I think.'

'For the warmth of your coat, no doubt,' Florence replied teasingly, but she could not help feeling pleased, for she knew that she was looking her best in a black coat that was cut to show her figure to advantage, and a bonnet that framed her face in a very flattering way.

Mr Stapleton laughed, but did not press home his compliment, and instead concentrated on talking about Bath, its pleasant situation and its many interesting amenities. 'It is a far cry from what you were used to in Howton, I am well aware,' he said eventually. 'Yours was not a happy existence, I fear.'

Florence was touched by his concern, but

unsettled by the raising of the topic. Her life with her father held nothing which she remembered with affection, and she wanted to put the whole episode behind her. She did not want to be rude, however, so she merely said, 'Yes, you are right. I am glad that it is in the past.'

'And yet there are some happy memories of that time,' he pursued. 'Eight years ago, for instance, when we first met. I shall never forget that day.' He paused, then went on, 'You were so different from all the other young ladies present.'

'Badly dressed, you mean,' Florence interjected.

'No,' he protested, laughing. 'I mean that you were shy and gentle, yet very intelligent. You captured my interest immediately.'

It was on the tip of Florence's tongue to reply that she had been just as interested in him, but she was wary of committing herself so soon. After all, they had only just met again after eight years in which he had shown no sign of pursuing her. So instead, she said, 'But you left very quickly.'

'I sought an interview with your father,' he said, his face flushing darkly. 'He told me that you had another attachment and sent me away.' He looked at her.

She gave a tiny gasp, for this was not at all

what her father had said to her, but she simply murmured, 'I don't suppose he was very civil.'

'No, he wasn't,' he answered shortly. 'When you first revealed that you had been married, I wondered whether perhaps you had formed an attachment to your late husband, even then.'

She made no answer to this, but simply said, 'And then you yourself got married.'

'Yes, but it meant nothing to me,' he hastened to say. Then, looking harassed, he added, 'That must make me sound like a scoundrel. What I meant to say was that since I could not have you, I had to make do with second best.'

Flattering though the tone of the conversation might have been, Florence was not entirely sorry when she saw Lady Trimm and her daughters coming towards them, for she felt that they had been straying into rather deep waters. She noticed how the two girls straightened as they caught sight of Mr Stapleton, and she was not surprised. He was certainly a fine figure of a man. He had met the Trimms on his previous visit to Bath, and whilst the girls were asking him if his business had prospered, Lady Trimm raised the subject of Mrs Bridge.

'Someone, I cannot remember who, informed

me that she has left you,' said her ladyship.

'Yes, that is correct,' answered Florence, reflecting that news spread just as quickly in the confined society that was Bath as it did in a small village. 'She was only ever with me on a temporary basis.'

'So how are you to manage?' asked Lady Trimm. 'You surely will not stay in Laura Place on your own?'

'By no means,' replied Florence. 'My cousin Mrs Waring has kindly offered to reside with me until I find someone else.'

'You are fortunate indeed in your relations,' commented Lady Trimm.

'Yes, very fortunate,' Florence murmured, unable to think of anything else to say.

'Sir Vittorio has certainly settled well into our English pastimes. Apparently he and Lord Braintree are gone out of town to attend some sporting fixture.'

'A sporting fixture?' exclaimed Florence, unable to imagine Sir Vittorio enjoying any kind of sport. 'Of what nature?'

Lady Trimm lowered her voice. 'A boxing match, I understand. Horrid, is it not? I cannot imagine what the gentlemen find to admire in it. They are to be out of town for several days, I believe.'

'It is very kind of Lord Braintree to take my . . . my cousin about a little,' said Florence. In her heart, she was certain that Lady Trimm must be mistaken. She could not imagine the baronet even expressing the slightest wish to observe such a violent sport.

In this supposition, however, she was quite in error, for the two gentlemen had set out early that day to go to Marlborough, where the boxing match was to take place. They travelled together in Lord Braintree's curricle.

'We'll leave in good time,' the earl had declared, 'since we want to get a good place at the ringside.'

The baronet was ready and waiting when his lordship drove round to the Christopher to collect him, and sprang athletically into the curricle without any assistance from the waiting groom. He was warmly dressed in a thick greatcoat in a shade of grey, with the edges piped in black and, as always, he looked just that shade more stylish than anyone else. 'Shall we go?' smiled the earl, and Vittorio nodded his assent.

The unexpected friendship had sprung up between them initially after Braintree had revealed that he had visited Italy whilst taking the Grand Tour in his youth. The conversations that they had had during the visit to Wells had cemented this friendship. Opinions on various sights, cities and art objects had been exchanged, and they had found themselves to be very much in accord. It had only taken the discovery by the earl that the baronet used a mixture of snuff that was much to his taste, and a similar discovery by Sir Vittorio that his lordship's palate was excellent, to assure the success of the friendship.

'It ain't too cold for you, I hope?' the earl asked as they left the city. 'No doubt it would be warmer in Italy just now.'

The baronet shrugged. 'It is colder here,' he agreed, 'but I think that my English blood must be responding to the land of its origin, for I find the air very invigorating.'

Braintree laughed. 'If you get too cold, you could always take a turn in the ring,' he suggested. 'That'd warm you up.'

Le Grey laughed in his turn. 'It wouldn't be the first time I had fought,' he replied surprisingly, 'although my preferred weapon is a sword rather than my fists.'

They travelled on for a while in companionable silence, until the earl said 'Would you like to take the ribbons for a spell?'

The baronet looked at him quizzically. 'How do you know that I will not overturn you?'

'Will you?'

Vittorio laughed. 'Hand them over, and

see,' he replied, and taking the reins, he proceeded to guide Lord Braintree's pair with expert hands.

Braintree sat back and after a few moments, he sighed. 'Everything you do, you do well,' he remarked. 'What I would not give to be able to impress the ladies!'

'Do you mean ladies, or lady?' asked Vittorio.

The earl darted a look at him sideways. 'You're devilish acute,' he answered, impressed. He paused for a moment, then said carefully, 'I beg that you won't take offence, but . . . '

'But what?'

The earl paused again. 'Look, Vittorio, you are something of a ladies' man, aren't you?'

The baronet burst out laughing. 'Now what on earth is that supposed to mean?' he asked.

'Well, they all seem to be attracted to you. You know just what to say which will please. I suppose I want to ask you, what is the trick?'

'Trick?'

'Yes. How do you do it?'

'My friend, there is no trick,' replied Vittorio. 'Of course certain things help, unquestionably; to be well dressed, for example; to be properly shaved; to bathe a little more frequently than some of your countrymen are wont to do; all these are pleasing to ladies.'

'And, to be tall, dark and devilish good-looking,' added the earl quickly, 'not to mention speaking with that accent; which, by the by, I have noted is far less noticeable today!'

The baronet grinned impishly. 'Yes, well, I admit that I do make it a little stronger at times; strictly between you and me, the occasional hesitation over words is largely assumed.'

'I thought it might be,' agreed the earl. 'But I think it's a little late for me to adopt any kind of accent; even if I did, the only one I could manage would be that of my native Yorkshire, which would hardly come across as romantically as yours, bah goom!'

Vittorio laughed again. 'I think you are probably right,' he agreed. 'But there is far more to attracting a woman than looks, you know. The most successful man at attracting women that I ever knew had few looks to speak of and only a modest fortune. He did it by listening to everything that a woman said with flattering attention. And he *really* listened, because later, he would be able to refer to something that she had said before. Women like to feel that they are being attended to, but then, I think that that is true of men as well.'

The earl nodded. 'That is what I have tried

to do,' he sighed. 'But of course the one woman that one wants to impress never is impressed, is she?'

The baronet smiled wryly. 'How true,' he replied.

* * *

Mrs Waring arrived later that afternoon, and at once announced herself to be delighted with the room that had been allotted to her. It was not the room that Margaret had had, for Florence wanted to keep that room free so that Margaret would be able to come and visit. But it was still a very attractive room, decorated in shades of green. 'This is charming,' Mrs Waring declared. 'Quite charming! I am so glad that I am able to come to your rescue in this way, my dear cousin. And of course, you have rescued me too, for I am no great lover of hotels.'

Florence left her cousin to settle in to her room, but they met later on, just before dinner. 'Such a delightful house,' said her cousin who, in honour of her first evening, had dressed in a handsome blue silk gown with rather a low neck. 'How did you come by it?'

'Mr Chancery came himself and made enquiries,' Florence replied.

'That was very good of him,' replied Mrs Waring. 'They were very good neighbours to you, were they not?'

'Yes indeed,' answered Florence, with feeling. 'No one could have been more kind.' Suddenly, she found herself remembering that Margaret had expressed doubts about why Mrs Waring had approached Renfrew rather than Mr Chancery.

'I gather that you must have remained in the same village following your marriage,' her cousin went on.

Fortunately, Florence was spared the need to answer this immediately because Stevens came in at this point and announced dinner. Once they were sitting down, she felt able to say calmly, 'My marriage was tragically very brief. It was naturally to old friends and acquaintances that I turned when it came to an end.'

'But now you have a new relative — Sir Vittorio,' commented Mrs Waring. 'Is he like your husband in appearance?'

'There is a resemblance,' Florence conceded. 'Family resemblances are so incalculable, are they not? After you had visited us in Howton, I went to look at Grandmama's portrait and you are very like her, but I am not like her at all.'

'How interesting,' replied her companion.

'My husband is very like his father, but not a bit like his mother.'

As the meal continued, they talked about such neutral topics as family likenesses, the state of the Bath streets, and the kind of shopping to be found there. Then, after the meal was over, they went to sit in the small saloon, where Casper was stretched out in front of the fire.

'My goodness, it is very warm in here,' exclaimed Mrs Waring. 'Would it be possible, do you think, to ask for the fire to be made up less?'

'Out of the question, I fear,' answered Florence, bending to pat Casper who had come to greet her, his tail wagging. 'I love to be warm.'

'I see,' replied Mrs Waring, gracefully taking a chair a short distance from the fire. 'The dog certainly seems to like it. Do you always allow it to come into the principal rooms?'

'Yes, I do,' answered Florence, as she continued to pat the dog.

'Is it not rather expensive to keep the whole house as warm as this?' Mrs Waring asked.

'Perhaps, but I consider it money well spent,' said Florence calmly.

Stevens came in with the tea, and after the door had closed behind him, Mrs Waring said, 'I have a suggestion to make, which I hope will please you. We are cousins after all, are we not? Pray, call me Anne, and may I call you Florence? Or would you prefer Fee, or Firenza?'

'Call me Fee,' Florence replied, at the same time feeling rather strange as she said it. It seemed rather an intimate nick-name to give to someone whom she barely knew, even though that person might be a relative. But oddly enough, the name Firenza felt very special to her too, almost as though it had in very truth been a name used only by someone dear to her.

'I feel so fortunate that I have found you,' said Anne, sipping the tea that Florence had passed to her. 'Relatives are so important, aren't they?' She paused briefly, then went on, 'For that reason, I think it only right to speak to you about my fears.'

'Your fears?' asked Florence, puzzled.

Anne nodded. 'My fears for you,' she said. 'My dear Fee, has it not occurred to you how dreadfully vulnerable you are? You are a widow, practically alone in the world; you have a fortune at your disposal. Now you have a male relative who has appeared from nowhere, and you only have his word for the fact that he is who he says he is.'

Florence stared at her for a moment, then

laughed disbelievingly. 'My dear ma'am, we are living in the modern world! Here I am, in Bath, surrounded by people! You are speaking as if we were involved in a Jacobean melodrama.'

Anne Waring looked away self-consciously. 'I do not want to distress you,' she said. 'But please be careful. There is something dangerous about Sir Vittorio. Don't tell me that you are unaware of it. Furthermore, has he shown you any credentials? Might he not just be an adventurer, pursuing you for what he can get? Even if he is genuine, ask yourself this: what proof is there that there is any substance behind his appearance of wealth?'

Florence wrinkled her brow. 'I will not just dismiss what you say, for I see that you are really concerned, but I feel sure that you must be wrong. When I met him in Bath, he had no idea that I was here; he was as surprised as I was.'

Mrs Waring looked at her dubiously. 'Surprised, or a good actor? He is a mountebank; you can't deny it!'

Florence thought about the baronet's appearance and behaviour. 'No, I don't,' she said slowly. 'But Bath is full of people who are playing a part.' Including myself, she added silently.

Mrs Waring smiled. 'Perhaps I am making

171

too much of it. I do hope that I am. And after all, you are not friendless; you have me, now; and there are others with your best interest at heart — like Mr Stapleton, for instance. But pray remember this: if anything happened to you, who would be the one to inherit?'

★　★　★

It was a long time before Florence got to sleep that night. She tried hard to dismiss the things that Anne had said, but the more she tried, the more impossible it became to forget them. How she wished that Margaret was still here! She was the one person who was completely acquainted with all the facts of her deception. Her deception! How grubby it sounded now, when originally it had been designed as just a bit of harmless fun. Now she thought about it more carefully, she realized that she was making relationships with all kinds of people under false pretences.

Suddenly she recalled an elderly woman called Mrs Trench who had lived in the village, but who had died some years before. Mrs Trench had told everyone that her husband had died in action on board one of His Majesty's ships. She had even shown people his medals, although she would never allow anyone to look at them very closely.

When she died, it was revealed that in fact her husband had been executed for stealing other men's belongings on board ship, then trying to throw the blame on to someone else. The medals, when closely examined, were discovered to be false, and had been fashioned by Mrs Trench herself from buttons and ribbon that she had bought at the haberdasher's in the next town.

When her fraud had been revealed, a few people had been understanding; but most had been contemptuous of her behaviour. Many had been angry at the way that she had played upon their sympathies.

Florence got out of bed, walked to the window and stared out into the darkness. Her own fraud might be seen as being even more contemptible, for she was not even seeking to protect a dead man's memory: she was only conducting it for her own amusement!

It was all Vittorio's fault, she decided. If he had not appeared, bent on perpetuating a fraud of his own, she would not be in any of this mess. And yet, she conceded, Anne Waring would still have appeared, and she would still have found herself having to act a part in front of someone who was now, probably, her only living relation; a relation who, moreover, had already proved herself to be a true friend by alerting her to the danger in which she now stood.

Even while this thought came into her mind, however, her brow wrinkled as she tried to assess whether she really did stand in any danger from Vittorio. True, she was a wealthy woman, and were she really who she claimed to be, then a genuine Sir Vittorio would undoubtedly inherit her fortune if she died. That was the situation which Anne Waring, and probably all of Bath, would believe to be the case.

Of course, she knew that this was not so. She was not married and never had been, and her fortune, on her demise, would probably pass to Anne herself. But what if Vittorio believed otherwise? And what if, through some distant connection, he really was related to the Le Greys in some way? He might think that by engineering her death, he would gain her fortune. Naturally, he would find himself mistaken, but that would not benefit her very much if one day she was found dead with an Italian stiletto buried deep in her heart.

Shivering, she took her candle to the fire and lit it; and the resulting glow comforted her a little. There was one thing that seemed to conflict with her theory, and that was the demeanour of Sir Vittorio himself. If his plans included making away with her, it seemed strange that he should not seek to ingratiate himself with her more than he had, but she wondered whether perhaps he intended to intrigue her by his mysterious attitude.

After a long period of thought she came to a conclusion that brought her a degree of peace of mind. In the morning, she would seek to make arrangements to have her will drawn up, in which she would leave her money to Margaret Bridge. That at least, would give Sir Vittorio, or whoever he was, no reason to destroy her for the sake of her money.

That decided, she blew out the candle, got back into bed and, because she was still somewhat unsettled, she did something quite unprecedented: she patted the bed, called 'Come on then', snuggled down with the comforting weight of Casper against her legs, and soon afterwards fell asleep.

10

The following day was bright and fine, and after a reasonable night's sleep — when at last she had been able to settle down — Florence awoke feeling much more optimistic. The unpleasant ideas that had worried her so much in the dark watches seemed to be too absurd to be even contemplated. Of course Sir Vittorio was not a double-dyed villain! He was simply a rogue with an eye to the main chance. His intimidating behaviour towards her was undoubtedly nothing more than an attempt to frighten her into giving him money. Well, he would soon find out that it would not work! Let her but encounter him in the Pump Room, and she would give him a piece of her mind!

One part of her night's reflections still seemed to make sense, however, and that was that it would be wise to make a will. If anything happened to her, she would like to feel that Margaret Bridge was provided for, and this would certainly not happen unless she set it down. It would therefore be necessary to send for Mr Renfrew so that she might instruct him.

Florence joined her cousin in the breakfast parlour, which felt rather chilly as she entered. She did not realize why at first, until she saw that the fire had been damped down. 'Stevens, why has this been done?' she asked, wrinkling her brow.

'It was on my orders, I'm afraid,' said Mrs Waring apologetically. 'It felt uncomfortably hot when I came in, you see.'

'Well, now it appears to have gone rather the other way,' remarked Florence. 'Make the fire up again, will you, Stevens?'

'Very good, my lady,' replied the butler.

'I do hope that you do not feel that I was exceeding my authority,' said Mrs Waring, after Stevens had gone.

'Not at all,' Florence answered politely, whilst thinking the opposite. She helped herself to coffee. 'You must understand, Anne, that I really cannot bear to be cold.'

'Nor can your dog, it seems. Does he always come into the room where you are eating?'

'Yes always.' Florence smiled down at Casper, who had followed her in, and was now stretched out in front of the fire. 'He likes his creature comforts. Have you ever had a dog, Anne?'

'No,' replied Anne. 'I do not care for

animals in the house very much, although Casper, I am sure, is an exception.'

'And what of Mr Waring?' asked Florence. 'Is he an animal lover?'

'No, we are of one mind in that matter. Fee, have you given any thought to what I said last night? About protecting yourself from Sir Vittorio?'

'Why yes, I have thought about your words,' answered Florence. 'But I have come to the conclusion that you are being far too anxious. We are hardly living in seclusion here. What possible harm could he do me?'

Anne's cheerful face took on a serious expression. 'Fee, we discussed this last night. He is a plausible rogue, and I am convinced that he means you harm! Do have a care!'

'Yes, of course, I will,' replied Florence. 'I am quite sure that you are exaggerating, but even so I have decided to take certain measures. I shall send for Mr Renfrew, my lawyer and make a will in favour of Mrs Bridge.'

'Mrs Bridge?' exclaimed Anne in surprise.

'Why yes,' replied Florence. 'She is my very good friend and she has no other resources. I cannot think of a better way of disposing of my worldly goods. If I do that, it will certainly stop Sir Vittorio from having designs on my wealth.'

'Yes, of course,' answered Anne in surprised tones. 'It is a wise decision, I suppose.' She did not sound particularly convinced however, and this conversation did something to dispel the good humour with which Florence had greeted the morning. She was very glad when the time came for them to rise from the breakfast table and make ready for the morning's activities.

The likelihood, of course, was that they would go to the Pump Room, and as Florence prepared to go out, she was suddenly conscious of a strange sensation; one which she had not felt for some time, and had never expected to feel again: It was boredom. The realization that that was what she was feeling brought her up sharp. What was she thinking of? By great good fortune, she had been plucked from poverty and an endless round of tedious drudgery, and she was now beginning to be bored! Surely she was not one of those females who could never be satisfied with their lot?

She tried to analyse why it was that she was feeling like this. Was it because she was tired of the Pump Room, and the same faces? She pictured to herself those who would be there that day; Lady Trimm of course, and her two daughters; elderly Captain Nesbitt and his spinster sister: Mr and Mrs Weybourn; and then there would be a yawning gap where she might expect to see Lord Braintree and Sir Vittorio.

This realization did indeed give her pause for thought. She could not possibly be bored because she knew she would not be seeing the wicked Italian, could she? On the other hand, there was no denying that the anxiety of what he might say or do was certainly enlivening to any social occasion. No, there must be another reason for her feeling of *ennui*, surely?

Was it perhaps because Margaret had gone? This last circumstance ought not to affect her so much, for she had always known that Margaret would have to go back to Mrs Chancery before very long, and after all, she now had Anne to bear her company. But Anne was not such an old friend as Margaret, and no doubt she would soon have to go as well, for unlike Margaret, she had a husband to think of.

This line of thought led Florence to wonder about the nature of Mr Waring. He must surely be a very complaisant husband, for he seemed to be quite happy for his wife to spend long periods of time away from him. Yet this complaisance did not seem to give rise to a great deal of affection on his wife's part, for she seemed strangely reluctant to speak about him. Florence resolved to try and find out more about him on another occasion.

It was as she was descending the stairs that the doorbell sounded, and she was pleased to hear Mr Stapleton's voice enquiring if the ladies were at home. 'We are indeed,' she said before Stevens could reply to this enquiry, 'but we are about to go to the Pump Room, if you would care to join us.' At this point, Mrs Waring came down the stairs, so Florence went on. 'But I am forgetting that you have not yet met my cousin. Anne, this is Mr Stapleton, an old acquaintance of mine. Mr Stapleton, this is my cousin, Mrs Waring.'

Both of them made noises of polite gratification, Mr Stapleton adding, 'I am rather disappointed I must tell you, Mrs Waring, that Lady Le Grey has described me as a mere acquaintance. I had hoped to have been promoted to the status of friend by now.'

'You see, I don't like to presume,' Florence answered smiling.

'Nonsense!' exclaimed Mr Stapleton, but with a warm smile.

Mr Stapleton declared that he would be delighted to escort them, and they soon set off together. 'I shall be the envy of all Bath, with two charming ladies on my arm,' he declared gallantly. 'Indeed, I've half a mind not to go straight to the Pump Room, but to parade around a little so that everyone will see how fortunate I am.'

Both ladies laughed at this absurdity. 'But you may escort us to Milsom Street later, if you wish,' Florence added.

'I shall be delighted,' he replied, but, as he smiled down at her warmly, Florence received the distinct impression that he would be far from displeased if Mrs Waring found a reason for being elsewhere.

The Pump Room was full of all the usual faces, apart from Lady Braintree and her son, and of course there was no sign of Sir Vittorio, so Florence felt quite free to enjoy Mr Stapleton's company. Perversely, however, she would have been quite pleased to have been able to show the wicked Italian that a presentable man could find her attractive.

Mr Stapleton, with the good manners which were clearly an essential part of him, was very happy to chat with Lady Trimm and the Misses Trimm, and with any other person who came within his orbit. His chief interest though was reserved for Florence, and by his manner, he did not care who knew it. For someone who had had it drummed into her that she was plain and unattractive, this was heady stuff indeed, and Florence could not help her heart beating a little faster when he turned that delightful smile upon her.

As she had hoped, when it was time for them to leave, Anne found a reason to linger in the Pump Room, and so Florence found herself walking to Milsom Street with just Mr Stapleton for company. 'How much I like your cousin,' he declared. 'She is so admirably tactful.'

Florence laughed. 'I do not know her well as yet, but she seems very amiable.'

'It is kind of her to stay with you since Mrs Bridge has been obliged to leave. How long do you think she will be able to remain?'

'I don't know,' Florence replied. 'I suppose I ought to look about me for a companion, or advertise, perhaps. I have hopes that Mrs Bridge may return to me eventually, but I must not count on it, and in the meantime my cousin has her husband to consider.'

'Have you no idea what his sentiments may be?' he asked.

Florence shook her head. 'Anne does not seem to want to talk about him very much. I suppose there are some people who want to keep their family life very private.'

'That must be it,' he agreed. Then, after they had walked along in silence for a little while, he ventured, 'It has been so long since we first met, yet having you lean upon my arm in this way seems very natural to me.'

She blushed, but could not think what to say in response. She did not know what his intentions might be, and she did not want to appear foolish by making assumptions about them.

'I cannot tell you how happy I am to have found you again,' he continued, after a short silence. He paused in front of the window of a jeweller's shop. 'To picture the wares inside gives me such hope,' he murmured. 'Dare I imagine that one day, when you are out of mourning, you might permit me to purchase something for you from this shop?'

His words were tantamount to a proposal. She looked up at his face, bent earnestly to hers, and suddenly she wanted to be done with this foolish masquerade, and tell him the truth. She opened her mouth to do so, when from behind her she heard the last voice that she had expected or wished to hear.

'*Bon giorno*, Firenza,' it said. She spun round to find Sir Vittorio standing behind her. He bowed elaborately, his grey greatcoat swirling about him revealing the stylish cut of his crimson brocade coat.

'Good day, Cousin,' she replied, curtsying. 'I am surprised to see you back in Bath. I had understood that you were away for some days.'

'But no,' he replied. 'Braintree returned this morning. I hope that you are glad to see me again. And I see that Signor Staplewood has been kind enough to, ah, deputize for me.'

'Stapleton,' the other man corrected, with gritted teeth.

'I beg your pardon; Staple*ton*,' answered Sir Vittorio. 'You must forgive my English.'

Something about the expressions of the two men made Florence realize that they were not destined to be friends. While polite enquiries were exchanged about the nature of the boxing contest, the various activities that had taken place in Bath recently, and the weather, the atmosphere of hostility became almost tangible. Eventually, Sir Vittorio said politely, 'It is kind of you, *signor*, to escort my cousin, but now that I am here, you may safely leave her in my protection.'

Florence took a deep breath, but said nothing. What *could* she say? Modesty forbade that she should say that she would rather proceed with Mr Stapleton. No doubt a lady more versed in the arts of polite flirtation would be able to convey her meaning, but she could not think of a way of doing so without appearing vulgarly forward.

Stapleton hesitated, then bowed politely. 'I need have no scruple in leaving you in the care of your cousin, ma'am,' he said, looking as if he meant precisely the opposite. 'Good day to you, sir.'

'Good day, *signor*,' replied the baronet, returning the courtesy in his usual practised fashion. Again, Stapleton hesitated, then with another inclination of his head, he turned and went back the way he had come. 'And now, if you please, Cousin,' said the baronet.

Florence had been watching the progress of Stapleton along Milsom Street, but now she turned to see that Sir Vittorio was holding open the door of the jeweller's shop. 'Sir?' she murmured.

'I have a fancy to purchase a little something for my newly acquired relative,' he said, smiling in a way that did not reach his eyes. 'Indulge me, pray.'

'Sir, I have no desire to be beholden to you for anything,' she answered fiercely in an undertone.

'Ah, but you will,' was the answer. 'If you wish to keep your reputation, you will do exactly as I say.' She stared at him. She longed to be able to sweep past him and go home, leaving him foolishly holding the door of the jeweller's shop; but she feared that he would indeed be capable of doing whatever he could to ruin her reputation in Bath. Now, she had another reason for not wanting this to happen; she did not want Gilbert Stapleton to know of her deception, until she could tell him about it herself. So, after one fulminating glance, to which he responded with a bland smile, she walked into the shop.

It seemed as if the baronet's idea of 'a little something' was vastly different from anyone else's, for he demanded that the jeweller produce sapphires for his inspection. 'The family diamonds, I regret, can only be given to my wife, but if I can purchase something fitting for you, my kinswoman, then I shall be satisfied,' he said.

'Sir, you are too generous,' she protested through gritted teeth. 'I cannot allow you to be so profligate in your spending.'

'Cannot allow?' he asked, his brows soaring. 'When I am the head of your family? I am your . . . ' — he snapped his fingers, his brows drawing together — 'what is that word?' he murmured. 'Ah yes! Protector! I am your protector, so I insist that I buy you something in keeping with your position.'

Florence stared at him. The jeweller obviously thought his uncertain grasp of English was genuine, but she saw by the baronet's expression that he understood exactly what he had said, and the nature of his innuendo, and she found herself wavering between a strong feeling of indignation at his astonishing presumption and a strange trembling sensation deep down inside to which she could not give a name. But for now, all she could do was wait while he hesitated between two hideously expensive necklaces, with ear-rings to match, and finally made his choice.

'Now, you will be able to adorn yourself as your beauty deserves,' he said at last, the transaction over.

'But not for a little while yet, Cousin,' she replied, with a hint of triumph. 'While I am in mourning, coloured stones are out of the question.'

He stared at her for a moment, his expression angry, before he smiled quite unexpectedly, and at once selected a pearl brooch from a case that was in front of him. Then he leaned forward and, slowly and lingeringly, fastened it to the front of her gown. 'Then have this to wear for now, my cousin, and when you are out of mourning, wear the sapphires, and think of me.'

Once outside the shop, she turned to him and said, 'How dare you? How dare you?'

'How dare I what?' he asked blandly. 'No one except for yourself would think that there was anything out of the way in your receiving a gift from your kinsman.'

'That is because I know you are not my

188

kinsman,' she replied, setting off at a furious pace, with which he had no difficulty at all in keeping up.

'Indeed! And how do you know that?'

She halted suddenly and turned to him. 'Because you are a mountebank and a charlatan,' she declared. 'I would like to know how you intend to pay for those jewels. Or are you going to disappear as suddenly as you came, leaving me with the bill?'

'Oh no, *cara*,' he replied, taking her hand firmly and tucking it in his arm, thus forcing her to walk along with him. 'I am very well able to pay for what I want.' She darted a look up at him, found that he was staring down at her, and suddenly found herself feeling breathless. 'I hope that you are attending the concert tonight,' he went on. 'I should very much like to see you wearing my brooch.' She said nothing in reply, and a few moments later, he said, 'Is that fellow Stapleton intending to be present?'

'I don't know,' answered Florence. Then some demon prompted her to add, 'I hope so.'

'You hope so, do you?' he asked, raising one brow. 'I must tell you, Firenza, that I do not care for him at all. I mistrust his motives.'

She stared at him again then burst out laughing. 'You?' she exclaimed 'You mistrust

189

his motives? By what right?'

'I am a man of the world, Firenza, and I know people as you do not.'

'Listen to me, Cousin,' she said insistently. 'I have known Gilbert — Mr Stapleton — for years. He is entirely trustworthy.' In the excitement of the moment, she forgot that her acquaintance with Mr Stapleton consisted of less than a dozen meetings altogether. 'But of course, trustworthiness is something that you would not understand.'

'Oh, I understand it, Firenza,' hissed Sir Vittorio, bending his head down closer to hers. 'Just as I understand its opposite; which is why I understand you so very well.' She made as if to pull her hand from his arm, but with his other hand, he kept hers in a steely grip, so that she could not move away from him without an unseemly struggle in the street. 'You do not deceive me at all,' he went on. 'You are an adventuress; an unscrupulous adventuress with an eye to gain whatever you can get. Well, wear my brooch tonight, *cara*, or I shall have something to say about it, and since you do not want it as a gift, be quite sure of one thing: I will find a way of making you pay for it.'

To her relief, they had reached the corner of Laura Place. She pulled away from him, and this time, he allowed her to extricate herself from his grip. He bowed politely, but she did not remain to acknowledge this courtesy. She picked up her skirts and fairly ran to her own door, his low laughter ringing in her ears.

Anne was in the hall when she arrived, and she smiled, saying archly, 'Well? Did you enjoy your walk with Mr Stapleton?'

'Ooh!' exclaimed Florence, stripping off her gloves. 'That man! That detestable man!' She hurried up the stairs, Anne at her heels.

'But what on earth has he done to annoy you so much?' asked her cousin, puzzled. 'I thought that you liked him; that you were pleased to see him again.'

Florence stared at her blankly then, as realization dawned upon her, blushed deeply. 'Not Mr Stapleton,' she hastened to say. 'I don't mean him.'

A look of comprehension crept into Anne's eyes. 'Sir Vittorio,' she declared.

'Precisely,' answered Florence. 'The . . . the baronet.' For some reason that she could not explain to herself, either then or later, she did not want to use the nickname, 'the wicked Italian', that she and Margaret had used between themselves.

'So what did he do to annoy you so much?'

Florence stared at her cousin. Suddenly, she knew that she could not tell her about the sapphires which in any case she intended to return as soon as possible. 'Oh, he came upon us in the street and surprised me,' she replied, conscious that this sounded a very mild offence, which scarcely warranted the high rage in which she had been when she had entered the house. 'Then he insisted on escorting me home, quite against my wishes.' She turned to unfasten her cloak and unobtrusively opened the top drawer of her dressing table and put the jewels inside.

'And Mr Stapleton just let him?' asked Anne. 'Well, I must say, I think the less of him for it.' She glanced curiously at the drawer as Florence closed it, but did not say anything.

'It was rather difficult for him to do anything else,' replied Florence, as she sat down in front of the mirror in order to attend to her hair. 'After all, when Sir Vittorio claimed the right of a relative to escort me, he could not very well object.'

'And so he just walked off tamely,' answered Anne tartly. 'I'm very disappointed in him.'

'He will have a chance to redeem himself tonight at the concert,' Florence said soothingly. It occurred to her that, strangely enough, her cousin seemed to be more annoyed at Mr Stapleton's defection than she was herself, and she said so.

Her cousin laughed a little self-consciously. 'I daresay I cannot understand properly how it was, not having been there,' she said. 'But as you have observed, he will have a chance to speak to you again tonight. Let's hope he doesn't make a mull of it. That's a lovely brooch you are wearing, my dear cousin. Is it new?' She leaned forward to examine it.

'What this?' Florence replied, hoping that she was not blushing. 'No, it is not new. It was given to me by Victor.'

'It's charming,' replied Anne. 'You must take great care of it. It looks valuable.'

Anne left soon afterwards, and Florence congratulated herself on having got over an awkward situation very smoothly.

Since she had no other engagements that day, she had time to read a letter which had come to her from Margaret Bridge that morning. She was a little surprised that her friend had written so quickly after her departure, but suspected that she was missing Bath, or, to put it more accurately, one inhabitant of Bath, namely Lord Braintree. She opened it with pleasurable anticipation, only to be shocked and saddened as she read the opening paragraphs.

My dear Fee,
    You will be surprised, I know, to hear

from me so quickly, and very sorry to hear the news that I have to tell, but I felt sure that you would want to know that Miss Le Grey has died. The end was quite peaceful, I believe, and the burial took place only just before I arrived here. I was surprised that Mrs Chancery did not inform you, but I don't think that anyone apart from myself was really aware that you thought of her as a friend. (Also, much though it pains me to reveal it, I'm afraid that my employer is rather dilatory in her correspondence!) I know how sorry you must be, for she was a very real friend to you when you needed one. At the moment, Mr Renfrew is trying to trace anyone who might be related to her. You don't suppose, do you, that it would be necessary to tell Sir Vittorio? After all, he might actually be some kind of relation of hers, even if a low, unscrupulous one.

The Chancerys are all well and, as I suspected, Mrs Chancery hardly missed me and says that the children seem to get on very well without any lessons at all. I have not yet broached the subject of leaving her permanently to come and live with you, but I will do so very soon.

How is everyone in Bath? (Lord Braintree, Florence thought to herself.) I

*keep thinking about the fun that we had
together. Please send my regards to any of
our acquaintances, if you think it proper.*

*With my very best wishes, my dear
friend,*

Margaret Bridge

Florence sat for some time with the letter on
her knee, her mind ranging back over the
years, remembering the occasions when she
had taken refuge with Miss Le Grey after her
father had been especially cruel. In particular,
she thought about how the elderly lady had
encouraged her to find a new life for herself,
and to invent a new identity. She could not
help shedding tears at this news. Had she still
been living at home with her father, the death
of Miss Le Grey would have meant that she
would have lost half her friends at one stroke.
How her father would have crowed!

Thoughts of her father had the effect of
banishing melancholy. She sat up, straightening her shoulders. No one would have the
chance to crow over her if she could help it.
She would not allow her fear of what Sir
Vittorio might do to frighten her! After all,
she was by no means defenceless. Margaret,
though at a distance, would continue to be a
good friend, Anne was clearly ready to
support her against him, and Gilbert

Stapleton would no doubt stand by her.

For the first time, she allowed herself to think about the things that Stapleton had said to her just before the baronet had interrupted their tête-à-tête. At the time, it had occurred to her that he was stating a definite intention to propose to her at a more proper moment. Reflection upon this incident did nothing to change her views, and she was at a loss as to how to respond to him. She had become quite accustomed to the idea that at her age, she might well never marry, and had certainly never expected to meet Mr Stapleton again, and find him single, or, at any rate, a widower. Nor would she ever have supposed, in her wildest dreams, that if she did meet him again, he would prove to have been so attached to her that he had never forgotten her. It was flattering, but it made her feel rather guilty, for although she also remembered him, and not without fondness, she had not treasured his memory in quite the same way.

She tried to imagine how she would have responded had he actually proposed, rather than simply hinted at it, and she came to the very unwelcome conclusion that Sir Vittorio's interruption had been very timely. It might be the case that given time, she would be ready to agree to be Mr Stapleton's wife, but as yet it was too soon for her to say. She did not feel that she knew her own mind.

On one thing, however, she was perfectly determined, and that was that she was not going to accept Sir Vittorio's sapphires. He had closed her fingers quite firmly around the case as they had parted, and she had had no option but to take it, unless she was to fling it down in the street. Whilst such a course of action would undoubtedly serve him right, she told herself, it would certainly be seen by someone, and cause just the kind of gossip and speculation that she was anxious to avoid. He had told her that he would be at the concert that night; very well, then, she would take the sapphires with her and insist that he have them back. She was still in a puzzle as to why he had bought them in the first place.

It was as she was preparing to go out that evening that she remembered the brooch. That, too, she would return to him. In some ways, she was sorely tempted to wear it, for it would have gone very well with her ensemble, but she put it down. That would be to embark upon a slippery slope that would surely lead to her destruction.

Briefly, she recalled the threat that he had made — that if she did not wear it, he would have something to say, and that she would be made to pay for it. No doubt this was a further threat to expose her, and a warning that she must pay for his silence by keeping silent herself about his false identity. As she paused in thought, her eye was caught by the letter from Margaret telling of Miss Le Grey's death. The name might not be hers by birth or even by marriage, but in some senses Miss Le Grey had entrusted her with it, and she had not stolen it, whatever the wicked Italian might be implying. She would show him Margaret's letter. Her very openness in that respect would surely convince him that she had nothing to hide, and there was no way in which he could harm the old lady now. Then she would return all the jewellery with thanks and ask him to leave her alone.

Having made this resolve, she went downstairs, conscious that she was looking her best in a black lace gown with a low neck, her only ornaments being a fine string of pearls which had belonged to her mother, and which she had never allowed her father to see for fear he might take them away.

Anne was waiting for her in the hall, and she, too, was in looks, in a sky-blue gown trimmed with silver lace. 'My dear Fee, I don't think I have ever seen you look better. Is it the thought of seeing Mr Stapleton that is putting such roses in your cheeks?'

Florence blushed, for in fact it had been the thought of doing battle with Sir Vittorio rather than encountering her faithful lover that had been to the forefront of her mind. But Mrs Waring, seeing this as evidence of interest in her long lost sweetheart, smiled with satisfaction.

The Assembly Rooms were already filling up nicely when they arrived, and Mr Stapleton was one of the first to greet them, coming towards them with a ready smile on his handsome face. He was looking as well-turned out as any man present, in a coat of dull gold with a tawny-coloured waistcoat embroidered in cream, and Florence could feel that many a young lady was regarding her enviously. It was a very pleasant sensation.

'My dear Lady Fee,' he declared, bowing over her hand. 'What a pleasure to see you again; and you too, of course, Mrs Waring. You cannot imagine what chagrin I felt when your cousin carried you off this afternoon; I am glad to see that he conveyed you home safely.'

Florence managed to summon up a smile. 'My cousin can be rather . . . masterful, at times,' she replied, 'as I expect you have realized.'

'That did occur to me,' he replied, ruefully, inclining his head to Mrs Waring as she excused herself in order to go and speak to an acquaintance. 'I trust you will not accuse me of discourtesy towards your kinsman, but I did wish him other-where today.'

'You are not alone in that,' replied Florence frankly. 'I quite frequently wish him other-where.'

He looked at her curiously. 'Is there any way I may serve you in this matter?' he asked her, dropping his voice slightly. 'You know that I am yours to command; that I would willingly do anything — '

'Now that is an offer of which I feel sure you should avail yourself, Firenza,' said a familiar voice. Florence turned to look at Sir Vittorio, who had approached them unseen. Dressed in black shot silk with a silver waistcoat and, as usual, with his linen dripping with lace, he cut an elegant figure, drawing many a female gaze. Comparing the two men, Florence told herself that she preferred Mr Stapleton's more restrained style, but there was no question that the wicked Italian was impressive in a way that was all his own. 'Your servant, Signor Stapleson,' he went on, bowing with panache.

'Stapleton,' the other man corrected, bowing curtly, but managing to say with an assumption of easy good humour, 'Sir Vittorio, you are not my favourite person today, I fear.'

The baronet raised one eyebrow. 'No doubt because I robbed you of your fair companion earlier,' he hazarded. 'But you must forgive me, *signor*. The rights and privileges of a male relative are new to me, and I am determined to enjoy them.'

'But I am the first to greet your cousin tonight, sir, so must claim the pleasure of finding her a place.' Florence looked from one to another. She would have been less than human if she had not enjoyed the sensation of having two such attractive men vying for her attention.

Sir Vittorio inclined his head. 'If I allow you that pleasure for now, *signor*, then you may be sure that I shall claim her later.'

Florence was aware of his eyes on her bodice, and she suddenly thought of the brooch. In the end, she had decided not to bring the jewellery that he had forced upon her as she could not fit them into her reticule without making it look disagreeably bulky. Furthermore, she had realized that to find a place where she could speak to him privately at the Assembly Rooms would be exceedingly difficult, if not impossible. Little though she might relish the prospect, she would have to ask him to call at the house.

Before she could lose her courage, therefore, she said, 'I would be grateful,

Cousin, if you would call upon me tomorrow as there is a matter upon which I would like to consult you.'

He raised his brows, and Florence gained the impression that he was genuinely surprised. 'Then naturally, my dear Firenza, I am at your disposal.'

'And so am I,' murmured Mr Stapleton, after Sir Vittorio had moved away. 'My dear Lady Le Grey, I would be a fool if I did not realize that you hold that man in fear and aversion. If you want me to be present at tomorrow's interview, then naturally I shall be there.'

'Thank you for your concern,' replied Florence in the same low tone, 'but I believe I need not trouble you. I assure you that I am quite capable of dealing with my own kinsman whom, you may be sure, I may regard at times with annoyance, but certainly with neither fear nor aversion.' She had answered instinctively; straight away, she realized that she had spoken the truth.

'I beg your pardon,' said Stapleton in a mortified tone. 'I did not mean to interfere.'

Florence's expression softened. She had not intended to snub him. 'You are very kind,' she replied, 'but you must permit me to manage my own affairs. Come and take me driving in the afternoon to console me for having had to endure an interview with my over-bearing relative.'

'You may count upon me,' he promised. After that there was no time for further conversation before the music began.

Delightful though the performances were that evening, Florence found herself unable to keep her mind on the music. Her gaze kept being pulled to the tall, dark, elegant figure of Sir Vittorio. He was sitting to her right, and slightly in front of her, so that she had a good view as he sat politely giving his attention to the younger Miss Trimm, who by the expression on her face was very well satisfied to have the handsome Italian at her side. Florence could not decide with which of them to be more annoyed, Sir Vittorio for turning his deceitful smiles upon an innocent young girl, or the innocent young girl for being such a fool as to fall for his wiles. As she watched, he took Miss Maria's fan from her and proceeded to agitate it for her benefit. 'Mountebank,' she snorted to herself, then instantly wondered who else she had heard describing him in that way.

After the concert was over, Vittorio excused himself to Miss Maria, and strolled over to Florence, who was standing on the other side of the room. She watched as he turned to address one man, stepped back to allow a lady to pass, and bent his handsome head to hear what someone else was saying. For the first time it occurred to her that his deportment displayed athletic grace rather than effeminacy. My goodness, his shoulders are broad, she thought to herself; then could feel that she was colouring at the very idea.

When he reached her side, she said, waspishly, because it was the first thing that came into her head, 'I trust you returned Miss Maria's fan to her. I don't think it was your colour.'

He laughed; he sounded as if he were genuinely amused. 'You may be right, cousin,' he replied. 'Why, are you feeling a little warm? Shall I borrow it again in order to cool you down? Or may I use yours?' So saying, he took her hand, lifted it, and removed her fan from her wrist in one smooth gesture.

'Do not be absurd, Cousin,' she said, trying to laugh. His touch had for some strange reason, possibly fear, caused her heart to jump into her throat. Her voice came out sounding rather breathless and she told herself that she was annoyed because of the effortless mastery with which he had taken the fan from her.

'Indeed, Cousin, you are rather warm; I can see it,' he answered, his voice still sounding amused. He shook out her fan, and agitated it gently in front of her. 'The language of the fan, Cousin,' he murmured. 'Now what do you think I am saying to you?'

'Something insulting, I expect,' she replied, wondering why, with the gentle breeze from the fan caressing her face, she should actually be feeling hotter.

'You are unjust, Cousin,' he protested. 'I can be very gallant at times, I assure you.'

Anne approached them at this point, and Vittorio casually folded her fan and handed it back. 'At what hour shall I wait upon you tomorrow, Firenza?' he asked.

'At about eleven o'clock, if you please,' she replied. Then, because some devil prompted her, she added, 'Mr Stapleton is to take me driving later in the day, so I would like to get our interview over and done with.'

'Business before pleasure,' he replied, showing his teeth. 'How wise.'

As they were riding home in the carriage that they had hired for the evening, Anne said, 'Was this interview with Sir Vittorio of your seeking, or has he pressed it upon you?'

'I requested it,' Florence replied.

'For any particular reason?'

Florence hesitated. She was glad that it was dark inside the carriage so that her cousin could not read the expression on her face. Naturally, whilst living in the house Anne would be bound to find out a certain amount about her concerns; but this close questioning from one whom she had not known for very long, all things considered, seemed rather impertinent. She could not imagine Margaret, a much older friend, asking such a personal question, and Anne's obtrusiveness made her answer with more reserve than she might have done otherwise.

'To discuss family business,' she said eventually. This seemed to silence Mrs Waring, who said no more on the subject, and apart from goodnight wishes, nothing more was said between them before they parted.

One other thought occurred to Florence that night; she had not yet sent for Renfrew, and really ought to do so before long.

11

The following morning, however, Florence was surprised to make two discoveries. The first was that yet again, the fire in the breakfast parlour had been damped down, whilst Casper had been banished to the hall.

'I beg your pardon,' Anne murmured, 'but I really find it hard to enjoy my breakfast in a warm room. And I felt sure that the dog would be happier outside, waiting for you.'

Other than asking Stevens to build up the fire again, and bending to pat Casper, Florence made no reply to this, although both incidents made it clear to her that having Mrs Waring to live with her could only be a short-term arrangement. The next thing that surprised her, however, was when Mrs Waring said, 'Now do not argue, my dear Fee, but I have decided that I must be present when you speak to Sir Vittorio. It will be quite unsuitable for you to see him alone.'

Florence stared at her. 'I cannot think why you should say so,' she replied, in astonished tones.

'We have already agreed, have we not, that he is a dangerous man?' answered Anne patiently. 'Who knows what he may do?'

'Anne, he is my kinsman,' said Florence indignantly, forgetting for a moment that this was a lie. 'There is no impropriety in my seeing him alone.'

'My dear Fee, I would never accuse you of impropriety,' Anne assured her. 'It is your safety that concerns me, and for that reason, I must insist on being present when you see him.'

'You are very kind, Anne, but this is my house, Vittorio is my relative, and I will see him alone. He is not going to do me a mischief in my own home with my servants within call. There, I have been uncivil and I didn't mean to be, but the business that I need to discuss with him is private and I must see him alone.'

'Very well,' replied Anne, looking offended. 'If you put it like that, what can I say? But be assured, Cousin, that I, too, will remain within call.'

But not within eavesdropping distance, Florence said to herself, and she resolved to make sure that Stevens kept Anne away from the door of the book-room. She had no desire for anyone to know anything about the sapphires and the brooch, but even had the jewellery not been in question, she would have refused Anne's suggestion. She had no intention of admitting to anyone that she found Sir Vittorio intimidating. Furthermore, she was quite sure that if she were to confront him with another person present he would assume that she was doing it because she *did* find him intimidating. She was determined not to give him that satisfaction.

Her one fear was that despite her wishes, Mr Stapleton would appear in order to defend her. She had no desire for the two men to confront one another in her saloon, for doubtless in such a meeting their dislike for one another would not by any means be diminished. Furthermore, however attractive she might find Mr Stapleton, she did not want him to fight her battles for her — particularly this one.

Shortly before eleven o'clock, Anne Waring reappeared. 'Fee, are you quite sure that you do not want me to be present?' she pleaded.

'Quite sure,' Florence answered, trying to sound reassuring rather than irritated. 'If it is any comfort to you, then I will tell you that I intend informing him that I am changing my will in Margaret's favour. Then he will have nothing more to hope for from me.'

Anne blenched visibly at this news. 'For God's sake,' she exclaimed, 'do not do any such thing! Do you not realize that to give him such news would be to sound your own death knell?'

At this unpropitious moment, the doorbell rang, and both women jumped. It was Florence who recovered first. 'For goodness' sake, don't be so melodramatic,' she declared. 'Take yourself off to the library, if you have an appetite for something sensational.'

Anne cast her a reproachful look and flounced out and, moments later, Stevens showed Sir Vittorio into the salon.

In honour of his visit, she had taken particular care with her own attire, telling herself that she could not possibly be shown up by a man as fastidious as he. She was therefore dressed in a gown of black figured brocade, with a petticoat of fine black silk, and she was conscious of looking her best. The baronet was dressed in the darkest of dark purple, his thick black hair tied back neatly and enclosed by a black velvet bag.

He bowed with his usual grace, and wandered towards the fire. 'Whenever I find myself thinking that you are a shameless adventuress without any redeeming features, cara, I remind myself that at least you know how to keep a house warm,' he remarked. 'I cannot bear to be cold.'

'Neither can I,' she replied. Then suddenly, in her mind's eye, it was as if she could see her father seated by his meagre fire, attending to his own needs and grinning maliciously if he thought that he had done her any hurt. She had believed that she had put all the distress and misery behind her, but it came back to her all of a rush, and she gave a gasp as if someone had struck her.

'Firenza?' questioned the baronet, his tone concerned. 'What is it?'

She looked at him blankly, still in the past. 'Why did he hate me, Vittorio?' she asked him. 'What was the matter with me?'

'Who do you think hated you?' he asked. 'Your husband?'

'My husband?' She stared at him for a moment. 'No . . . no,' she answered. 'My father; my father hated me.'

'Sit down,' he said, conducting her to a chair, then ringing the bell. 'Wine for your mistress,' he said when Stevens came. 'She is agitated.' He walked over to the fire and stood looking down at her, one foot on the fender, his arm along the mantelpiece. 'What makes you think he hated you?' he asked her curiously.

'Everything he ever said and everything he ever did,' replied Florence baldly. 'Forgive me; I have no wish to speak of this.' To her horror, she heard her voice crack, and could feel a prickling at the back of her eyes. She knew that whatever happened, she must not expose her weakness to this ruthless man. She closed her eyes briefly, and to her amazement, after a moment, she could feel a firm hand gripping her shoulder reassuringly.

Stevens came in with the wine, and Vittorio poured out two glasses and took one to Florence. He sniffed appreciatively at his own glass. 'From the Rhone, I think,' he murmured. 'A good wine.' He was silent for a moment, watching her sip from her own glass. Eventually he said, 'I know nothing of your father except what you have told me, but I must beg you to consider, *cara*, that perhaps his dislike of you shows a fault in him, rather than in you. Perhaps he in his turn is to be pitied rather than hated for this reason.'

She stared up at him, shaken equally by the novelty of this observation, and by the fact that it was he that had made it.

At this point, Casper stood up, stretched and wagged his tail, and proceeded to demand attention. Florence half expected so immaculately dressed a man to brush the dog aside for fear that animal hairs would spoil his clothes. Instead, Vittorio put down one shapely hand to tickle him behind his ears, and Florence watched him in some surprise. Sensing her bewilderment, he smiled up at her and said, 'I like dogs; this is a very fine fellow indeed.'

'Sir, whatever can have happened?' Florence asked, half her mind still occupied with the extraordinary feeling of liberation that his words concerning her father had given her. 'We are in agreement.'

'I suppose it was bound to happen, given time,' he replied. 'Doubtless it will not last. What is his name?'

'Casper,' replied Florence.

The baronet took hold of the dog's chin gently. 'And are you as wise as your name indicates, hmm?' he asked him. Casper wagged his tail enthusiastically, as if to give assent to this question. After a moment or two, Vittorio straightened and said, 'But pray tell me, Firenza, why you have requested my presence here today?'

'For two reasons,' she answered, pulling herself together. 'The first is to return these.' She picked up the box with the sapphires in it and the pearl brooch and held them out to him. 'Were I really as unscrupulous as you say I would doubtless keep them. But I have far too many scruples and far too much virtue to do so.'

'But if you were my kinswoman — as you say you are — you would be prepared to accept gifts from the head of your house, surely.'

'Even if we were related — which, sir, I

strongly doubt — I would still never accept such jewels from you. It would be quite improper. But why I am bothering to tell you this I have no idea, for you know it perfectly well. When you gave me these yesterday, it was purely in a spirit of mischief.' Her tone, which had been calm and reasonable, had become angry and impatient by the end of this speech, and she looked up at him with a stormy expression in her eyes.

'But, my dear Firenza, how can you say such a thing?' he asked her, his expression puzzled but his eyes gleaming. 'To bestow jewellery for such motives would be the act of a madman. Anyway, I made it very clear that I felt some responsibility towards you.'

'Yes, I know very well what you said,' she replied crossly. 'Believe me, *signor*,' she went on, with heavy emphasis, 'that whatever you understand by the term 'protector', it means something very different in English!'

Swiftly, he was at her side. 'Oh, but I do not think that it does,' he purred, catching hold of her upper arms.

Suddenly, Anne's warning came into her mind and she made as if to pull away from him, crying, 'Don't touch me!'

'What is this?' he demanded, continuing to hold her lightly but firmly. 'Do you think that I intend you violence?'

'I don't know,' she replied swiftly. 'But I must tell your sir, that if anything happens to me, my money is to go to Mrs Bridge.' Her will had not yet been made, but he was not to know that.

'I have no interest in your savings,' he answered, pulling her into his arms. 'You have captured my interest; *you, cara,* believe me. I am in no doubt as to the purpose for which you are best fitted. The sapphires, unlike the diamonds which are intended for my wife, will serve to . . . stake my claim, I believe is the term, and this will act as a deposit.'

'No,' she panted, as he lowered his mouth to hers.

'*Si,*' he replied before he kissed her. Since his last embrace in the Chapter House, she had been telling herself severely that she must have been mad to allow such insolence; that he had taken her by surprise; that if he dared to attempt such a thing again, she would kick his shins very soundly and fight for all that she was worth. Now, however, with his arms about her, and his mouth moving against hers with such assurance, her every instinct seemed to demand that instead of fighting against him, she should wrap her arms around his neck. Before she could fully return his embrace, however, he drew back and murmured, 'Your life is about to enter a new and exciting chapter, my little adventuress.'

Undoubtedly, he would have kissed her again, but for the fact that they both heard the door handle turn, and Florence tore herself free, so that when Stevens entered to announce Lord Braintree, she was sitting in a chair by the fire, and Vittorio was carefully examining the sapphires through his quizzing glass. At once, the memory came to her of how Stapleton had surprised them and they had sprung apart in just the same way. She could not help it; she gave a little choke of laughter and, looking up, her eyes brimful of mirth, she saw that Vittorio was glancing at her sideways, the sapphires in his hand, her amused expression returned by one on his own face.

'Lord Braintree,' exclaimed Florence, getting up, turning her giggle into a smile of welcome. 'This is an unexpected pleasure. Have you only just returned to Bath?'

'Just this morning,' he replied, bowing to her and to Vittorio, which courtesy the other man returned. 'Vittorio; you returned safely, then.'

'But did you imagine, my dear George, that I would become lost in the countryside without you to guide me everywhere?' asked the baronet. His voice was full of good humour, and Florence contrasted the marked cordiality which existed between the two of them to the antipathy that had been so palpable between the baronet and Mr Stapleton.

'By no means,' returned the earl. 'Those look like fine stones,' he remarked, looking at the sapphires. 'May I?'

The baronet shrugged and handed them to him, and Braintree groped for his own quizzing glass. 'Yes, very fine,' he said eventually, handing them back. 'Are they yours, or Lady Le Grey's?'

'They are Firenza's,' Vittorio answered, but since Florence said 'my cousin's' at the same time, it was not surprising that Lord Braintree looked puzzled.

'I have bought them for Firenza, to mark the fact that she is a member of my family, but she does not wish to accept my gift,' replied the baronet, with what Florence considered breathtaking audacity. 'Tell me, George, is it improper to accept such a gift by way of an addition to the family jewels, shall we say, when the gift is bestowed by her natural protector?'

Again that word. Suddenly, Florence felt her blood begin to boil.

'I think it can probably be allowed,' answered the earl thoughtfully. 'Of course, were you not related, then the lady's reputation would be completely ruined by such a gesture; but since you are her kinsman, such a gift, though somewhat extravagant, can, I think, be allowed.'

'You please me very much, my friend,' said Vittorio, smiling at Florence in a way which made her think of a cat about to pounce. 'I understand perfectly, and know that Firenza will now be in no doubt as to the spirit in which I offer this gift. But now, my dear, I must take my leave of you. I am sure that George will keep you very well entertained. Lock up those sapphires carefully. There are many rogues about, or so I am told.'

With another elaborate bow he was gone, and Florence stared after him fulminatingly. 'That man!' She exclaimed. 'That wretched man! Oh, he puts me all out of temper!'

She had spoken in haste; now she saw that Lord Braintree was looking at her in some surprise, and she smiled apologetically. 'I have a dislike of being beholden to anyone, whoever they may be,' she explained.

'I understand,' answered the earl, smiling with a warmth that made Florence understand why Margaret was so drawn to him. 'You must allow him to spoil you a little, you know. He has very few family members left in Italy, and he is probably enjoying having a relative to look after.'

'Probably,' agreed Florence, reflecting upon the strange *naïveté* which the earl seemed to display towards the wicked Italian when in other situations he appeared to be worldly wise.

'I wonder,' said the earl, colouring a little, 'I was hoping that I might see Mrs Bridge. Can you tell me, is she within, or has she gone out already?'

Florence stared at him. So much seemed to have happened since Margaret had left that she had forgotten that he would not be aware that she had gone. 'I am afraid that you have missed her,' she began.

'So she *has* gone out already,' put in the earl. 'I thought she must have done. Pray tell me, when do you think she will be back? Will you let her know that I have called?'

'I did not mean that, Lord Braintree,' replied Florence. 'I meant that she has left Bath.'

'Not left altogether?' exclaimed Braintree, his expression one of shock and consternation. 'This is most unexpected. What on earth could have prompted her to leave?' He stared at Florence as if he half expected her to admit to some kind of cruelty committed against the gentle Mrs Bridge.

'You are shocked, my lord, I can see.' He did not deny it, but walked to the window and stood looking out, his hands behind his back. Florence rang the bell and when Stevens came, she asked him to bring another glass. There was no sign of Anne, and for that she was thankful. There was more than a hint of inquisitiveness about Anne that made her reluctant to share any secrets with her, particularly when they were not her own. She was not yet sure how discreet she could be.

'It is quite simple,' answered Florence. 'Mrs Bridge only came to Bath as my friend to oblige me; she still has a post as governess in the house of Mr and Mrs Chancery, and she has returned there to fulfil her obligation.'

'Oh,' replied Lord Braintree, still looking not a little crestfallen. 'It had never occurred to me that she would not remain in Bath. I had very much wanted to approach her on . . . on a certain matter.'

'Yes, Margaret told me that you were looking for a companion for your mother.'

He stared at her. 'I beg your pardon?'

Florence repeated herself. 'She understood that you might want her to fill that position.' Looking at his horrified expression and making one or two assumptions of her own, she added, 'I gather that that is not the case.'

'Not by any means,' he declared. 'Lady Le Grey,' he went on, after taking a deep breath, 'my reason for seeking out a companion for my mother was so that I might be free to pursue my own inclinations. It is my very earnest desire to ask Mrs Bridge to be my wife. What do you think? Will she accept me?'

While inwardly whooping, Florence contented herself with replying, 'That is not for me to say, my lord. You will have to ask her for yourself.'

He got up from his chair, and strode across to the window. 'I cannot believe that she did not understand me,' he said. 'I thought that I had made myself perfectly clear.'

At this point, Stevens returned with the glass, and poured wine for his lordship. After he had gone, Florence said, 'Mrs Bridge is a lady, Lord Braintree. She would never dream of making any assumptions about your intentions.'

He coloured. 'No, no indeed; of course not! Oh how I wish I had spoken earlier! But it is not too late, after all. If only I have not given her a disgust of me through my crassness! Lady Le Grey, can you furnish me with her direction? I must seek her out without delay.'

Florence sat at the little table in the window and wrote down Margaret's direction on a piece of paper. 'There you are, my lord,' she replied, handing it to him.

'Thank you,' he answered, taking hold of it as if it were something precious. 'I shall leave immediately. I shall ask your kinsman, Sir

Vittorio, to bear me company. Do you have any idea where he might have gone?'

To her great annoyance, Florence could feel herself blushing. 'I'm afraid not,' she answered. 'He may have gone back to his hotel, perhaps.'

'That's a good thought,' replied Braintree eagerly. 'I'll go and see if I can find him.' He bowed and was on the point of leaving when Florence stopped him on impulse.

'Lord Braintree,' she said.

'My lady?' His manner was perfectly courteous, but Florence could sense in him an impatience to be gone.

'I won't keep you for long,' she said apologetically.

'I beg your pardon,' he said ruefully, and came back towards her. 'In what way may I serve you?'

She smiled, bit her lip, looked away, then said all of a rush, 'Why do you like him so much?' He looked at her uncomprehendingly, so she went on, 'My . . . my cousin, why do you like him so much? I know that I am only seeing things from one side, but it seems to be that you and he are . . . are . . .'

' . . . Quite the opposite of one another?' suggested the earl with a smile.

'I suppose so,' she agreed.

'We are very different,' he responded. 'But

we have a good deal in common. I have visited Italy, although not for some time, and so we have that link between us.'

'Yes, but . . . ' Florence protested; then could not think how to complete her sentence.

Braintree seemed to understand what she was trying to say, however, and he said carefully, 'Don't be fooled by that manner of his, ma'am. He's by no means the effeminate butterfly that you might suppose. In my estimate, he is very much a man to be reckoned with.'

After he had gone, Florence picked up the sapphires and looked at them again, before putting them away. She was still determined not to keep them, but Braintree's words rang true: Vittorio was a man to be reckoned with and if, for some reason, he was determined that she should keep them, he could make it difficult for her to return them.

And yet, she thought to herself, and yet, at the beginning of that interview, she had been given a glimpse of a man who could be understanding, gentle and sympathetic. She was bound to acknowledge, little though she wanted to do so, that it would be dangerously easy to be seduced by such a man as that.

12

Mrs Waring was delighted when she heard that Sir Vittorio had gone out of town once more. 'All the better,' she declared. 'It will give you more time to enjoy Mr Stapleton's company.'

Florence agreed, but in a rather abstracted way. It had occurred to her that Vittorio's absence would provide the perfect opportunity for her to return the sapphires and the brooch. She would have them wrapped and taken round to his hotel with a note, saying that he had left some property by mistake. The thought of doing this did make her hesitate, for it hardly seemed a safe way of treating such valuable jewellery. But she told herself that if she wrapped them up carefully, took them herself, then told the hotel that the package contained a book that the baronet had left, then it would be much less likely that anyone would wish to steal it. Besides, even if it was stolen, it would just be his own stupid fault for forcing such a gift upon her and refusing to allow her to return it.

Mr Stapleton appeared, as agreed, to take her out for a drive after lunch, and was warmly welcomed by both Florence and Anne. 'You both look so delightful, that I wish I could take you both up,' he said, smiling, 'but the curricle I have hired will only take one passenger, unless you are prepared to be squashed.'

'By no means,' replied Mrs Waring spiritedly. 'I can have a turn another day. Dear Fee needs an outing to improve her spirits. I fear she has been inflicted with another visit from her kinsman, today.' She pronounced the word 'kinsman' as if it were a term of abuse.

Stapleton looked concerned. 'I hope he has not distressed you,' he said, his face serious.

'Not at all,' replied Florence, feeling irritated. She had not liked the way in which Anne had spoken so disparagingly of her hostess's relative in front of a man she hardly knew. 'All I need is a change of scene.'

'Then let it be done,' replied Stapleton. 'I am entirely at your service, my lady.'

Once they were driving out of Bath, however, he raised the subject again, although in a roundabout way. 'I am so pleased that you have Mrs Waring staying with you,' he said. 'She seems an altogether delightful person.'

'I feel very fortunate to have found her,' Florence replied. She could have said that she and Anne differed as to the temperature at which they liked rooms to be kept, that Anne did not seem to care for Casper, and that she could be overbearing at times and rather nosy, but she did not want to seem critical, and after all she was very grateful that Anne was helping her out of a difficult situation.

'I am sure that she is entirely to be trusted,' he went on. 'It is such a comfort to me that you have one relation in whom you may repose complete confidence.'

Florence did not reply. She could not think what to say.

Eventually, Stapleton went on, 'I know you will not approve of my saying more, but I cannot be silent upon this head. My dear Lady Le Grey, pray have a care with regard to Sir Vittorio. I cannot rid myself of the idea that he may cause you some harm.'

'You are very kind to be concerned, but I would really rather not discuss this matter,' Florence replied, thinking of the groom perched behind them.

As if in response to this, Mr Stapleton reined in the curricle and said, 'Shall we walk for a little? The views are very fine up here on the Downs. Lowson, go to their heads.'

The groom sprang down to take hold of the horses, and, after a moment or two's hesitation, Florence alighted with the assistance of Mr Stapleton's hand. She felt quite sure that he wanted to raise the subject of Sir Vittorio's wickedness, but she could not think of a good reason for refusing to get down. Furthermore, if the groom's absence meant that he could speak frankly, then so too could she when she refused to say any more. It was very strange, but although she was delighted to abuse Vittorio herself, she felt rather annoyed when other people did so. She could only put it down to some strange, misplaced 'family' feeling; or perhaps to the kind of loyalty that one adventurer must feel towards another.

As they began to walk, she confined her observations firmly to the excellent views to be found as they looked back towards Bath, and for a time, Mr Stapleton responded in kind, but soon he reverted to the previous topic. 'If only I had the right to protect you,' he said fiercely. 'I cannot tell you how helpless it makes me feel to know that you are at the mercy of that . . . that viper!'

To defuse the situation, Florence pretended to misunderstand him and, looking down, exclaimed, 'Oh good heavens, are there snakes about?'

'You know what I mean,' he replied impatiently.

'Sir?' queried Florence with a touch of hauteur in her voice.

'I beg your pardon,' he answered in an agitated tone. 'But I cannot bear to think that he has the right to have influence over your life.'

'Forgive me, sir, but I am of age. Neither he, nor any other person, has that right unless I choose to give it to them.'

'Then give it to me,' he said hastily.

'To you?' She did not immediately understand what he meant.

'Yes. Be my wife, Florence.' He bit his lip and turned his head away. 'Forgive me. I know I have spoken too soon, your mourning is not yet over. But my feelings are such that . . . in short, I cannot bear to wait any longer before addressing you. If we were married, I could protect you from that scoundrel.'

Florence stared at him. She had been aware that his interest in her was growing, but had certainly not expected a declaration at this stage. She remembered something that had occurred to her and that she had put to the back of her mind, namely, that before she could accept anyone's declaration she would have to tell him the truth about herself.

He clearly misunderstood the reason for her hesitation, for he said, 'I know he is your relation, but I also know that he is not to be trusted. Where has he come from? Who knows him? The only person who vouches for Sir Vittorio Le Grey is Sir Vittorio Le Grey.' He paused. 'Be careful, I beg of you. I know your cousin feels the same.'

'My cousin?' In her confusion, she could only think of Vittorio.

'Your cousin Anne — Mrs Waring, I should say.'

'I appreciate the concern that you both show in my welfare,' Florence assured him. 'But as for anything else, you are quite right that it is too soon, and I am not prepared to discuss this matter further. Pray take me back to Laura Place, sir.'

'I have offended you,' he murmured. 'Will you forgive me?'

'You have not offended me,' she replied, 'but you have confused me. Let us speak of other things.'

He obliged her, and for the rest of their walk and during the journey back, he talked of indifferent matters, but there was an undercurrent of tension between them that reminded her that he had not forgotten what had been discussed between them.

On their arrival back at Laura Place, he got down from the curricle and walked with her to the front door. 'I shall say no more on a certain subject since that is your wish,' he murmured, taking hold of her hand and raising it reverently to his lips, 'but pray believe that I am your obedient servant, now and always.'

Anne was in the hall when she went in, and she could almost have suspected that she had been lying in wait, so timely was her appearance. 'Well?' said Mrs Waring eagerly. 'Did you have an agreeable drive?'

'Yes, thank you,' replied Florence. 'We went up to the downs, and had a splendid view of the city.'

'Oh, good,' answered Mrs Waring, sounding as if she had been expecting to hear something far more interesting. 'And was Mr Stapleton very charming?'

'Quite as charming as one would expect,' said Florence, mounting the stairs.

'Shall I ring for tea for us?' asked Anne. 'Then you can tell me all about it.'

Florence turned on the stairs. 'I think I'll just have a little rest in my room, if you don't mind, Anne,' she replied. 'I'll be down later.'

She was aware of Anne's disappointment, but she was not prepared to talk about the conversation with Mr Stapleton just yet, or even at all, perhaps. She wanted to think about it a little more for herself first.

Once in her room with the door closed, she rang for tea, and when it had arrived, she sat down in front of the fire to think about what had happened. First of all, it was impossible not to be flattered by Mr Stapleton's interest. She had clearly made much more of an impression upon him all those years ago than she would ever have suspected.

She reminded herself that he had come to visit her at The Laurels, and that her father had sent him away. Her father had sneered at her, telling her that Stapleton had only been interested in her money. She was now able to put a lot of what he had said down to spite, but she could not help thinking that a man with a genuine interest in her would have tried a little harder to see her as Margaret had once suggested, and, although she hated herself for being so suspicious, she had to bear in mind the fact that he was courting her now in earnest, knowing that she was a wealthy woman.

Of course, she was still a wealthy woman whether she called herself Lady Le Grey, or whether she returned to being plain Miss Browne, but what would Mr Stapleton think of someone who had practised a deliberate deception upon the good citizens of Bath? Furthermore, how would he feel about his well-meaning warnings concerning Sir Vittorio, when he realized that the gentleman who had been behaving towards her in such a masterful and possessive way was not in fact related to her at all?

One thing was clear: if she did decide to tell Mr Stapleton the truth, she would have to get away from Bath first. Then, if he still wanted to marry her after her deceit, she could return eventually as Mrs Stapleton, and no one need know the truth.

She put down her cup, and stared into the fire. How handsome Mr Stapleton was! How tall and well made! He was surely every woman's dream. Why, then, was she thinking about marrying him in such a calculated way? She recalled how he had kissed her hand when he had brought her back. What a romantic gesture it had been! How charming! How unexciting. Unexciting? Now where had that idea come from? And if Mr Stapleton's salute stirred her so little — which surely must mean that she was demented — what exactly did she want from a man?

In the most illogical way, her thoughts strayed to Sir Vittorio, and the liberties that he had chosen to take with her person. Of course she did not want Stapleton to seize her in the Chapter House, or hook his fingers into her bodice, or kiss her in her very own house with visitors arriving at the door — did she? After all, Sir Vittorio was the rudest man alive, and his behaviour towards her only became remotely excusable if he did in truth believe her to be an adventuress, as he had always declared. Surely, if there was the slightest chance that he believed her to be truly Lady Le Grey, he would never behave so disrespectfully.

As an adventurer himself, he might possibly behave in a casual manner towards one whom he suspected of being cast in the same mould. Unfortunately, there was one other entirely plausible explanation for the insolence mixed with anger which had characterized his attitude to her, and that was that he was really Vittorio Le Grey, genuine owner of that name, legitimately outraged because some unknown female had purloined it.

The very idea made her shudder. For a brief moment, she remembered that sympathetic pressure of his hand on her shoulder and she toyed with the novel idea that he might be prepared to listen to her story without instantly condemning her. No sooner had the idea occurred to her than she instantly dismissed it. The owner of such a proud name would show no mercy to one who had brought it into disrepute.

She remembered Miss Le Grey. She had always stated quite categorically that she was the last of her name, and that with her, it would die out. What if she had been mistaken? What if there had been some other relative that she had forgotten, but whom the name or appearance of Sir Vittorio might call to mind? Unhappily, the old lady was dead now, so it was too late to ask her.

Memories of Miss Le Grey and the neighbourhood in which she had lived reminded her that Lord Braintree was to go there, and had perhaps already set off. Suddenly she clapped her hands to her mouth. He had declared the intention of inviting Sir Vittorio to go with him: the baronet would meet the Chancerys, who knew that Florence Browne was in Bath, but who, unless Margaret had divulged the whole truth to them, which was unlikely, knew nothing about Lady Firenza Le Grey! Now what was she to do?

★　★　★

Vittorio, who had taken just as much of a liking to Lord Braintree as had the earl to him, was sorely tempted to go with him, but at first declined. 'I have business here in Bath that needs to be concluded,' he declared. 'Furthermore, it is possible that my aunt, who is also travelling here from Italy, may be arriving any day, and I want to be present when she appears.'

'That's disappointing,' Braintree responded. 'I had had hopes that you might be able to keep my spirits up on the journey. Besides,' he added craftily, 'I thought that you might be interested to see where your relative, Lady Le Grey, grew up.'

The baronet looked suddenly attentive. 'Did she grow up in that place? I did not know.'

'Mrs Bridge let it slip in conversation on one occasion,' replied the earl. 'Why don't you come? It might give you a clue as to why she is so fascinating. That is, if you don't mind leaving Stapleton with a clear field . . . '

'It doesn't matter to me what progress Stapleton makes,' snapped Vittorio. 'Of course I will come.'

'I dare say your business will wait,' murmured the earl, hiding a smile.

★   ★   ★

It did not take Florence long to decide upon her course of action; she must leave Bath, without delay. Whether Sir Vittorio was genuine or not was now irrelevant. The merest amount of investigation on his part — and she had no doubt that he would indulge in some — would reveal that she was

235

not who she claimed to be. Then, doubtless he would feel free to denounce her to all and sundry and shower jewels upon her and probably insist that she become his mistress. A shiver ran through her at the very idea; disgust, she told herself. Before she could think any further about the matter, she went to find Anne. Her cousin was seated at a writing-table in the book-room, busy with her pen, but she stopped as soon as Florence came into the room and got up to come towards her.

'You find me writing to my husband,' she said, smiling. 'It is rather long since we parted, and he will be missing me; indeed, I must think about returning to him soon.'

'Perhaps now would be a good time,' said Florence without preamble. 'I find myself longing to leave Bath almost immediately, and must begin making plans at once.'

'Immediately?' exclaimed Anne, her face the picture of consternation. 'But why?'

'Believe me, there are reasons,' answered Florence, trying to sound unconcerned.

'Do they concern your cousin?' asked Anne, her eyes narrowing.

Florence turned away so that the other woman could not see her expression. 'Certainly not,' she replied untruthfully. 'I scarcely think of him from one day's end to the next. I have simply become weary of the place.'

'Of course I shall help you all I can,' her cousin declared, 'even though I am not entirely convinced of all that you say.'

'Thank you,' said Florence warmly. 'Will you give orders for the house and my things to be packed up as soon as may be? I have an errand which I must undertake without fail.'

'But can I not do that for you?' asked Anne. 'Surely it would be better for you to give the orders yourself.'

Florence hesitated, but then decided that she could not leave the delivery of the sapphires to another. 'I shan't be long,' she declared. 'But I cannot entrust this task to anyone else.'

'Where will you go?' Anne asked.

'Perhaps to Buxton, although I haven't yet completely made up my mind,' Florence replied. Then, thinking that it might sound odd that she was leaving one watering place simply go to another, she added, 'I have never visited Derbyshire.'

Anne smiled slyly. 'Of course, Mr Stapleton's estates are in the North,' she murmured.

Deciding against replying directly to this, Florence said simply, 'If you can find out how long it will take to pack everything up, will you ask Stevens to have a post chaise ordered for me on the first possible day? Tell him that I shall want him to look after Casper until I am settled somewhere.' She had not taken the step of purchasing a carriage of her own whilst in Bath, judging it to be unnecessary when it was perfectly possible to walk nearly everywhere, and hire conveyances easily whenever they were needed.

It did not take her long to wrap up the sapphires and the brooch, and to make the whole parcel look like a book. It took her three times longer to write the note that she felt should go with them. In the end, she simply inscribed these few lines;

I am not what you think me. Your sentiments and your insults dishonour you as much as they dishonour me. Pray do not insult me with such gifts again.

That done, she sealed the note and tucked it under the string with which the parcel was wrapped. Then having put on her outdoor clothing, she went downstairs. She was just leaving the house when Grieves, the footman, came in.

'Where have you been?' she asked him, thinking that all the servants would have plenty to do if she and Anne were to leave Bath very soon.

'Taking a note for Mrs Waring, my lady,' he answered self-consciously.

Florence nodded. That would be the letter to her husband which Anne had been writing earlier. Strange that she should still choose to send it when no doubt their departure from Bath would mean that she would be reunited with him quite soon. Probably she did not want to waste effort and paper.

As she walked through the Bath streets on her way to the Christopher, Florence could not help reflecting that this might be the last time that she would do such a thing. With what high hopes had she come! How foolish she now felt, obliged to leave because of her own deception! What had seemed a piece of harmless innocent fun had become a falsehood that threatened to make her look absurd and pathetic! If only Sir Vittorio had not come, she sighed to herself. Then she might have met Mr Stapleton again, confessed to him the true state of affairs, and their romance, killed by her father, might have been reignited without this awful stumbling block of her own creating.

Strangely enough, however, this idea failed to capture her imagination at all. She thought again of Sir Vittorio. What would their first meeting have been like if she had been introduced to him as plain Miss Browne?

Would he have bowed politely and turned his handsome head away, or would he have bent that burning gaze upon her, and spoken so audaciously that she was obliged to catch her breath?

On arriving at the Christopher, she went inside and, attracting the attention of a waiter, entrusted him with the package. 'It is most important that it should be placed into Sir Vittorio's hands personally,' she told him.

'Am I to tell him who delivered it, ma'am?' he asked respectfully.

'Yes,' replied Florence, deciding that this would be the very last time that she would use the name. 'You may tell him that it is from Lady Le Grey.'

There was the sound of rustling behind her and, as the waiter withdrew, bowing politely, an imperious voice said, 'And who may that person be, *signora*, for I am of that family, and I know beyond the shadow of a doubt that no such person exists.'

Florence turned to be confronted with a haughty-looking lady of mature years of about her own height and very upright bearing, who bore considerably more than a passing resemblance to Sir Vittorio. Like Florence, she was dressed entirely and very expensively in black, her clothes were in the height of fashion, and she carried a beribboned cane. Florence's heart sank in dismay, for this lady's appearance confirmed what she had already been suspecting; here was a genuine aristocrat of the highest rank; if she was indeed of Vittorio's family, then he must be one too.

Standing a short distance away from them, Florence could see a small group of people to whom she had been introduced in the Pump Room, and they were watching the unfolding scene with some curiosity. She could have wished them to be in any other place at this moment.

'Well, *signora*, are you going to explain yourself?' the lady asked.

Florence straightened her spine. This might be her last appearance as Lady Le Grey, and she was determined not to disgrace herself. 'I am Lady Le Grey,' she replied in calm tones that were completely at variance with the way in which her stomach was churning. 'In what way may I serve you, madam?'

'You may come with me into this parlour,' said the other, 'and there you will explain to me the meaning of this performance.'

'Performance?' repeated Florence, her colour heightening. 'I do not understand you, madam. After all, I am not the one who is making a spectacle of herself in the entrance of a hotel.' Nevertheless she did follow her into the parlour, in order to save attracting any more attention to their interview.

'But I think that you understand me perfectly well,' she replied, her glittering smile making her look more like Sir Vittorio than ever. 'What word other than performance would be appropriate with regard to the work of an actress?'

'You insult me, madam,' answered Florence, 'and you do so, furthermore, without doing me the courtesy of informing me to whom I am speaking. Or do you not have a name that you can give me?'

The lady drew herself up so that she was even straighter than ever and fire flashed from her magnificent dark eyes. 'I have a perfectly good name, which is, unlike yours, all my own,' she declared. 'I am Constanzia da Sforza, and Vittorio Le Grey, whom I am meeting here this day, is my nephew.' She took a step closer to Florence. 'I know for a fact that no Lady Le Grey exists; so who, *signora*, are you? And, which is more to the point, where is he?'

Her questions reminded Florence so much of those which the baronet had addressed to her when they had first met, that her anger swelled up to leave no room for fear. Furthermore, her mind latched on to one vital fact which her questioner had so foolishly revealed. 'Does it not occur to you, madam, that there is one very good reason why I might know where your nephew is when you clearly do not; why I have brought a gift for him; and why I bear his name?'

For the first time, Florence had the satisfaction of knowing that she had disconcerted her companion.

'You cannot mean . . . ' began Signora da Sforza, staring at her. 'A woman like you . . . '

'But I thought that you knew exactly who I was and what I meant,' Florence retorted, buoyed up because for a moment or two she held the whip hand. 'I will leave you to your reflections for now, madam. You may wallow in your lurid imaginings until you discover the true state of affairs.' So saying, she swept past the other lady regally and left the hotel, bowing imperiously to her acquaintances from the Pump Room as she did so.

The satisfaction that she felt from having given a good account of herself carried her all the way to Pulteney Bridge, where she paused, and stood looking down into the water, where a single craft was making its way from beneath where she was standing. She had certainly burned her boats now, she reflected. She had been unpardonably insolent to a lady who was quite clearly exactly who she claimed to be. Furthermore, she had as good as told Signora da Sforza that she was married to Sir Vittorio Le Grey. How could she possibly face her again? Worst of all, how could she possibly face *him*? Whatever would he think of her now? His anger and his suspicion she could bear with her head held high, but his pity and his contempt?

Impatiently she strode on, angrily brushing away the tears that had suddenly come into her eyes for no reason that she could conceive. She would go elsewhere, perhaps to another watering place, as she had intimated to Anne, and this time she would be plain Miss Browne, and seek to be nothing else, which was why, however kind her cousin might be, she must go alone.

When she arrived back at the house in Laura Place, her cousin was there and, to her surprise and annoyance, Mr Stapleton was also present. He eyed her with concern, and took her hand. 'My dear Lady Le Grey, you look distressed. May I be of assistance?'

Florence stared up at him, pulling herself together. It was inevitable that Sir Vittorio would discover her deceit, but she did not want Mrs Waring and Mr Stapleton to learn of it until she chose to tell them. Just now she did not feel ready to make explanations, and, in any case, Sir Vittorio deserved to be the first to know.

'No, I am not distressed,' she replied, forcing a smile to her lips. 'But I have much to think about at present.'

'I happened to call in, and Mrs Waring has told me that you plan to leave Bath,' said Mr Stapleton. 'Is this not a sudden decision?'

'I suppose so,' answered Florence. 'But I am quite determined upon it.'

Mr Stapleton's firm jaw hardened. 'If I believed that that scoundrel had been menacing you, then I should call him to account,' he declared forcefully.

Suddenly, Florence was terribly tired of the whole business. 'Oh, for goodness sake,' she exclaimed in exasperated tones. 'He is not a scoundrel! Why do we have to discuss him as if he is the centre of the universe? Can you not leave the matter alone?'

Stapleton flushed. 'I beg your pardon,' he said in subdued tones. Florence noted that he glanced quickly towards Mrs Waring, who looked rather annoyed. At once she realized how rude she had been.

'No, I must beg yours,' she answered, smiling in rather a strained manner. 'You are very good to be concerned. But forgive me, Mr Stapleton, if we are to leave Bath as soon as may be, then I must bid you good day and beg to be excused.'

'I shall not delay you,' he replied, his tone

humble after her reproof. 'But allow me to serve you by escorting you to wherever you wish to go. It is my earnest desire to serve you in whatever way you may permit.'

'You are very kind,' said Mrs Waring. 'I am sure that my cousin is very grateful for your kind offer, and we will send word if it is needed.' He bowed and took his leave. 'What a delightful man he is,' Mrs Waring remarked, after he had gone. 'So handsome, and so devoted to your interests!'

'Yes indeed,' agreed Florence, setting her foot on the bottom step. 'How is the packing proceeding? How long before it will all be done?'

'You will be able to leave first thing in the morning,' answered her cousin, walking up the stairs with her. 'Since you took the house furnished, there is very little to bring apart from your personal effects. Stevens says that he can see to the shutting up of the house and follow later with the dog. I have bespoken a post chaise for you for eleven o'clock.' She paused briefly. 'Have you definitely settled on Buxton?'

Florence shook her head. 'I'm not sure,' she replied. 'Buxton or some other watering place.'

Mrs Waring made a face. 'And have to suffer another lot of dowdies?' she asked incredulously. 'Sad stuff! Fee, I have a better idea, and pray, don't eat me.'

'I shan't,' answered Florence. They had by now reached her bedroom and she went in and began to take off her hat, wishing that her cousin would just go away.

'Today, after you had announced that you wanted to leave Bath, I added a line or two in my letter to my husband to the effect that I might be bringing a visitor when I returned to him.'

'A visitor?' questioned Florence.

'You, you silly thing,' replied Anne laughing. 'It will solve your problems perfectly, and will be charming for me as well, to have you to stay.'

'You are very kind, but I would not wish to impose,' said Florence.

'Nonsense! It will be no imposition, I can assure you,' exclaimed Anne warmly. 'And it will give you time to think about what to do next, without worrying about prying eyes.'

'Let me give you my answer in the morning,' suggested Florence.

'Oh, very well,' Anne shrugged and Florence sensed that she was not very pleased. 'Far be it from me to force you into doing anything. I only wanted to be helpful.'

'I know you did,' answered Florence, suddenly feeling guilty for not being more appreciative of this kind offer. 'It's just that I have so many things on my mind at present.'

After Anne had gone, Florence acknowledged reluctantly that, unfortunate though it was, she had never really warmed to her cousin. Perhaps it was that touch of inquisitiveness that repelled her, or maybe it was the habit that she seemed to have of always trying to cool the rooms down. Florence told herself that she was being unreasonable, but she knew that she would never feel able to confide in Anne in the way in which she had been able to confide in Margaret Bridge.

All the same, she told herself, it was very comforting to have two people like Mrs Waring and Mr Stapleton looking out for her interests. She was sure that Mr Stapleton would prove to be more than a match for the wicked Italian. Except, of course, that he wasn't wicked after all; he was a gentleman with a proud name, who had sought to take steps to prevent it from being dragged in the mire by a sordid adventuress! She closed her eyes in an effort to block out the pain.

Oh, that he could have met and admired me in an ordinary, respectable way! she thought to herself, getting up, then pacing restlessly about the room. But then, of course, he would never have seized her and kissed her in the Chapter House, or here in the saloon of this very house. At the very memory of his kiss, she began to feel dizzy.

At once, she sat down on the bed, her eyes widening with disbelief. By the greatest irony, it suddenly became clear to her that she had been in love with Vittorio almost from the very beginning. It had only been her determination on the one hand to think him a villain and on the other to prevent him from thinking her an adventuress that had stopped her from seeing it sooner.

So much had he captured her imagination that even the appearance of Gilbert Stapleton, with all the reminders that he had brought of love that might have been, had failed to alter her allegiance. She had been pleased to see him again and her vanity had been flattered by the attentions of so masculine a man. The memories that he had given rise to, of a time when her mother had been alive, had moved her, as had his professions of continued interest in her; but he had not touched her heart. That had been stolen by a foppish, effeminate-looking Italian, whom Stapleton could probably knock down with one hand tied behind his back!

It was no use repining. Now that she had insulted his aunt, the baronet would never forgive her. Her iniquities were too many. But she would not take the obvious way out by marrying Stapleton. It was unfortunate for him, but from now on, Florence could not help but connect him with Bath and all that had happened there. She felt much the same about Mrs Waring. She smiled ironically. She had spent such a lot of time in the past wishing that she could have some relations; now that she had found one, she had come to the conclusion that she would as soon be without her.

She would thank them both for their kindness, but from here on she would go alone, find a new place and make new acquaintances among the ranks of those who had never even heard the name of Vittorio Le Grey. She knew that she was running away like a coward, but she could not help it.

★　★　★

The following morning, when Florence awoke, the serving maid who brought her chocolate told her that everything had been packed. 'There's just your travelling things laid out for you, my lady, then your night things to be packed away and it'll all be done.' Florence thanked her. She had from the beginning decided not to employ an abigail, judging that since she had been managing without one for most of her life, she could certainly manage without one now. It would at least be one less person to worry about uprooting, she concluded.

On going into the breakfast-room, she found that the fire had not even been lit. 'It seemed a little foolish, when we are to leave so soon,' Anne remarked. 'I have told Stevens not to light fires in any of the other rooms either.'

Feeling a little annoyed, but trying not to show it, Florence said, 'I can understand your decision, but you might perhaps change your mind later. I have definitely decided, Anne, that I will leave alone. You are, of course, welcome to stay on in this house until Stevens has finished here, but I did get the impression that you wanted to leave very soon as well.'

On hearing her words, Mrs Waring looked not a little put out. 'By no means,' she declared. 'I cannot allow you to leave all alone and unescorted, and I am convinced that Mr Stapleton will not allow it either.'

Florence waited for Stevens to leave the room before saying, 'Anne, I have made my mind up about this. I am truly grateful to you for all your help, indeed I am. But I am resolved to go alone. Do me the justice of accepting that I know my own mind in this.'

For a moment, her cousin stared at her in a

way that could only be described as hostile. Then she shrugged and said, 'Oh very well, please yourself. But do not blame me if I, in my turn, have errands to run this morning. Oh and by the way, pray do not bother to make arrangements for me to stay here. I have no wish to batten upon you and shall remove from this house when you do.'

'It would not be battening, as you express it,' said Florence, rather annoyed at being put upon the defensive simply because she wanted to determine her own fate. Not wanting to argue over the breakfast table, especially when Stevens might return at any moment, Florence said no more on this subject, and instead remarked that the day was bright and clear, not at all unpromising for travelling. She was grateful that Anne seemed to take her cue, and responded with a little anecdote about a journey that she had taken in the North country recently.

'Make sure that the local staff are all paid off well, if you please, Stevens,' said Florence, when the meal was over.

'Very good, my lady,' he responded. Florence smiled. Dear Stevens! Not once had he slipped up with regard to her supposed title.

She turned to Anne. 'Forgive me if I go upstairs to finish getting ready,' she said, softening her voice, because she was aware that she had sounded a little harsh before.

'Of course,' replied Anne, smiling back. She was still smiling when Florence climbed the stairs.

13

On finding the only hostelry in Howton quite unable to put them up for even as much as a night, Lord Braintree and Sir Vittorio repaired to Gloucester, where they found a coaching inn, ready and able to accommodate them.

Lord Braintree, with an eagerness that would not have disgraced a man half his age, was all for setting out for Tall Chimneys immediately, but Sir Vittorio would not allow him to do so. 'My friend, would you address your lady hungry and with your dress in disarray from your journey?' he asked quizzically.

The earl looked down at his coat, which was certainly somewhat creased from sitting in the coach. 'Perhaps I had better change,' he said doubtfully, with the air of one conceding a doubtful point.

'Indeed you had,' agreed Vittorio. '*And* eat.'

'Eat? I haven't time to eat,' protested his lordship. As if taking fright at this decision, his stomach gave a rumble of protest. The baronet said nothing, but simply raised one brow, and the earl was obliged to laugh. 'Oh, very well,' he agreed. 'But bespeak something that won't take too long, there's a good fellow.' He stared at his companion, who was looking far more well groomed than a man who had sat in a coach for several hours had any right to be. 'How do you do it?' he asked. The baronet laughed and shrugged in a very continental style.

'Go and change,' he said. 'I will bespeak a dinner for you that will suit your purpose.'

Although Lord Braintree resented having to spend this time changing when he would much rather have gone to see Mrs Bridge, his mirror told him that he was not looking his best. The landlord very obligingly arranged for the clothes that his lordship had brought to be pressed, and after the earl had discarded his soiled shirt and washed the grime of the journey from his face and hands, he began to feel glad that he had given the time to refresh himself.

It was a little over half an hour later that the earl came downstairs, feeling much more appropriately dressed to face his lady, in a puce coat with a waistcoat of a lighter shade. The landlord showed him into a private parlour and announced that soup would be served 'as soon as the foreign gentleman was ready'. Recalling the unfailingly immaculate appearance of the baronet, Lord Braintree looked at the clock, then at his watch, and wondered how long he would have to wait.

He did Sir Vittorio less than justice. Only five minutes after the earl himself had appeared, and before he had had a chance to do more than swallow half of the glass of excellent sherry that the landlord had pressed upon him, the door opened and the baronet entered, looking as if he had stepped straight out of a band box. 'How do you do it?' the earl asked again, shaking his head.

Once more, the baronet laughed. 'Shall we eat?' he said.

The meal was excellent, but simple, as the earl had requested, and they enjoyed a delicious vegetable soup followed by a steak pie with vegetables, and, because neither man had a sweet tooth, the meal was rounded off with a fine plate of cheese. The red wine that the landlord offered them was very acceptable, but the earl nobly resisted the temptation to send for another bottle. 'I need all my wits about me tonight,' he insisted.

They did not linger when the meal was over. 'Come, then,' said the baronet. 'You will give me no peace until we have found your lady.' They sent for their carriage, and achieved the short journey in a brief space of time, arriving at Tall Chimneys just after the tea tray had been brought in.

Mr and Mrs Chancery were the only occupants of the room and Lord Braintree, baulked of his prey at this crucial moment, could not think of anything to say. It was left to Vittorio to step forward and introduce himself and his companion.

'You must forgive this intrusion,' he said, 'but we were fortunate enough to make Mrs Bridge's acquaintance in Bath, and chancing to be in this part of the world, we decided to call and see how she does.'

Even Mr and Mrs Chancery, surely the most easy and accommodating of people, must have found it strange that an English peer and a half-Italian baronet had made a special evening call purely in order to renew their acquaintance with the governess of the house. If they did think so, however, they did not say anything to that effect. Mrs Chancery merely remarked that Mrs Bridge would shortly be coming downstairs with the children, and, as if on cue, the door opened, and two demure young girls entered, followed by their governess.

Lord Braintree fixed his eyes upon her, and to him, after a few days' deprivation, she looked more beautiful than ever. She did not see him at first, absorbed as she was in making sure that the two girls made their curtsies, but when she did catch sight of him, her colour went alarmingly, then came back in a rush, and she raised her hand to her throat.

'Margaret, my dear, here are Lord Braintree and Sir Vittorio, come to see how you are,' said Mrs Chancery.

'I . . . I am well,' she stammered. 'It is very kind of you to call upon me.'

'I could not keep away,' said Lord Braintree in heartfelt tones.

Unfortunately, by this time Mrs Bridge had remembered with what high hopes she had encountered his lordship on one occasion, and how bitterly she had been disappointed, and she was determined not to risk incurring any further hurt. She therefore guided her two charges to sit down at one end of the room, and sat with them, taking out her needlework.

Lord Braintree, baffled by these tactics, looked at Sir Vittorio in an imploring way, but the baronet merely raised his brows and grinned impishly, before engaging his host and hostess in conversation. Braintree, therefore, determined not to be put off, seated himself with the schoolroom party.

'I trust that you are in good health, Mrs Bridge,' he began. 'I was very sorry to discover that you had left Bath before I had had an opportunity to say goodbye to you.'

'My place is here, as you see, with Rebecca and Stephanie,' Margaret replied, in an even tone that belied the turmoil in her heart. 'I could not continue to remain in Bath, leaving Mrs Chancery in the lurch.'

'Besides, we were missing her, weren't we Stephanie?' piped up the elder of the two girls. The younger one nodded her head. 'Would you like to hear about what we have been learning, my lord?' Rebecca went on. 'We have been studying the history of the Roman empire. Did you know that the Romans heated their houses by lighting fires under the floor?'

'Yes, I did know it,' replied Braintree, anxiously hoping that the child would not now feel bound to tell him all that she had learned so far.

'I know lots of other things about the Romans,' she went on enthusiastically, thus appearing to dash all his hopes.

At this point, Margaret stepped in, however. 'Perhaps his lordship could come to the schoolroom another day so that you can show him your drawings,' she suggested. Then, turning to the earl she continued, dropping her voice a little, 'I hope that Lady Le Grey is well.'

'Very well, but missing you, I believe,'

replied Braintree. 'She is not the only one to be doing so.'

Margaret looked up into his face, and catching the ardent expression upon it, looked down again. 'You are very kind,' she said. 'How is your mama?'

'She is well, thank you.'

'Is your mama still alive?' asked Rebecca.

'Yes, indeed she is,' replied the earl.

'I would have thought that she must be dead by now,' answered Rebecca, with the disastrous frankness of childhood.

'Would you indeed?' said Braintree ruefully. He could have wished the child other-where. If there was one thing he did not need at the moment, it was a child telling him in as many words what an unattractive prospect he must be.

'That was not very civil, Rebecca,' said Margaret. As the child begged his pardon politely, the earl glanced at his beloved, saw that she was trying to hide a smile and at once suddenly felt that he might have reason to hope. With this in mind, therefore, he said to Rebecca, 'My mother is alive and well, and is happy at the moment for I have succeeded in finding a new companion for her.'

Margaret's head came up with a jerk at that moment. 'But I thought . . . I was under the impression . . . '

'You thought that I wanted you to be my mother's companion,' filled in the earl gently.

'But Mrs Bridge could not be a companion for your mama, because she is our governess,' declared Rebecca.

'Perhaps it's just as well, then, that I do not want her to be my mother's companion,' Braintree replied, smiling at Margaret, in his expression a feeling that she could not mistake. 'I have quite another role in mind. With your permission, ma'am, I would very much like to return tomorrow morning so that I may tell you what it is. Will you allow me to do so?'

Margaret looked into his face, and his ardent expression almost caused her heart to skip a beat. 'Another role?' she whispered. 'But you cannot mean — '

'Yes I do; with all my heart,' he replied. 'May I come and see you tomorrow?'

She bent her head, but he heard her whisper, 'Yes, you may.'

'Then I am satisfied,' he replied, rising to his feet, and turning to join the others. Had he been feeling less euphoric, he must have noticed that some of Sir Vittorio's easy charm and address had deserted him, but, to be fair, his mind was on other things, and he was hardly aware of what he was saying as he conversed with Mr and Mrs Chancery. The two men only stayed for a little longer before taking their leave.

Once inside their carriage, Vittorio said, 'By your beatific expression, I take it that I am to wish you joy?'

'I'd be a coxcomb to say yes,' the earl replied. 'But she has given me leave to call upon her tomorrow. She would surely not encourage me thus if she intended to refuse me.'

The baronet shook his head. 'One can never tell with women, my friend,' he said solemnly. The earl began to look anxious, but his friend clapped him on the shoulder. 'I am only joking with you,' said Vittorio in quite another tone. 'My friend, I could not be more pleased. But, by your leave, ask your lady a question or two for me in the morning.'

'For you?' asked Braintree, puzzled.

'Why yes,' replied Vittorio, looking very self-satisfied. 'I should very much like to know how it is that in Bath, she was living as companion to Lady Le Grey, whereas she left this village to go to Bath as companion to a Miss Florence Browne.'

'Miss Browne? But how can this be?' asked Braintree, his brow wrinkling. 'I have never met such a lady.'

'Ah, but I think you have,' declared the baronet. 'It is my belief that Miss Browne and

Lady Le Grey are one and the same.'

'You mean that Miss Browne married before she reached Bath? But no, that could not be, so — '

'Exactly,' Sir Vittorio interrupted. 'Miss Browne is not married and never has been. She is, as I have always suspected, an adventuress and a thief.'

'A thief?'

'She has stolen my name, my dear George.'

There was silence for a moment. Eventually the earl said, 'How did you find this out?'

'As simply and easily as you could imagine,' answered the baronet. 'Whilst you were discovering Mrs Bridge's sentiments, I was in conversation with Mr and Mrs Chancery. They enquired about Miss Browne, about whether she had managed to settle down happily after Mrs Bridge's departure, and if she was happy with the house in Laura Place that Mr Chancery had procured for her. There can be no doubt about it.'

'My God!' exclaimed Lord Braintree. 'I cannot believe it! Why should she want to be so deceitful? And what chance made her choose your name?'

'It was no chance,' Vittorio replied, his tone changing from ironic amusement to grim disapproval. 'There was an elderly lady living in the village who died very recently. She was called Miss Le Grey, and believed herself to be the last of her name. That actress's deception could perhaps be excused under some circumstances, but that she should plot to keep me apart from an elderly relative, who died alone needlessly, I cannot forgive. And she shall pay for it.'

★ ★ ★

It occurred to Florence that it would be very discourteous of her to leave Bath without saying goodbye to Lady Trimm, and to one or two others. She did not really want to go to the Pump Room again, but as she had entered Bath society in that very place, it seemed fitting that she should go to say goodbye. After all, she told herself, she had not done anything really wicked. She had called herself by another name, that was all. She had not conspired to defraud anyone, or cause hurt of any kind. She could still hold her head up high. Perhaps in time to come, when she was feeling braver, she would write to Lady Trimm and tell her the true story of her identity.

She would invite Anne to go with her, to make up for leaving her behind. Then once in the Pump Room, she would explain to Lady Trimm that Mrs Waring might be staying on in the Laura Place house on her own, and crave her kindness on Anne's behalf. That would surely convince Anne that her decision did not reflect upon her in any way.

When she went to Anne's room, however, there was no sign of her, and a request that one of the chambermaids seek her out yielded the rather surprising news from Stevens that she had gone out, without saying when she would return. In that case, Florence decided, she would go to the Pump Room alone. She hoped that Anne had not taken offence at her announcement that she would leave Bath without her. She had appeared to do so at first, but later had seemed to have become reconciled to the idea. The likelihood was that she had suddenly realized that she needed something from the shops, and had hurried to get it before the time came for the chaise to leave.

As Florence walked to the Pump Room, she reflected that this would be the last time that she would make this journey. What a lot had happened since the first time she had gone there! Inevitably, this reflection brought thoughts of Vittorio to her mind, and she tried hard to repress them. It would not do to start thinking of him now. Better to wait until she was on her way; then, in the privacy of her chaise, she would be able to think about what might have been, and if the tears started to fall there would be nobody to see.

To her relief, Lady Trimm was indeed there with her daughters, and she was sorry to hear that Florence was leaving. 'My dear Lady Le Grey, this is a very sudden decision, surely,' she said concernedly. 'The loss of your company will leave a gap in our little society here.'

'You are very kind,' replied Florence, feeling very foolish at the sensation of prickling at the back of her eyes. 'But the departure of Mrs Bridge has rather unsettled me. I have decided to travel about a little, perhaps to some other watering place.'

'You must write to me,' said Lady Trimm, 'and please promise to come back when you are tired of travelling.'

'Perhaps I might,' agreed Florence, adding silently, when I have confessed about my real identity and been forgiven.

'Is your cousin to go with you?' asked her ladyship innocently.

'No, I intend to go alone,' answered Florence. She was thinking of Anne Waring.

'Perhaps you may not be allowed to do so,' suggested her ladyship. 'Here he is, now.'

With a feeling of impending doom, Florence turned round to face Vittorio Le Grey. For a moment, he paused in the doorway, then strode across the room towards her, with a leisurely, panther-like grace. Now that she knew the truth about him, the idea that he was anything other than an aristocrat of a long and distinguished lineage seemed completely absurd. He was dressed today in dull red brocade with a black waistcoat of watered silk and, as usual, his hair was immaculately tied back at his neck. The very sight of him made her heart beat faster, but as he drew near, she could see by the expression in his eyes that this would be an encounter unlike any they had ever had before.

As he reached them, he swept a magnificent bow. 'My dear Lady Trimm,' he exclaimed. 'How pleased I am to see you once more! But I beg of you, introduce me to this *signorina*.'

Florence could feel her face turning to fire. Lady Trimm looked puzzled, as well she might, stared at the baronet, looked around as if the advent of some other lady had taken place and escaped her notice, and then stared at him again.

'But . . . but Sir Vittorio, I . . . You must explain yourself,' she stammered.

'*Certamente*,' he replied. 'I had been told that a relative of mine was here, but it is not so, for there is no one present in this room with any connection to me or to my family.'

Florence stared at him. As usual, his flamboyant presence had attracted some attention, and since he had not lowered his voice, those in the immediate vicinity were easily able to hear what he had to say.

'But . . . Lady Le Grey,' murmured Lady Trimm.

'There is no such person, my lady,' replied Vittorio. His words were addressed to the baroness, but his eyes were fixed on Florence, and they were as hard and as unforgiving as agate. 'There is, however, a Miss Browne; a plain, undistinguished creature, who has, through deceit and the unscrupulous use of my name, managed to worm her way into this society. Would you like to meet her?'

Florence did not wait to hear any more. She turned, picked up her skirts and fairly ran for the door, but she had reckoned without the baronet. With a murmured '*mi scusi*' to those around, he was after her, and he caught her up just outside the door, grasping her arm, and swinging her round to face him.

'What do you want,' she asked him, staring into his face, her expression at one and the same time angry and miserable. 'Haven't you done what you wanted to do?'

'What I wanted?' he exclaimed. 'This has nothing to do with what I want.'

'Of course it has,' she replied scornfully. 'You wanted to drag me down from the very beginning. Deny it if you can.'

'I don't deny it,' he answered. 'But do you not deserve to be dragged from a position that was not yours to claim?'

'I wanted no position,' she stormed. 'I had no idea you existed.'

His expression took on a look of contempt. 'I say you lie, Firenza,' he replied.

'It's true,' she replied desperately. 'How could I have known about you? I thought that Miss Le Grey was the last of her name, and so did she.'

'Ah yes, my kinswoman,' he put in. 'The kinswoman about whom I have only just learned, who died alone and friendless before I, as head of her family, could offer words of comfort and support. The kinswoman about whom you knew, but never told me!'

'Oh no,' she whispered, as she looked up at him. It had never occurred to her that he would feel like that.

'Are you starting to feel that your adventure is just a little sordid?' he asked her, pulling her closer to him. A small crowd of interested spectators had gathered about them, but they were both quite oblivious to anything except for one another. 'Does it not strike you, Signorina Browne, that such a sordid adventure can have only one ending?' He dropped his voice to a purr. 'Your deceit has been exposed. You have my sapphires. You know that I desire you. Surely there is now only one logical step?'

He was suggesting that she become his mistress and although, because she loved him, she was sorely tempted to belong to him in the only way that was open to her, she knew that she could not bear to keep seeing the contempt in his eyes. With an inarticulate cry, she tore herself free and ran in the direction of Laura Place, dropping to a walk when she became out of breath, and completely ignoring the interested gaze of passers-by.

Once back inside, she was thankful for the continued absence of Anne. In her present state, she hardly felt that she would have been able to avoid that lady's curiosity. She hurried up to her room. It looked quite strange now, largely bare of her own belongings.

She could feel tears coming to her eyes, but again she firmly suppressed them. The chaise would be at the door at any time; Anne no doubt would reappear; there were the servants to be faced; all in all she could not afford to give way to her emotions now. Heaven knew, she had had enough practice in concealing what she was feeling during the time that she had had to live with her father. She could surely do so for a little longer.

When she was almost ready to go, there was a knock at the front door. Her heart skipped a beat, and she wondered for a moment, whether the baronet had come to apologize. Then she told herself that it was much more likely that if he had pursued her, it would be to upbraid her further. When a maid came upstairs to tell her that Mr Stapleton had arrived to see her, she did not know whether to be glad or sorry. She must be in a desperate way if she could acknowledge that she would rather see Vittorio than any other man on earth, whatever mood he might be in, she acknowledged ruefully.

She looked round once more at her room for the last time, and went downstairs and into the saloon, where Mr Stapleton was waiting, his hat and cane in his hand. He came forward, took hold of her hand and kissed it. His gentle courtesy came as something of a relief after the savagery of Sir Vittorio Le Grey.

'You will be angry with me for disregarding your wishes,' he said. 'But I have made myself free on purpose to escort you to wherever it is you want to go.'

Florence smiled wanly. 'You are very kind,' she said, 'but I had made up my mind that I should go alone.'

'Will you tell me why?' he asked her gently.

She walked over to the window. 'I suppose I owe you that,' she said in a low voice. 'Much has happened to me in Bath; much that has been unexpected and . . . disturbing. That is why I feel that I need to escape completely, and leave every association behind.'

'Including those who have come to know and love you?' he asked.

'Forgive me,' she answered, turning to look at him, her expression pleading. His own face was serious.

'Is there then no chance for me?' he asked her.

She shook her head. 'I can offer you no hope,' she replied.

His face took on a set expression. 'There is someone else; I believe I know who it is. He is not worthy of you.'

She blushed and turned away. 'You are mistaken,' she answered. If only he knew!

'I beg your pardon. I did not mean to intrude. Forgive me for saying so, but it seems to me that you are in need of a friend. Even though you can give me no hope, can I not prevail upon you to permit me to escort you to wherever it is you wish to go? I

272

promise I will not press my attentions upon you any further.'

She smiled up at him. In truth, she felt sorely in need of a friend at this time. 'You are very good,' she said. 'Thank you, Mr Stapleton, I will accept your kind offer, but only until I have found somewhere to stay for the night.'

'So be it,' he replied, bowing. 'May I be the bearer of any orders for your driver, my lady?'

She opened her mouth to correct his mistake, but then closed it again. He did deserve an explanation of her deception because he had been so kind, but there was not enough time to give it properly. 'Just ask them to head north,' she said.

What would her father have thought? He had been so convinced that she would always be despised and unsought; yet in one day she had rejected a proposal of marriage, and another proposal, this time from the man she really loved, of a far more dishonourable nature. She could have laughed if she had not been feeling so sad.

Conscious that it was now time for her to leave, she went once more to look for Anne, but she was nowhere to be found. Puzzled, she rang for Stevens. 'I cannot think what might have occurred, except that when I made it clear that I did not want her to come with me, she did not seem very pleased,' she said.

Stevens looked puzzled. 'But she has gone, my lady,' he said. 'Just after you went out, she returned briefly and gave orders for her trunk to be taken back to the Christopher, where she had been staying.'

'Did she leave no message?' asked Florence, wrinkling her brow.

'No, my lady. She said that you had already made your farewells.'

'I see,' sighed Florence. She would have liked to have said goodbye to Anne in a more cordial way, but it could not be helped. 'Never mind, Stevens. I shall send for you as soon as I have decided what to do.'

'Very good, my lady,' answered Stevens. 'Will you be safe travelling on your own?'

'Quite safe,' replied Florence, bending to pat Casper, whose tail was wagging uncertainly. He seemed to sense that he was about to be parted from his beloved mistress. She almost decided to take him with her, but then she remembered that she did not know where she would be stopping for the night.

As if sensing her concern, Stevens said, 'Don't worry about the dog, my lady. I shall look after him well.'

'I know you will, Stevens,' answered Florence. 'For your part, don't worry about me. I have Mr Stapleton to escort me for the first bit of my journey. Oh, and Stevens,' she added, turning on the doorstep.

'My lady?'

'It will be Miss Browne from now on,' she said ruefully. 'I am resolved to be done with subterfuge.'

The carriage had stopped a couple of doors on, and Florence, not wanting to insist that the driver backed up his horses, hurried along the street and mounted the steps as a servant held back the door for her. Mr Stapleton on horseback was waiting on the far side and, as she approached, he gave a cheerful wave. As she climbed inside, however, there was a surprise awaiting her, for Mrs Waring was seated in the far corner, dressed in travelling clothes.

'Anne!' exclaimed Florence. She could only suppose that she had not made her wishes sufficiently clear to her cousin about travelling alone. The door closed behind her and the carriage moved off. 'What are you doing here?' she asked. 'Stevens said you had gone.'

'Ah yes,' Mrs Waring agreed. 'You will have to forgive me.' She was looking more than a little smug, and Florence began to feel annoyed.

'Anne, I have valued your company very much,' she said, 'but I think that I made it

275

clear that I needed some time to myself.'

'Yes, you did,' agreed Anne, 'but I'm afraid that that wouldn't suit me at all. Now we need to stop briefly, but I must ask you to remain in your seat whilst we do so.' Mrs Waring knocked on the roof, the horses began to check, and Florence, by now feeling thoroughly annoyed, made as if to get to her feet. 'Pray sit down again, Cousin,' said Mrs Waring firmly. Florence faced her and found herself looking into the barrel of a pistol.

Willing herself not to be frightened, she said, 'Anne, I have no idea why you have chosen to take this crazy course, but perhaps you are not aware that Mr Stapleton is escorting me.'

To her amazement, her cousin started laughing and, while Florence still sat with her eyes fixed on the gun, the door opened, and someone else got in. 'For God's sake, Anne, put that thing away,' said a voice she recognized, and she turned in horror to look into the face of the man who had joined her cousin in conspiring against her.

14

After Lord Braintree had seen Sir Vittorio off back to Bath, he found that he had some time to spare before he could decently arrive at Tall Chimneys so, after checking the immaculate state of his neckwear for the hundredth time, he called for the chaise in which they had arrived — Vittorio having returned to Bath on a hired horse — and asked to be taken to Howton.

In the summer, no doubt it would have its pretty side, but in the winter, the place struck him as being rather bleak. Leaving the chaise at the Bull and Gate, he began walking along the village street, looking about him as he did so. Just as he was wondering where Lady Le Grey, or rather, Miss Browne, had lived, a gig pulled up next to him and a big, hearty-looking man, who by the nature of his physical wig and the bag next to him appeared to be a doctor, leaned down towards him.

'May I help you, sir?' the man asked him. 'You look a little lost.'

'No, I am not lost, but thank you for your concern,' replied Braintree. 'I am expected at

Tall Chimneys later, but as I was a little early, I decided to look around the village.' He paused briefly, then went on, 'I have an acquaintance, a Miss Browne, who used to live here, and I was wondering which house she lived in.'

'I am acquainted with Miss Browne myself,' replied the other. 'I am Doctor Surrey, and I attended both her mother then later on her father in their last illnesses. I trust that Miss Browne is well?'

'Yes, she is well,' replied the earl. 'I'm Braintree, by the way. Is the house where she lived around here?'

'It's just behind you,' replied the doctor.

Braintree turned to look at the place where Florence had grown up. There was nothing about it that invited; in fact, its appearance was repellent more than anything else. 'It looks pretty bleak,' he observed. 'Is there no one living there now?'

The doctor shook his head. 'Believe me, it looked just as bleak when it was occupied,' he said, 'and a bleak time of it Miss Florence had too. A life of thankless servitude is how I would describe her former existence. I do trust that her life is happier now?'

'I believe so,' answered the earl, wondering what Vittorio would do to destroy that happiness. 'But I see that it is time I was on my way. It has been a pleasure to meet you, Dr Surrey.'

'And you too, my lord,' answered the doctor genially. 'Please give Miss Browne my kind regards when you see her. She is a lady who has my deepest respect.'

In a thoughtful mood, the earl got back into the chaise. What was it that had caused Miss Browne, who was probably respected by the whole village community, to take part in a masquerade that had earned Vittorio's contempt? It was possible that Margaret would know, he reflected. But then, thinking of Margaret turned his mind to the errand upon which he was bound and, for the time being, any reflections about Florence were completely forgotten.

Mr Chancery received him very warmly and was delighted to hear about the purpose of his visit. 'My wife seemed to know in what quarter the wind stood, and she told me last night,' he confided. 'It beats me how women can work these things out, but there's no denying that they can.'

'From my conversation with Mrs Bridge, it seems to me that there are no male relatives for me to approach in order to ask for her hand,' the earl surmised. 'And so I thought that you, sir . . . '

'Nothing to do with me,' replied Mr

Chancery. 'Margaret Bridge is of age and can answer for herself. She is an excellent woman, and the children will miss her, but neither my wife nor myself would do anything to stand in the way of her happiness. You will be married from this house, of course.'

When Margaret came downstairs, she was shown into Mr Chancery's own study, and there she found Lord Braintree waiting for her. He had been busy preparing speeches and arranging and rearranging the different component parts of his declaration, but when he turned round and saw her, she looked so pretty and smiling that every word went out of his head. He simply hurried over to her and took her in his arms saying, 'Margaret, my dearest, how could you ever have thought that I intended you to be my mother's companion, when I want you for my very own?'

As a proposal, it certainly lacked elegance, but Mrs Bridge could not find fault with it, and instead proceeded to reassure him that his sentiments were returned as fully as he could ever wish.

When at last they emerged from the study, both looking flushed, happy, and, it must be admitted, just the tiniest bit dishevelled, Mr Chancery's butler conducted them to the saloon where his master had ordered champagne. Both Mr and Mrs Chancery were ready and waiting with warm congratulations.

Mrs Chancery was all for a long engagement, so that Margaret's trousseau could be prepared, but Lord Braintree was not prepared to be so patient. 'I have waited to marry for longer than most men because I wanted to find the right woman,' he said. 'Now that I have found her, I don't intend to waste any more time.'

Most of the talk was of wedding preparations, but eventually Mrs Chancery sighed and said, 'This is all so delightful, but not at all what I expected. I had quite thought that when dear Margaret went to Bath, it would be Miss Browne who would come back engaged.'

'Ah yes, Miss Browne,' murmured Lord Braintree, glancing at Margaret. She glanced down, blushing, for in the excitement of the earl's proposal, she had quite forgotten the part that she had played in Florence's deception.

'Is she happy?' Mrs Chancery asked. 'Is the arrangement with her cousin working out? If anyone deserves some happiness, it is she.'

This was the second time that day that the earl had heard such sentiments expressed. 'I believe it is,' he replied, 'although I do not think that she is finding Margaret easy to replace.'

Margaret ventured to look at him and saw that, although she must tell him about her part in Florence's adventure, she was already forgiven. That being the case, she ventured to say, 'Is Mr Stapleton still proving attentive?'

'Stapleton?' said Mr Chancery rather sharply.

'It cannot be the same,' murmured his wife.

'Yes, that's right,' agreed Margaret. 'Though now I think of it, the name will be familiar to you, for I believe that she met him at this house.'

'Yes, she did,' agreed Mr Chancery, 'much to my regret. Unfortunately, he is a distant relative, or we would have refused him house room. He was something of a fortune hunter even then, and he made Miss Browne the object of his gallantry.'

'But how could that be?' asked Margaret, wrinkling her brow. 'Florence had no money, and no prospect of any until after her father died, and even then it was a complete surprise, even to her.'

'Yes but you see, there were one or two rumours flying about to the effect that Cuthbert Browne was a wealthy miser. I suppose that Stapleton must have heard some of them.'

Margaret looked thoughtful. 'So when Mr Browne sent Stapleton packing, it must have been one of the few good turns that he did his daughter.'

'Yes indeed,' agreed Mr Chancery. 'After Stapleton left us, he travelled north, and was soon married to a wealthy young woman, who died within a year of their marriage.'

'Surely Florence would not be taken in by him again?' said Mrs Chancery in anxious tones.

'If he had to marry for money years ago, perhaps now he is genuinely in love with Florence, and desires to marry with true affection as his motive,' suggested Margaret. 'After all, he has his fortune.'

Chancery shook his head. 'Just because he has married one fortune does not necessarily mean that he will be satisfied,' he told her. 'You have no notion of how expensive some men can be, and I have recently heard that he has other calls upon his purse.'

'Well I am placing my hopes in Mrs Waring,' said Margaret. 'She seemed to have a true concern for her cousin's welfare.'

Mr Chancery stared at her for a moment, then got up saying, 'Excuse me', politely to the assembled company.

After he had gone out, the conversation turned to wedding plans once more, and to the question of where the couple would live once they were married. It was while Lord

Braintree was describing his principal residence that Mr Chancery came back in with a letter in his hand.

He sat down rather heavily, and said, 'I would like you to hear this. I thought that there was something familiar about the name of Waring, and now I think I have the solution, little though it pleases me. This is a letter from my nephew, Gregory Bruford, who lives in London.' He searched to find the paragraph then read out:

You may be interested to learn that Stapleton is in town, and living as expensively as ever. He has a new mistress in tow, a Mrs Waring, who is a widow, and as expensive as he is, so no doubt he'll be looking for more ways to finance himself. No one appears to know how or when Mr Waring died, by the by.

There was a moment's silence. 'It cannot mean anything,' said Mrs Chancery doubtfully. 'After all, neither Mrs Waring nor Mr Stapleton knew beforehand that Miss Browne would be in Bath, did they?'

'Which of the two of them appeared first?' asked Mr Chancery. They all looked at Margaret and she thought hard. 'Mr Stapleton,' she said positively. 'He was in Bath for some days before Mrs Waring arrived. It was not until after I had decided to leave Bath that she came. Yes, and I remember her saying that she had been to see Mr Renfrew, who had told her where to find Florence; so her arrival could not have had anything to do with Stapleton.'

'I'm not convinced of that,' murmured Braintree. 'Her meeting with Stapleton could have been chance, but I dislike the way in which both of those people have reappeared in her life within such a short period of time. I intend to return to Bath to make sure that all is well.'

'And I think that you should go too,' said Mrs Chancery to Margaret. 'If she has been imposed upon by two people in whom she has placed her trust, then she may need a woman to comfort her.'

'And I shall pay Renfrew a visit to make further investigations,' said Mr Chancery. 'It would be very interesting to discover if Mrs Waring did indeed visit him as she said, and if she did, what she found out.'

Margaret turned suddenly pale. 'Pray heaven they have not discovered that she is really not a widow at all.'

Mr and Mrs Chancery looked puzzled as well they might. 'Not a widow?' faltered Mrs Chancery.

'It was an innocent deception,' Margaret faltered. 'Florence had had such a dull life that she longed for adventures so she pretended to be a widow. Everyone in Bath believes her to be one.'

'But if Mrs Waring has discovered the truth from Renfrew, then she will realize that she is Florence's next of kin,' said Mr Chancery slowly.

'Come my dear,' said Braintree, in his voice a note of determination that Margaret had never heard before. 'Your friend may be in grave danger.'

★ ★ ★

After Vittorio had confronted Florence, he returned to the Christopher with one thing on his mind: he wanted to get thoroughly drunk. It was not a thing that he did very often. Of a long and distinguished family of vine growers, he believed that wine was to be savoured, not to be swilled down, but on this occasion he was in search not of pleasure but of forgetfulness. The proprietor ventured to mention that there was a package for him, but he waved his hand dismissively. 'Later,' he said. 'Send a bottle of something red and drinkable to my room, and when I have finished it, send some more.'

'Very well, sir.' Blue-devilled, if ever I saw it, the proprietor thought to himself.

Once in his room, Vittorio loosened his neck-cloth, pulled his ribbon out of his hair and threw himself down into a chair next to the fire. Well, he had done it; he had sent that unscrupulous little adventuress packing. That would teach her to make free with his name, and to doubt his own word and honour. He had achieved all that he had planned to do, and the look of distress in her eyes had left him in no doubt whatsoever that his words had hit home. Why then did the recollection of that scene give him so little satisfaction? Why was it that, quite contrary to reason, he was left with the feeling that he was the one who had behaved dishonourably, and that she was the one who had been insulted?

'*Accidente!*' he exclaimed. 'Where is that *buffone* with the wine?'

The next moment, the door opened, but it was Guido, his manservant, who held the tray, and he also had a message for his master. '*Signor*, there is a gentleman who would have speech with you,' he said, setting his burden down.

'*Dio*,' growled Vittorio. 'Tell him to go to hell and not to bother me.'

'*Signor*, it is *il conte* Braintree.'

'Braintree? Then by all means send him in,'

287

answered Vittorio. 'If there is one other thing that the day lacks to make it a perfect representation of Hell, it is the opportunity to witness another man's joy.'

Guido hesitated for a moment, then said 'Your pardon, *signor*, but there is something else: your aunt, *la contessa*, has arrived.'

The expression that greeted this announcement was so crude that it was perhaps merciful that Vittorio spoke in his own language, so that all Braintree heard as he entered was a mouthful of Italian. 'Come in, *Giorgio*,' said the baronet. 'Let us celebrate together.'

Seeing Vittorio more dishevelled than he had ever seen him before and taking due note of the bottle on the table, the earl said, 'How many of those have you had? Are you drunk?'

'Alas, not yet,' replied Vittorio. 'But let Guido bring another glass and we can get drunk together. I hope that your sudden return to Bath does not mean that your errand did not prosper?'

'No, no it prospered,' answered his lordship. 'Margaret is an angel. But it is not concerning her that I have returned to Bath. It is concerning Miss Browne, whom we have always known as Lady Le Grey.'

Again the baronet swore. 'I am done with her,' he declared. 'She is a liar and a cheat and I want nothing to do with her.' He poured himself a glass of wine. 'To the future!' he exclaimed, raising his glass.

Braintree came closer, placed the palms of his hands on the top of the table and leaned over it. 'Vittorio, listen. This is important. Miss Browne — '

' — may go to hell for all I care,' the baronet interrupted rudely. 'Is that the only subject you wish to raise, because if so, you might as well take yourself off.'

'Vittorio, she may be in danger,' insisted the earl. 'It seems certain that that fellow Stapleton and her cousin are working together, and I am convinced that they mean her harm.'

'Then she will discover what it means to experience hurt rather than to inflict it,' he replied calmly. 'She is justly served.'

Braintree stared at him for a moment. 'Is that really all you have to say?' he demanded. 'Do you really refuse to help her?'

'Why should I?' asked Vittorio, draining his glass and pouring himself another. 'After what she has done — '

'What she has done!' exclaimed Braintree incredulously. 'And what exactly has she done to hurt you? She borrowed your name; she refused to take you at your own high estimate; she would not be cowed by you, or bow down to you; she refused to explain herself. She showed herself to be a proud woman; a woman of dignity. If you ask me, Le Grey, your chief complaint against her is that she has hurt your damned pride.'

The baronet stared at him, his glass frozen in his hand. Before either of them could speak, however, there came to their ears the sound of an imperious voice proclaiming, 'It is of no use making excuses, fellow! My nephew is here; that servant downstairs told me so. I demand to see him!'

'*Dio*,' exclaimed Vittorio, putting down his glass, and attempting to rectify his appearance.

A moment later, an imperious lady entered, dressed all in black, ready for travel, and carrying a beribboned cane. Her face was the very picture of fury.

'Zia Constanzia,'Vittorio exclaimed, bowing gracefully. 'I am rejoiced to see you well.'

'You do not see me well at all. *Briccone*! Scoundrel!' she exclaimed, snatching her hand away before he could kiss it. Then she looked round and saw Lord Braintree, who had stood back in order to allow her free access to the room. She might have been very angry, but never would Constanzia da Sforza neglect the courtesies. 'This gentleman is, I believe, unknown to me, but I must gather,

Vittorio, from your untidy appearance that he is an intimate of yours.' She smiled at the earl in what Vittorio recognized as being her most gracious manner. His lordship, meeting her for the first time, could feel the very marrow in his bones freezing.

'Of course,' replied Vittorio. 'may I present to you the Earl of Braintree? George, this is my aunt, the Contessa da Sforza.'

Braintree bowed in his best manner, and since he was still very well-groomed because he had been to propose to Margaret that morning, her ladyship was pleased to approve.

'I am happy that Vittorio seems to have found a friend with some maturity and position,' she said. 'However, I wish to have a private conversation with my nephew, so — '

'Aunt, I am constrained to remind you that this is my room. Braintree is here about important business.'

'It must be very important indeed if it means that you feel able to neglect your aunt,' declared the *contessa*. 'Here I am, in a foreign land, a helpless female — I beg your pardon?'

Vittorio had given a snort of laughter. 'Nothing, Aunt. Please, go on.'

'Helpless in so far as I do not know this place at all, I was going to say,' she went on with great dignity. 'The least I might have expected would have been that my nephew would be here to greet me. But no! There is no sign of him. Even now you behold me in travelling dress, ready to seek you out.'

'But I am here,' he said soothingly. 'And, when I have finished this matter of business, I will be entirely at your service.'

'You will be entirely at my service immediately,' she declared, her black eyes snapping as she banged her cane on the ground at the same time as she spoke her final word. 'You have caused me nothing but trouble and distress and I insist that you pay attention to me.'

'And so I will,' replied Vittorio.

The countess sat down and threw up her hands. 'This business is not, I trust, anything to do with the brazen female who spoke to me with such boldness yesterday?'

Vittorio glanced swiftly at Braintree, then turned his narrowing gaze back upon his aunt. 'Which female might this be?'

'She came here, yesterday, to this very hotel. She faced me down! Me, Vittorio! So proud she was! In her effrontery, she called herself Lady Le Grey, and when I challenged her, she announced herself to be your wife!'

'What?'

The countess's eyes slid away from his.

'She implied it. Why are you laughing?'

'You wouldn't understand, Zia Constanzia.' He sighed and turned to Braintree. 'I suppose it would do no harm to make sure that all is well,' he conceded. Braintree's features relaxed in relief.

'Am I to understand that you are intending to pursue this shameless woman?' demanded the *contessa*.

'I merely intend to make sure that no harm has come to her,' Vittorio replied.

'Then I wash my hands of you,' declared her ladyship. 'Come and find me when you have returned to your senses.'

After she had gone, Vittorio called for Guido, and invited Braintree to come through to his dressing-room whilst he set his appearance to rights.

'What made you change your mind?' asked the earl, whilst Vittorio was tying a clean neckcloth.

The baronet thought for a few moments, then said, 'I looked at my aunt in all her pride and intolerance and I saw myself. But my friend, she *has* wronged me. I cannot promise to do more than enquire into her well-being.'

'It is all I ask,' answered the earl.

When they reached the hall downstairs, they found Margaret waiting for them. 'Oh George,' she exclaimed, quite forgetting correct forms in her anxiety. 'I very much fear that Florence may be in danger. She left with Mr Stapleton as her escort, and Mrs Waring is nowhere to be found.'

'You mean that she has gone out shopping, or on some other errand?' asked Vittorio.

'No. Stevens told me that she left with all her belongings when Florence went out to the Pump Room.'

The baronet had the grace to colour a little. 'Did he say where she had gone?'

'Apparently, she was going to return to the Christopher.'

Vittorio stared at them. '*Mi scusi*,' he said, before going to speak to the proprietor. A moment later he came back to them. 'She has not returned,' he said, his face set. 'Where was Stapleton staying?'

'At the White Hart,' answered Braintree.

'I think that the manner in which Stapleton left his hotel would be worth investigating; it might give us a clue as to where he has gone. I would also like to know whether a lady had ever visited him there, and what her appearance might have been.'

'We could do that, could we not, George?' suggested Margaret. 'I might find a way of gaining information from the housekeeper, or the chambermaids, perhaps.'

Vittorio nodded. 'I'll send for Biagio, my

groom,' he said. 'Between us, we'll find out what route the chaise took on the way out of Bath. We will meet back here as soon as we have discovered anything.'

An hour later, when Braintree and Margaret got back to the hotel, they found that Sir Vittorio had already returned and had gone up to his room. The proprietor conducted them into a side room and a few moments later, coffee was brought. 'Will we have time to drink this?' Margaret asked anxiously.

'I don't know, my love,' answered the earl, as he poured out a cup for her. 'But I'm ready for it, and I'm prepared to attempt a few mouthfuls, at least.'

In the event, it was about ten minutes before the baronet came downstairs. He was dressed with as much care as ever, but his costume was much plainer, consisting of buckskin breeches, boots of a shininess that is seldom seen, and a plain black coat. He was also carrying a sword.

'They have gone east,' he said. 'Biagio is saddling horses for us even now. Have you discovered anything?'

Braintree nodded. 'Stapleton left this morning, as we know. It was quite a sudden decision; he gave notice yesterday.'

'Has he asked for his room to be kept?'

'No, he hasn't.'

'Did he give any indication of where he was going?'

'No, but apparently he seemed to be in a good humour; very pleased with himself, as the landlord put it.'

'Any news of a woman visiting him there?'

'That was what I managed to find out,' put in Margaret. 'I quizzed the housekeeper a little about Mr Stapleton and his 'gallant reputation'. It seems that a woman has been seen visiting him very discreetly. She is quite short with fair hair and a full figure.'

'Mrs Waring, without a doubt,' exclaimed Vittorio. 'We must be gone. Are you coming with me, George?'

'Of course.'

'I must come as well,' declared Margaret. 'Fee may need me when we find them. Oh George, I pray that they have not discovered that she is still single!'

As the implications of this remark sank in, Vittorio lost some of his colour. 'There is not a second to be lost,' he said. 'The hotel has a carriage for hire. I'll give orders for the horses to be put to. Follow as soon as you can.'

The trail that Biagio had picked up led them out of Bath in the direction of Chippenham. They rode in silence, and Vittorio had a chance to think about some of the things that he had learned over the past few days.

Firstly, it seemed clear that Florence had not taken his name for any financial gain. By Mr Chancery's account, she was a wealthy woman because of an unexpected bequest from her father, and she had never had any expectations of inheriting from Miss Le Grey.

The second thought that occurred to him was an extremely novel one. What if she had been convinced that *he* was the unscrupulous adventurer? After all, she had been told for years that there were no more Le Greys. What if she thought that he was claiming the same in order to gain an advantage for himself? The one thing he found it hardest to forgive was the fact that because of her reticence he had not been able to meet Miss Le Grey. But if she had thought that he was not to be trusted, then, naturally, she would seek to protect her friend from such a man.

When all this was over, he would like to sit down with her and ask her why she had indulged in this masquerade. But for now, she was in danger, and that danger may have been increased immeasurably because of his immoderate words to her in the Pump Room.

Suddenly, almost without his realizing it, the need to rescue her had become more important to him than her money, her deception, his name or anything else.

15

'No! I don't believe it!' exclaimed Florence, staring at Gilbert Stapleton.

He looked away, avoiding her eyes. 'What else could we do?' he asked. 'We need the money.'

'My money?'

'Of course your money,' declared Mrs Waring scornfully. 'You don't imagine we have any of our own, do you?'

'I don't understand,' Florence murmured.

'Try not to be dense,' said Mrs Waring patiently. 'You had two chances to oblige us and you failed miserably in both of them. The first mistake you made was to get married. Why did you do that, Fee? It would have been so much easier if you had remained single, then all I would have had to do was dispose of you.'

Florence willed herself not to shudder visibly. How glad she was now that she had not chosen to confide either in her cousin or in Mr Stapleton! Thank God, as well, that neither of them had heard about the baronet's denouncing her in the Pump Room.

'How very tiresome of me not to consider your circumstances when deciding whether to marry or not,' she said contemptuously.

'Oh, hold your tongue,' snapped Mrs Waring. 'The second tiresome thing you did was to refuse to fall in love with Gilbert. I really cannot see why you did not. He is, after all, exceedingly handsome, are you not, my darling? And he has his fair share of charm and address. It would have been so much simpler if you had just accepted his suit.'

Florence glanced from one to the other. 'You have been in conspiracy together right from the beginning,' she said slowly.

'Clever girl,' replied her cousin. 'Yes, Gil and I are lovers.'

Florence looked directly at Stapleton. 'What of the time when we first met, all those years ago?' she asked him curiously. 'It couldn't have been my money then. I didn't have any.'

'You might have had,' he replied, his gaze not quite reaching her eyes. 'There was a rumour that your father was a rich miser. But when I went to see him . . .'

Perilous though her situation was, Florence could not help laughing. 'And to think I believed that my father had never done me a good turn,' she declared. 'He served me

300

better than he knew when he sent you packing.'

Stapleton did glare at her then. 'Damn you,' he snarled.

'Oh never mind, Gil,' interrupted Mrs Waring, who was clearly the stronger of the two. 'She can talk all she likes, it won't make a whit of difference in the end. By the way,' she went on curiously, 'was your father a rich miser, or did you marry money?'

'It was my father's,' Florence replied. Then, anxious to change the subject, she asked, 'What of Mr Waring? What does he say to all this? Is he a conspirator too?'

Anne laughed. 'I am a widow, Cousin,' she said. 'Waring has been dead for years.'

'Then why do you and Gilbert not marry?' Florence asked.

'You really don't listen, do you? We need money; your money, to be precise.'

'How did you know I had any?' asked Florence curiously.

'It was quite simple,' answered Mrs Waring. 'Gilbert's visit to Bath was a coincidence. The fact that you were employing a companion seemed to indicate that you had come into money. A few discreet enquiries confirmed it. That's irrelevant now anyway. Once you are married to Gilbert, your money will be his. What a mercy you didn't get round to sending for Renfrew.'

Florence stared at her, then at Stapleton. 'You cannot possibly imagine that I would consent to marry him after this episode, do you?'

Stapleton laughed softly. 'Consent? Why should we need your consent?' He seized hold of her arm, twisting it until she cried out in pain. 'You'll do exactly what we want — sooner or later.'

He released her, and she shrank back into the corner of the seat. Glancing again from one to the other, she could not see in either face the tiniest shred of pity. She could only hope that an opportunity for escape would come later. 'Where are you taking me?' she asked.

'To a charming, out-of-the-way place where you will be married to Gil without loss of time,' said Mrs Waring. 'Don't think to get any help from the clergyman. He is very old and very deaf.'

'How can you do this?' Florence asked her, mystified. 'I was prepared to share my home with you. I would have helped you . . . '

'Oh charity,' sneered Mrs Waring. 'How you would have enjoyed aping the great lady! Well, I don't want to receive humbly whatever crumbs you feel like giving out. You don't know what it's like — '

'On the contrary,' answered Florence, her voice icily cold. 'I know exactly what it's like. Use whatever excuse for your greed you can find, but don't pretend that I've lived in affluence all my life whilst you've suffered.'

'Shut up,' snapped Mrs Waring. 'You'll go through with this or — '

'Or what? You'll kill me? No you won't, because if anything happens to me, my money will go to my kinsman, and he will certainly be revenged upon you.' It was not true, but they were not to know that. A fleeting memory came back to her from she knew not where, and she added, 'Have you never heard of the vendetta, Cousin?'

Anne looked a little shaken, but she said scornfully, 'That mountebank! What can he do?'

'Mountebank!' exclaimed Florence, in her voice a tone of dawning realization. 'Of course! You both described him in exactly the same terms, and I never thought of it until now.'

'So what if we did?' replied Anne carelessly. 'By the time he arrives — if he arrives — you will be married to Gilbert.'

'My gentle bride,' Stapleton said smoothly, taking hold of Florence's hand in order to kiss it.

Florence snatched it away angrily, and

rubbed it against the skirt of her coat.

'So ungrateful!' declared Anne mockingly. 'And when you have such a handsome bridegroom to attend you!'

Florence looked Stapleton up and down and he reddened. 'Handsome, yes; I'll give him that,' she replied coldly. 'What a pity that when you've said that, you've described the best thing about him.'

'Damn you,' he said, staring at her angrily. 'You're as haughty as that kinsman of yours.'

The mention of Vittorio somehow renewed her courage. 'So I should hope,' she declared. The name of Le Grey might only be a borrowed one, but she would not do anything to bring it into contempt.

'She can say what she likes,' said Anne. 'It won't change anything.'

Where were they going? Florence asked herself. Wherever it might be, it seemed to her that there would a better chance of escape when they arrived. Here, in the coach, outnumbered by two to one, and one of them a strapping man, whilst the other held a pistol, escape would be well nigh impossible. She would just have to be patient. One thing did occur to her: if they forced her to marry and she did so in the name of Le Grey, would the ceremony be valid? It was a very faint hope indeed, but it cheered her a little.

She was settling back into a corner in order to rest and build up her strength, when there was a muffled shout from outside, and the coach lurched to a halt.

'What the — ?' exclaimed Stapleton. Moments later, the door was pulled open by a curious-looking moustachioed fellow, who bowed courteously.

'If you will please to alight,' he said in thickly accented English.

'The deuce we will,' declared Stapleton.

At that moment, Vittorio came into view, sword in hand, very plainly but nevertheless immaculately dressed, and bowed politely.

'Vittorio!' exclaimed Florence, her feelings a mixture of hope and relief for herself, and fear for his safety at the hands of two people whom she would not hesitate to describe as a ruthless pair.

'Cousin,' he said politely, bowing in her direction. 'Signor Stapleworth,' he exclaimed, 'I am rejoiced to find you. I would, however, be grateful if you would be so good as to explain where you are taking this lady?'

'It is quite simple,' replied Stapleton. 'We are going to a wedding.' He smirked. 'Our own, in fact.'

'Then I fear that I am the bearer of bad tidings,' Vittorio went on. 'There will be no wedding today, for weddings are beyond my power to provide.' He grinned widely. 'Funerals, however, I can certainly arrange. Please step down.'

'No!' exclaimed Anne involuntarily.

Vittorio stared at her straight-faced, in his eyes more than a hint of menace. 'I assure you, *signora*, that I intend to use this sword, either in a fair fight, or to skewer anyone not brave enough to face me. Now step down, *signor*.'

Stapleton looked him up and down. 'Popinjay!' he exclaimed contemptuously. 'So be it, then. Perhaps this may be a richer haul than we ever imagined,' he threw across to Anne. 'Kill the last male Le Grey and she might inherit more than we dreamed.' He paused in the act of stepping down, looking doubtfully at Vittorio's sword.

'Do not fear,' said the baronet politely. 'I will not start a fight when you are not ready. That and other treacherous actions, such as kidnapping and extortion, I leave to those unworthy of the name of gentleman.' He turned to his groom. 'Biagio, you will attend the ladies. Braintree, I rely upon you to see fair play.'

The earl nodded. 'It will be done,' he said, and proceeded to take out another sword so that Stapleton could compare its length to the one which Vittorio already held.

'Vittorio,' uttered Florence, leaning towards him. He turned. 'Be careful.'

'*Naturalmente*,' he nodded, inclining his head.

'Bastard!' Anne spat, as he turned away. Then she looked at her cousin. 'I suppose you imagine he has a chance,' she said contemptuously. 'Gil is an expert swordsman, you know. He will carve him into pieces.'

Florence stared at her, but did not say anything. To see Vittorio for the second time since she had realized that she was in love with him had caused her heart to lurch alarmingly. Now, he was risking his life for her, before she had had a chance to say that she was sorry for appropriating his name, and for doubting his honour and his word; if Stapleton killed him, she would never have a chance to do so.

The duel was to take place in a clearing at the side of the road. In a few moments, the two men had removed their coats, waistcoats and boots, and their white shirts gleamed in the light of the gathering dusk. Florence could not help noticing that Vittorio's shoulders had a breadth that would have surprised many who thought of him as just a dandy.

Braintree gave the signal, and the fight began. Florence had read about duels in the poetry and the novels that she had delighted

307

in devouring for as long as she could remember, their tales of adventure being at one time her only escape from her miserable life of servitude. Nothing that she had read, however, had prepared her for the speed of what was taking place, or its sheer savagery.

If asked, she would have found it impossible to choose between them. Stapleton, being a little taller, had the longer reach, but it seemed to her that Vittorio was the lighter on his feet; and if Stapleton was an expert swordsman, the baronet was surely no less capable. Oh that those who had thought of him as a fop, a dilettante, a mountebank, could see him now!

As the duel progressed, she was vaguely conscious of the sound of a conveyance, but she was far too caught up with what was taking place before her eyes to look around and see who might have arrived. The pace of the duel suddenly increased; there was a moment of lightning sword play, Vittorio thrust forward with all his strength, and Stapleton staggered back, his hand to his shoulder.

'No!' screamed Anne, and Florence whirled round in surprise. So absorbed had she been with the progress of the fight that she had completely forgotten the presence of the others. Before either Florence or Biagio could do anything to prevent her, Anne threw herself out of the coach and hurried forward. It was only at this moment that Florence remembered the gun.

This time, it was her turn to scream 'No!' But the sound of her cry was smothered by the sound of Anne Waring's gun, and Vittorio fell to his knees, then to the ground. Before Florence could do more than step down from the carriage, another gun roared, and this time, it was Mrs Waring who fell. Florence turned to see Signora da Sforza standing by the chaise that had just arrived, a gun in a hand that was rock-steady.

Florence flew over to Vittorio, and fell on her knees next to him, breathing his name. His eyes opened. 'Ah! The adventurous . . . Miss Browne . . . ' he murmured, before he lost consciousness.

'Keep away from my nephew, you hussy,' the contessa commanded. Florence looked up at her. She was still holding the pistol in her hand. 'You made him put his life in danger. You, and you alone; and for what? Go now; leave him to me.'

'But . . . ' Florence stood up, took a step towards her accuser, then turned back towards the baronet. He lay motionless on the grass, his usually immaculate appearance dishevelled, and with an ominous red stain spreading across the front of his shirt.

'Go, I said,' repeated the countess. 'It was only his misplaced sense of honour that brought him to your aid. Go back to your own class of person, actress that you are, and leave him to his own.'

By this time, the countess's servants were hurrying to Sir Vittorio's aid. Stapleton was sitting on the ground, clutching a pad of some kind to his shoulder, and watching, whilst Biagio examined Mrs Waring, who lay very still on the ground.

Florence looked round helplessly, but at that very moment, Margaret came hurrying towards her. 'Oh my dear Fee, my poor dear Fee,' she exclaimed. 'You are safe. Thank God, thank God!'

'I may be, but what of Vittorio,' demanded Florence. 'Margaret, I must help him, but I am not permitted . . . ' Her voice cracked.

Braintree hurried across to them. 'I am sending Biagio to fetch another conveyance from Corsham,' he said. 'I think that the best thing now is for you both to go back to Bath to Laura Place.' Florence opened her mouth to protest, but Braintree forestalled her. 'The countess will not let anyone else near him just now, and you will allow that if anyone is capable of organizing his care, it is she.'

Margaret added her voice in agreement to

his. 'Braintree is right,' she said. 'And I know that he will come and tell us the moment that there is any news.'

'Of course,' agreed the earl.

Florence looked towards the baronet reluctantly. She knew that her friends were right. The countess was undoubtedly taking control, and was related to him. She, Florence, had no rights with regard to his care that anyone would acknowledge. She nodded, took a step towards the chaise, paused, turned, then ran back towards Vittorio and, before anyone could say or do anything to prevent her, she knelt down and pressed a kiss to his brow. 'Get well, my darling,' she whispered. Then she stood up, and returned to the chaise where Margaret was waiting.

★   ★   ★

On the evening of the duel, Braintree came to the house in Laura Place, his face grave. After ensuring that both ladies were sitting together on the sofa, Margaret holding Florence's hand, he said 'My dear Miss Browne, I have news which I fear may distress you,' he said.

'Go on,' whispered Florence, turning quite white.

'I am afraid that your cousin is dead,' he said.

Florence stood up. 'Oh God, Vittorio,' she cried. Her knees buckled, and had Margaret not caught hold of her, she would have fallen to the ground.

'Quickly, there is brandy over there on the sideboard,' urged Margaret. Braintree hurried to pour some and bring it to Florence. 'She has been so used to calling him her cousin that she must have thought that you meant him.'

Florence soon began to come round, and obediently took a sip of the brandy. 'Vittorio,' she murmured again.

'No, *not* Vittorio,' Braintree assured her. 'I mean that Mrs Waring, your real cousin, is dead. She was taken back to the inn at Corsham where Vittorio and Stapleton both lie, but when the doctor came to treat her, the bullet had pierced a vital organ, and she died soon afterwards.'

'She behaved unscrupulously towards me, and I know that she would have ended my life without compunction; but I cannot be glad at the news of her death,' said Florence in low tones. 'I have no relations at all now.' She paused in thought for a moment, then remembered another vital matter. 'Vittorio?' she uttered, fixing her eyes on Braintree in an expression of painful intensity.

'Vittorio is gravely ill, there is no doubt,'

answered Braintree. 'But Mrs Waring was not as good a shot as the *contessa* and he is holding his own. I promise that I will ride over every day, until he is out of danger.'

'And Stapleton?'

'He will be dealt with,' answered Braintree grimly.

★ ★ ★

Once back in Laura Place, Florence proceeded to live like a recluse. To no one did she advertise her presence, telling Margaret to inform everyone that she had left town permanently, and would soon be sending for her servants. Any exercise that she took, she took at night, wandering up and down the garden, pacing its length over and over again until Margaret and the staff began to be really worried about her. The only thing that saw her become at all animated was the daily bulletin that Braintree brought, as he had promised.

For several days, the baronet hovered between life and death, and there were times when the earl concealed from Florence the very fine nature of the thread from which his life hung. Then one day his lordship came with the glad tidings that orders had been given for the baronet's room at the

Christopher to be prepared, and a nurse ordered to attend. She wept tears of relief on that day, but still she could not bring herself to leave Bath. She wanted to be sure that he had turned the corner.

Eventually, the day came when Braintree said to her, 'Fee, my dear,' (she had become Fee to him during the weary days of waiting for news), 'I am not sure how to tell you this.'

'He is worse?' she faltered, losing all her colour.

'No, he is not worse,' he answered gently. 'He is making a good recovery, but now the *contessa* is talking about taking him back to Italy, so that he can complete his return to health in a warmer climate.'

This news helped her to make her decision: she would leave Bath. Before she did so, however, there were two things that she had to do. The first was to write down for him exactly what she had done and why. One day, when the earl arrived, she sent him out driving with Margaret so that they might have some time alone together. That done, she went to the book-room, sat down at the desk there, and prepared to write Vittorio a letter. She told him about her childhood, her meeting with Stapleton, her mother's death, her father's cruelty, her hopes and dreams, her unexpected inheritance, her decision to take a different name; everything. She closed by asking for his forgiveness. She did not tell him of her love; that was a burden that he could do without.

The second thing that she knew she had to do was to try to see him again. That decision made, she sealed up her letter, walked in the direction of the Christopher, and waited until the *contessa* had gone out with her maid, for Braintree had told her that now the baronet was getting better, his aunt was taking exercise every morning.

Heavily veiled, she walked into the Christopher and went upstairs, judging that if she looked assured enough no one would stop her. Her plan to find Vittorio's room was quite simple. She would wait until someone emerged from one of the rooms and she would make some comment about trying to be quiet because she had heard that there was a sick Italian gentleman who needed to rest. The person to whom she spoke would, she hoped, give some indication as to where the gentleman might be. If not, she would simply have to try the ploy again.

The first person who emerged was a dark-haired man who looked like a valet, and Florence congratulated herself on her luck. A servant would be much more likely to know what she was trying to find out than a wealthy guest.

Her plan proved to be both triumph and disaster. The man looked at her solemnly, and said 'I am Guido, *signora*. Sir Vittorio is my master, but he is much better.'

She stared at him, and suddenly she started to tremble, and she could feel the tears coming into her eyes. 'Truly?' she whispered.

'*Veramente*,' he agreed. 'May I ask if I am addressing Signora Le Grey?'

She gave a little laugh that turned part way through into a sob. 'Yes, I am she,' she replied. 'Or more correctly, I am Florence Browne.'

'He has spoken of you,' said Guido. 'Can I help you in some way?'

Her idea of seeing Vittorio seemed presumptuous now. He had spoken of her. She could guess the kind of things that he must have said. She took the letter that she had written out of her reticule and handed it to Guido. 'Will you give this to him when he is well enough to read it?'

Guido nodded. 'Do you have any message for him?'

She shook her head. 'No message. But you will take care of him, won't you? He is . . . ' — she gulped — 'very dear to me.'

'*Certamente*,' he replied. 'It is my job.'

She hurried down the stairs and left the hotel, crossing the road just as the *contessa* came back.

'Who was that woman?' her ladyship asked Guido, whom she met in the hall.

'What woman, *signora*?' Guido asked.

'Never mind,' she replied, before going upstairs.

16

When at last Vittorio was permitted to get up, he was astonished both at how weak he had become and at the length of time for which he had been ill. His aunt, who had always seemed to him to be someone for whom the honour and dignity of his house mattered more than anything else, showed such relief at his recovery, that he taxed her weakly with having some affection for him.

'Naturally I was concerned for you,' she declared haughtily. 'You bear an old and honourable name. It would be a cause of regret to me if that name should be lost.'

Since Guido had told him that the countess had sat by his bed night after weary night, he was not fooled by her show of indifference, and instead took hold of her hand and raised it to his lips.

'*Grazie, Zia Constanzia*,' he murmured, smiling at her.

'Foolish boy,' she scolded, snatching away her hand, but not before he had caught a glimpse of a smile.

He did attempt to ask her about some of the others involved on that dreadful night, but she remained tight-lipped, refusing to discuss, as she said, such dissolute and murderous persons. He was therefore very relieved when Lord Braintree was ushered up to his room. Because of the assistance that he had rendered the countess, he was allowed to pay a visit before anyone else was permitted even to enter the sick-room.

'George!' he exclaimed. 'What pleasure to see you.'

'How are you?' Braintree asked, shaking hands with him very gently.

'Weak as a cat, but alive, thank God,' replied Vittorio. 'I'm glad you've come, for I'm desperate for news. What happened after I was shot? Where is everyone?'

Braintree looked at him for a moment with narrowed eyes, then said, 'Mrs Waring was killed by the *contessa*'s bullet. Stapleton has made a full recovery and is awaiting your pleasure.'

'What of the authorities?' asked Vittorio.

'I think you will find that your aunt put them very firmly in their place.'

Vittorio gave a shout of laughter, that turned into a coughing fit, and Braintree eyed him concernedly. When the coughing had subsided, he fidgeted for a moment or two with the bedclothes and said, 'What of Firenza?'

319

'She is well,' answered the earl, 'but she has been very anxious.'

'About Stapleton?'

Braintree raised an eyebrow. 'Don't be absurd,' he said.

Vittorio grunted. At that point, Guido came in with wine for Lord Braintree. 'I trust you have a glass for me,' murmured the baronet. Guido set the tray down, went to the door, looked around cautiously, then took another glass from the inside of his coat. Vittorio chuckled. 'Seeking to avoid my aunt, I see,' he declared.

The earl eyed the wine doubtfully, but relaxed when he saw a little colour coming back into his friend's face.

It was after they had both drunk some of the wine that Guido came back into the room with two packages in his hand. Both were addressed to Vittorio in the same writing. 'This,' he said, handing over the package, 'was delivered to the hotel before you were wounded, *signor*.'

The baronet turned the package over in his hands, then tried to unfasten the string; but after a few moments, he said fretfully, 'I cannot. This string — George, open it for me.'

After a very brief hesitation, Braintree took the package and in a short time had undone the knot. He made as if to hand the package over to the baronet, but, as if exhausted by the very idea of opening it, Vittorio closed his eyes, and gestured to indicate that his friend should also take off the wrapping. As the earl did so, a folded paper fell, and came to rest on the bed next to Vittorio's hand.

The baronet picked up the paper and read the brief note that Florence had written.

'Do you want me to open this box?' Braintree asked.

'No need,' replied Vittorio. 'I know what is inside. What else do you have there, Guido?'

The manservant gave him the letter over which Florence had toiled for so long. 'This was handed to me in person by a veiled lady, while you lay in this bed, too weak to see anyone.'

Vittorio opened his eyes. 'Give it to me,' he said. The manservant put it in his hand. 'George, will you leave me now? I am tired and — '

' — and you want to read your letter,' smiled the earl. 'Of course, my dear fellow. I'll come and see you again tomorrow.'

Once he was alone, Vittorio took up the letter, but he was indeed more tired than he had imagined, and when the words began to dance before his eyes, he laid it down, and soon afterwards was fast asleep.

It was early evening when he woke again, feeling very much better. Conscious of a raging thirst, he rang the bell for Guido, but before the manservant came, Constanzia da Sforza entered.

'Ah, now you are looking much better,' she said, drawing close to the bed. 'Perhaps we may see you getting up by the end of the week. And here is the good Guido, I see.'

'You rang, *signor?*'

'I did. Bring me something to drink, will you?'

'No wine,' said the countess firmly. 'That is what tired you so much earlier.' As if wanting to change the subject, she wandered over to the window and began to comment upon the view to be had from the window in the daytime.

'Earlier . . . ' murmured the baronet. 'Earlier . . . ' He fumbled on the quilt, but failed to find anything. '*Zia*, there should be a letter here, a letter which Guido brought today, but I cannot find it. Can you see it anywhere?' He lifted his head as well as he could and tried to look around. His aunt had not moved from the window. '*Zia*,' he said more impatiently. 'Come and look. You know I cannot find it for myself. It might have fallen, or . . . ' In sudden suspicion, he noticed that she had walked over to the fire and was looking down into it. '*Dio*, you have burned it!' he whispered. 'You have burned my letter.'

She whirled round then. 'And if I have, it was entirely for your own good.'

'For my good?' he murmured disbelievingly.

'How could it be anything but good for you to forget that woman entirely?' she stormed. 'She has brought you nothing but grief! Nothing! And what has your response been? To run after her and nearly lose your life in defence of her non-existent honour.' He said nothing, so taking encouragement from this, she went on coaxingly, 'I have made arrangements for you to be taken back to Italy so that you can recover properly in the sun. The doctor approves this decision. Once back home, you will soon forget this woman.' Still he did not speak. 'There is a girl at home; a lovely girl of a good family,' she went on. 'I know her father will be glad to hear from you . . . ' She looked at his face and her voice faded away. His face was a mask of fury and, for the first time, to her great astonishment, she found herself in awe of her young nephew.

'You forget yourself, *signora*,' he said, his

voice like ice. 'I am the head of this family and you have very seriously displeased me.'

'Vittorio,' she began, but he would not allow her to finish.

'Silence,' he snapped. 'You will leave me now, but you will not remove me, or yourself, or anyone else to Italy without my express permission. Is that clearly understood?'

For a long moment, his aunt stared at him; then for the first time in her life, she made him a formal curtsy and withdrew.

Moments later, Guido entered with a tray, on it a jug of lemonade and a glass. At once, the manservant could see that something was amiss. 'Signor?' he questioned.

'She burned it,' said Vittorio. 'She burned my letter.' To his horror, he could feel, in his weakness, that tears were threatening to come.

'*Si, signor*,' replied Guido calmly. 'I thought that she might; which is why I took great care that she should not find both of them.'

'Both of them?'

'There was a little note with the package, if you recall,' said Guido. 'That was what she burned. The other' — he put his hand inside his coat — 'I have here.'

'Help me to sit up, and give it to me,' said Vittorio eagerly.

Guido did as he was bid. 'There is one other thing, *signor*,' he said, as he adjusted the baronet's pillows behind him.

'Well?' asked Vittorio, a note of impatience in his voice.

'The lady who delivered the letter asked me to care for you well, as you were very dear to her,' he said calmly. 'Is there anything else, *signor*?'

'Just my letter,' replied Vittorio smiling faintly.

*   *   *

It was another week before Vittorio was well enough to be up and about again, and still longer before he felt strong enough to travel. A period of convalescence was necessary, and from being one of those who attended the Pump Room merely to see and be seen, he became one of those who needed to drink the waters in good and earnest, and very nasty he found them.

To his surprise, he found that he had become an object of curiosity to all those who were present. Rumours were rife concerning all who had been involved in the events that had taken place on the day when he had been shot by Anne Waring. Lady Le Grey had eloped with Gilbert Stapleton; she had eloped with Lord Braintree; she had lost all her money and absconded, leaving her staff unpaid; she and Mrs Waring had both run away to the Continent; Mrs Waring had eloped with Mr Stapleton and Lady Le Grey had gone in pursuit; they were all dead; they were none of them dead. There was no end to the different versions that were going round. At least, Vittorio reflected, his appearance had succeeded in quashing another set of rumours, namely that he himself was dead or had eloped or absconded with someone.

Besides those who had been intimately involved with the affair, the only other person who knew the truth of the story was the local magistrate. He had been ready to accept that Constanzia had only fired at Mrs Waring in order to save her nephew from further injury, and so, to Vittorio's relief, his aunt would not be pursued by the law in connection with that matter. Those not connected closely with the business had been allowed to believe that Vittorio had been injured in a shooting accident. Mrs Waring had come to Bath very suddenly, and her equally sudden disappearance attracted very little comment.

Florence had been around for longer, however, and so, inevitably, Vittorio was asked about the whereabouts and well-being of his cousin. Undoubtedly some of those who approached him had heard him denounce Florence, or had heard rumours about it. Any enquiries about that scene he killed at birth by assuming his haughtiest manner, but the rumours and whispers remained. He silenced some of them by saying that she had gone to visit a friend who had suddenly been taken ill. No, he told them, he did not know when she would be back. Yes, they certainly did all miss her. *He* missed her, he acknowledged privately. She had undoubtedly made his life more exciting.

She had made her own life more exciting too. Her letter had touched him deeply. It was not that it had been self-pitying; quite the reverse. It had, in many ways, been rather gallant. But putting together the things that she did not say alongside the things that he had seen and heard in Howton, and the remarks that she had made to him in person about her father's hatred, her life until very recently had been one of drudgery, loveless-ness and sheer boredom. '*I could not endure the idea of being plain dull Miss Browne to the end of my days,*' she had written. '*If I did nothing about it, nobody else would do anything for me.*' In seeking a better life for herself, she had shown a spirit which would even excite the admiration of his aunt, if she could only be brought to acknowledge it. It had certainly excited his own, and he would like to tell her so. The problem was that he did not know where to find her. He had sent servants to enquire about her in Laura Place, but they had found the house shut up and everyone gone away. The only person who might perhaps have known anything was Lady Trimm, and she had left town to visit relations in Kent. Not for the first time, he chafed at his own weakness.

At last, he felt well enough to travel, and it was then that he saw fit to confide in Lord Braintree. 'I want to find Firenza,' he said bluntly.

'Why?' asked the earl. 'To distress her further?' He had by now heard the story of Vittorio's denouncing Florence in the Pump Room.

'No, not to distress her,' replied the baronet. 'I want to find her because . . . because she has come to mean more to me than I would have dreamed was possible,' he concluded eventually.

The earl broke into a smile. 'I hoped it would be so,' he said. 'I can take you to her.'

'You know where she is?' exclaimed Vittorio. 'You have known all this time, and you have not told me! *Che inganno!*'

'It wasn't deceit at all,' replied the earl, who had begun to pick up quite a lot of Italian in recent weeks. 'If you had asked me, I would have told you, but you didn't ask.'

Just a few days later, they left Bath. Before doing so, Vittorio found time to confront both his aunt and Gilbert Stapleton. It soon became clear that Mrs Waring had provided the energy and the planning behind their schemes, and without her, all the fight had gone out of him. Nevertheless, Vittorio could not forget what Florence had suffered at his hands, and was much inclined to have him punished as severely as the law would allow. Because Florence was the chief sufferer, however, it seemed right that she should have some say in his fate, so he decided to leave Stapleton to think about his situation. It would do no harm to let him sweat.

Constanzia da Sforza, too, was somewhat subdued. Although a dominant woman, she had great reverence for the position of head of the family, and once Vittorio chose to exert himself, she could do no other but obey. He made it quite plain to her that when he decided to be married, it would be to a woman of his own choice, and he would expect her to give the real Lady Le Grey the respect that was her due.

Once that had been done, they set off for the north, but before completing their journey, Braintree insisted that they visit

Howton. 'I want you to see exactly what kind of life she led,' he said.

'So this is where my Firenza grew up,' murmured Vittorio, looking around. He had passed through on a previous occasion, when the earl had visited Tall Chimneys in order to propose, but he had hurried back to Bath before he could see very much of the village.

'This is where she grew up,' agreed Braintree. 'I can show you where she lived, if you would like to see it.'

They drew up outside the Brownes' old residence and the baronet exclaimed almost involuntarily, 'What a bleak place! But I suppose that an unoccupied house always looks like this.'

At that moment, the door opened, and a slight, dapper-looking man came out. 'Can I help you, gentlemen?' he asked. 'I am John Renfrew, Miss Browne's solicitor. I have come to inspect the house.'

'Good day,' replied Braintree. He introduced himself, then said, 'And this is Sir Vittorio Le Grey.'

'Le Grey?' exclaimed Renfrew. 'Well bless my soul! I have had searches instituted for any member of the Le Grey family, for although Miss Le Grey always swore that she was the last of her name, she was very elderly and apt to be forgetful towards the end.'

'Signor Chancery knew of my existence,' replied Vittorio. 'He did not mention my name to you, then?'

'I do not often see him as he is not my client,' replied Renfrew. 'Doubtless he expected you would approach me yourself. He did call and see me recently to make enquiries concerning a relative of Miss Browne, but I had never met the lady, so I was not able to enlighten him.'

Vittorio and Lord Braintree glanced at each other, as if to say 'that solves another mystery'.

The baronet turned to Renfrew. 'My father was Sir Victor Le Grey,' he said. 'He quarrelled with his family, and they wanted nothing more to do with him. Perhaps that was what led to the misunderstanding. My mother was Italian and spoke no English, so my father remained in Italy until his death. It was only after the death of my mother that I decided to come to England and see whether any of my family were still alive.'

'Miss Le Grey died not long ago,' said Renfrew regretfully. 'So unfortunate that you were not able to meet her.'

'Indeed,' agreed Vittorio, rather tight-lipped.

'You will realize, sir, that I will have to ask for proof of your identity, before I can entrust you with your inheritance, although I fear that Miss Le Grey had very little to leave, and in any case she had made no will.'

'I am surprised that she left nothing to Miss Browne,' the baronet murmured.

Renfrew's eyes lit up. 'You know Miss Browne?' he asked. 'Such a brave young woman, and a comfort to Miss Le Grey. Yes, it is surprising that your relative made no provision for her. She fully deserved the good fortune that came her way, but it was no thanks to her father. He would have left her destitute. Do you want to see inside?'

'*Grazie*,' replied Vittorio. 'We were saying that an empty house always looks bleak.'

'It looked bleak when it was lived in,' Renfrew answered drily. 'Shall we go in?'

The inside of the house was as bleak as the outside, and Vittorio wrapped his cloak more warmly about him, for it was colder in the hall than it had been outside with the benefit of the wintry sun. 'What a desolate place,' he remarked looking round. 'I suppose it must have been more cheerful when the family was living here.'

'Not noticeably. Mr Browne was a miser, and the most unpleasant man I have ever met. He kept his family in poverty, and I have never seen it look any more cheerful than it looks today, apart from the fact that when Miss Browne lived here, it looked a little better because she kept it clean.'

'She kept it clean? With her own hands?' the baronet demanded.

'With her own hands. At least being busy meant that she kept warm, for Cuthbert Browne would never have fires burned except in his own bedroom and in the room where he chose to sit. Everyone else froze to death, or sat in the kitchen.'

They wandered around the house, but apart from the occasional comment, Vittorio surveyed the house in silence. He was trying to imagine what it must have been like for Florence to live here. He thought about a girl growing to womanhood in that bleak, cold house. No wonder she always wanted to be warm. Florence, he thought to himself. Florence. But even while his mind was saying those words, his heart was saying *bella Firenza*.

17

'Margaret, I wish I did not have to go out,' Florence complained. 'Honestly, if I had thought that you would be such a bully, I would never have asked you to come with me.'

They were standing in the hall of the small house which Florence had rented in Buxton, both dressed ready for the evening, and waiting for the carriage to be brought round to the door, so that they might go to a ball in the Long Room of the Old Hall. Although Florence had not yet taken the step of purchasing a carriage for herself, she had made an arrangement to pay a retainer to a local hostelry to ensure that they would provide her with transport whenever she needed it.

They had been in Buxton for several days. At first, Florence had continued her recent behaviour in Bath by acting almost as a recluse. Mrs Chancery, knowing that she would have to replace Margaret very soon, had happily released her, readily acknowledging that Florence's need was greater than her own. Margaret had allowed her friend to have her own way, but now she had come to the conclusion that it was time that she put her foot down. She had therefore declared that unless Florence made more effort to go out, she, Margaret, would go back to Mrs Chancery, 'for,' she had declared forthrightly, 'you do not need a companion if you are not prepared to be accompanied anywhere.' Florence had agreed reluctantly although not without protest.

'It will do you good to go out for the evening,' Margaret replied. 'You need to see some other faces.'

'I see plenty of other faces during the day,' Florence argued.

'Yes, at the shops or in the street,' Margaret agreed. 'That kind of encounter gives no opportunity for conversation.'

Florence looked doubtful, but at that point, the carriage arrived and Stevens came to open the front door for them.

'I hope you have an enjoyable evening, my lady; Mrs Bridge.'

'Stevens, I have told you that I am not 'my lady' any more,' Florence protested.

'You will always be 'my lady' to me, ma'am,' he replied, straightening his shoulders.

The Long Room had been in use as a ballroom in Buxton for some years, but extensive building was taking place in the town, the end result of which would be a magnificent crescent to house among other things a new ballroom. In the meantime, the town was undoubtedly far less impressive than Bath, and therefore very different from it, and this was felt by Florence to be an advantage. The disadvantage about living there, however, was that because it was a smaller place, it was much more difficult to blend into the crowd, and part of Florence wanted simply to disappear and melt away.

Despite the tone of her remark to Margaret, she was very grateful for her presence. Margaret was the one person who knew the story of the events of recent weeks; the one person to whom she could speak openly. How could she ever have explained to anyone else all that she had done and why? Looking back on her decision to create a new identity, it seemed to be completely absurd. Most importantly of all, however, Margaret was the one person amongst present company who knew Vittorio Le Grey.

Some of the time, she tried not to think about him. More frequently she thought about nothing else, wondering what he was doing and if he had fully recovered. Had his aunt indeed taken him to Italy as she had intended? She thought about the *contessa* who had defended her family's honour so fiercely, and who had shot Anne in order to protect her nephew. What must it be like to be the object of such loyalty! On the other hand, if he had not gone to Italy, had he found consolation in the arms of Maria Trimm? Her fingers clenched into claws at the very idea.

Soon after her arrival in Buxton, she had ordered some new clothes, and for the first time in many years they were neither black nor brown. This evening she was wearing a dark-blue dress of a simple cut, with a petticoat of a lighter shade. She looked well dressed but modest, and she flattered herself that no one would pay attention to her. There was to be dancing, but she had resolved not to take part in it. From now on, she told herself, I will be satisfied with being plain Miss Browne, dull by name, dull by nature.

'Come, this is better than sitting looking at one another's faces, is it not?' said Margaret.

'Yes perhaps,' agreed Florence. 'But if that wretched Master of Ceremonies tries to make me dance with anyone, I shall go home immediately.'

As the evening went on, almost against her will she found that she was beginning to enjoy herself. Some of the people there were very conversable, especially one Mrs Ross and her daughter, and in some way, perhaps in the close bond of affection between them, they reminded her a little of Lady Trimm and Dianne. The four ladies were talking together, when Florence felt in need of a drink of lemonade. She excused herself, stood up and began to walk across the room, for dancing was not taking place at that moment. Just as she had reached the centre, something made her turn towards the entrance and standing there, looking very much alive and twice as dandified as any other man in the room, was Sir Vittorio Le Grey. He walked towards her, the skirts of his pale-violet coat of watered silk swinging about him. He drew every eye in the room, and a palpable hush fell.

'There she is,' he declared. 'Do you see her?' Florence began to tremble. She wanted to run away, but somehow her legs would not obey her. 'Do you see her?' he declared again. 'She has insinuated herself amongst you as the modest Miss Browne, I imagine. So sweet! So innocent! Let me enlighten you *signori, signore*!' He strode right up to her then, seized hold of her, and turned her to face the shocked assembly, still holding her by the arms. 'This is not Miss Browne! This is the notorious Lady Firenza Le Grey! Oh yes, you may gasp! You may stare! She is no shrinking miss! She is an adventuress!' The assembled company glanced round at one another. Several thought of intervening, but there was something infinitely dangerous about the violet-clad figure that made them hold their peace.

For her part, Florence felt giddy as she swung rapidly from delight that he was so fully recovered, to bitter despair, and thence to crazy hope. The way in which he had denounced her had at first shocked her beyond measure, but as he had strode towards her, there had been a light in his eyes which had not had anything to do with hatred or contempt. Then, when he had seized her, his grip had been firm, but not ungentle, and his announcement of her to be Lady Le Grey — which he now knew very well she was not — convinced her that he had something other than revenge on his mind.

'Shall I tell you something else about this woman?' Vittorio demanded, pulling Florence back against him, so that his chin rested on the top of her hair. 'She has broken my heart, and quite without compunction. Well, never again! I shall not permit her to harm any other man in the same way. Ladies and gentleman, I shall remove this scheming adventuress from your assembly, so that you may be safe from her.' So saying, he turned her round, lifted her effortlessly in his arms, bent his head and kissed her on her mouth, taking his time, to the accompaniment of shocked exclamations, then strode out of the room, out of the building and towards a waiting chaise.

Any concerns she might have had about whether he had recovered his strength were easily stilled by the way in which he negotiated the step, and placed her inside before climbing in after her himself.

Thrilled by his touch and his kiss, but not daring to guess at his motives, she said, rather unsteadily, 'Sir Vittorio, what are you about? Pray, explain yourself.'

'Certainly' he replied, lounging back in his corner of the chaise. 'I'm abducting you, cara.'

'Abducting me?' she exclaimed, her voice coming out as a squeak.

'Have I not chosen the right word?' he asked her, his tone puzzled. 'I mean that I am carrying you off. I know that my grasp of English is not always good. You must forgive me.'

'I think that your grasp of English is far better than you pretend, and I feel sure that you understood exactly what you were saying,' declared Florence.

'But you sounded surprised; confused, even,' answered Vittorio. 'I wanted to make the position clear.'

'Thank you,' answered Florence. 'Would you mind telling me why?'

'Oh, for a number of reasons,' answered Vittorio easily. 'After all, you told me in your letter that you wanted an adventure.'

'You read my letter?' she exclaimed, her hand going to her throat.

'Every word,' he replied, his voice softening. 'I thought I would provide you with one; then, of course, you have purloined my name. I can't allow you to get away with that without doing something about it.'

Had she been mistaken, then, when she had seen that light in his eyes? Had his voice not softened at all? Now, because she could not see his face, she began to doubt what she had seen and heard, and suddenly she started to shiver.

'*Dio*, you are cold,' he exclaimed. 'I brought you away without collecting your cloak!' He leaned across to the opposite seat, picked up a cloak that had been placed upon it, and drew closer to her. 'Come here to me, *cara*,' he said. 'Let me wrap this around you.' She allowed him to do so. 'Are you warmer now?' he asked her. She nodded, but there was a cold feeling inside her that not all the warmth of the material could dispel. 'I am glad of that,' he replied, 'but we still have a problem. You see, *innamorata*, I am from Italy, and I cannot bear to be cold either. So what are we to do?'

'I don't know,' she answered wretchedly. Then she added, inconsequentially, 'I wish I always understood what you were saying.'

'Do you?' he murmured caressingly. 'Then let me offer a solution to both our problems.' Before she could protest he had caught hold of her and lifted her so that she was sitting on his knee. 'And now I will tell you what I mean. When I call you *bella*, Firenza, I mean that you are beautiful; and when I call you *bellissima*, I am telling you that you are most beautiful to me. *Cara, amata, innamorata*; my dear, my darling, my sweetheart; are these translations adequate for you, or do I need to demonstrate further?'

She hesitated. He uttered a low laugh and changed his grip on her, so that she was leaning back against his shoulder. Then his mouth was on hers again; this time she slid her hands up around his neck and kissed him back.

After a very long time, during which it was quite impossible to say anything, he drew back a little. She opened her eyes and saw by the light of the lantern outside that he was smiling down at her tenderly.

She reached up a hand to his cheek and

said longingly, 'Oh I wish that I could say something to you in a romantic language!'

'There is no need,' he answered. 'Just tell me that you love me, *cara*, and I shall be satisfied.'

'Oh I do,' she sighed. 'And I do believe I loved you from the beginning, even when I thought you to be an adventurer.'

'It was the same for me,' he said. 'Whatever logic may have told me about you, all I knew was that I was finding it increasingly difficult to keep my hands off you. I could not work out why you were deceiving everyone as to your identity. My suspicious mind could not credit that your motives were innocent, and yet I found myself falling in love with you.'

'I was so tired of being Miss Browne, all in brown, who had never done anything or been anywhere,' sighed Florence. 'I only wanted an adventure.'

'You certainly found one,' replied Vittorio. 'In fact, I would say that you found several. A long-lost cousin after your fortune, a former suitor trying to entrap you into marriage; two men fighting a duel over you; what more could you want?'

'No more; in fact, I could have done with rather less,' said Florence frankly.

'I know; I'm sorry, *cara*,' he said contritely.

'Sorry? For what?' she asked him. 'You

343

were right to be suspicious of me. I told myself that it was all right to appropriate your name because Miss Le Grey said that I might, but it wasn't really. I wasn't fair to you.'

'*Non importa*,' he replied. 'It doesn't matter. But I am sorry that I was never able to meet this lady who I think must have been my last surviving aunt on my father's side.'

'Vittorio, I am sorry for that too,' said Florence contritely. 'But at first, I was suspicious of you myself, and if you were some kind of a rogue, I did not want to expose her to your schemes. By the time I realized that you were genuine, she was dead.'

'Yes, I understand that now,' he replied. 'I have learned from others how greatly she valued your friendship, and I shall look to you to tell me all about her. What is more important is that I was so busy victimizing you myself that I failed to see that you were in imminent danger; for that I ask your pardon, *cara*. I mean to make it up to you for all that you have suffered, from your father, your cousin, that scoundrel Stapleton, and, of course, myself. Not to mention my aunt.'

'Your aunt, Constanzia da Sforza?'

'The same; I apologize on her behalf. I think that you will find her very contrite and ready to receive you.'

344

At that moment, the carriage drew to a halt. 'Where are we?' Florence asked, as she realized that there were now lights outside.

'We are at an inn a few miles outside Buxton,' answered Vittorio. 'You have not asked me my intentions, *cara*.'

She hesitated on the step, looking down into his face. 'I don't need to,' she said. 'What was my life until you came? I only want to be with you.'

He lifted her down, swung her round and kissed her. '*Te adoro*,' he declared. 'I adore you! Come, let us go inside, and I will tell you why I have brought you here.'

They went into the inn and were shown by a genial landlord into a private parlour, where there was a roaring fire burning. 'Ah!' she sighed.

He took the cloak from her shoulders. 'You will love Tuscany,' he said.

'Tuscany?'

'It is where my estates are; at least, some of my estates.'

Florence had the grace to blush. 'So, not a boy from the back slums, then,' she murmured.

'Not quite,' he replied, as he conducted her to a chair by the fire. 'Do you have any idea, *cara*, how angry you made me when you said that?'

Florence thought of how he had thrust her against the wall of the Chapter House. 'I think perhaps I do,' she answered, casting her eyes down. 'Perhaps I don't deserve to be taken to Tuscany.'

'You deserve to be taken to whatever place I choose,' he answered with an arrogant tilt of his chin. For a few moments, he stood looking down at her, then with a soft chuckle, went down on one knee in front of her. 'This is the accepted mode, I believe,' he said. 'Will you marry me, *bella Firenza*? And at once? I have with me a special licence, and a clergyman will come at my signal.' When she hesitated, he went on, 'It would solve so many problems, after all. You will never have to tell the inhabitants of Bath about your deception, for one, for you will in very truth be Lady Le Grey.'

'But you have already told some of the inhabitants that I was no such thing,' she reminded him gently.

He coloured. 'You made me so very angry,' he explained, 'and when I saw you there looking as lovely as I remembered, I lost all sense of reason. But it was you yourself who gave me hope that I might be forgiven.'

'When did I do that?' she asked, genuinely puzzled.

'When you told Guido that I was very dear to you.'

She blushed. 'Oh, that,' she said.

'And now, *cara*, before my knee becomes stuck to the floor, please halt this suspense and tell me that you will in very truth be my own Lady Le Grey.'

'I cannot think of anything else that I would rather be,' she smiled. He rose to his feet, pulled her into his arms and kissed her.

'After we are married, I will take you to Italy,' he told her, 'and I promise that if I can help it, you will never be cold again.' Once more he kissed her. After a brief interval he went on, 'I have some jewels with me in which you can be married; some rather fine sapphires.'

'Yes, why did you insist on giving them to me?' she asked, puzzled. 'You made me feel like a kept woman.'

His eyes twinkled. 'Why so you are, *cara*, for I intend to keep you and never let you go. Seriously, I don't know why I gave them to you. It was an impulse, born of the anger that seized hold of me when I saw you gazing at that shop with Stapleton.'

'I have observed that in his absence you get his name right every time, whereas in his presence, you could not get it right at all.'

'I wanted to annoy him,' Vittorio said frankly.

'Why?' she asked him, guessing at the answer.

'Because he had known you for a long time and because you had once been in love with him.'

She shook her head, and snuggled close to him. 'I knew him a long time ago, but I was never in love with him,' she confessed.

'You cannot imagine how glad I am to hear you say that, *Firenza mia*.' He paused. 'He is at this moment awaiting trial. I suspect that he may hang or, at the least, be transported for what he did.'

'Vittorio, no!' Florence exclaimed in shocked tones.

'You must consider, *cara*,' he said gently, his arm around her. 'He carried you off by force, and treated you brutally. No doubt he would have killed you, had his paramour told him to do so. He does not deserve any mercy.'

She sighed. 'Perhaps not,' she agreed. 'But Vittorio, you must remember that before I came to Bath, my life had very few bright spots. Gilbert Stapleton was one of them, whatever his motives might have been, and for that reason I will always be grateful to him. Can't you do something to soften his sentence?'

'Plead for him, you mean?' She nodded, and he smiled ruefully. 'I had a feeling you might ask me to do so. It will go against the grain with me, but at this moment, I can deny you nothing, *innamorata*.' This time, it was she who kissed him.

At that moment there was a gentle knock at the door and a vigorous black Labrador came bounding in and flung himself at his mistress, with all the enthusiasm of a dog who had been parted from his owner for all of three hours. He was followed by Margaret and Lord Braintree; to Florence, Margaret's expression looked decidedly sheepish.

'You knew!' declared Florence accusingly, even whilst she hurried over to embrace her friend. 'All the time you knew. No wonder you were so insistent that I should go tonight!'

'I knew that he meant to speak to you tonight, and that he intended to bring you here, but I had no idea that he would be quite so . . . so . . . '

'Extravagant?' asked Vittorio with a grin.

'Piratical,' retorted Florence. 'And you too, Lord Braintree!'

'Ah, but I am here for a purpose,' replied the earl, 'and, by the way, please call me George, since everyone else here does so. Margaret and I are here to be witnesses; or, alternatively, we will take you back to Buxton with us whilst Vittorio drowns his sorrows.'

Florence's face took on a thoughtful expression that was slightly marred by the twinkle in her eye. 'I think I'll stay,' she said. 'I have a fancy to be Lady Le Grey; besides, Stevens has never really got out of the habit of calling me 'my lady'.'

'Then if only for Stevens' sake, *Firenza*, you had better marry me,' Vittorio laughed.

'You shouldn't keep calling me that,' Florence said unconvincingly. 'Margaret invented it for me. In fact, I never even pretended that it was my real name at all — at least, not for very long.'

'So what was the explanation for your using that name?' he asked her, completely ignoring the presence of their friends as he gathered her close.

'I told everyone that my husband liked it,' Florence smiled.

'*Precisamente*,' replied the baronet, and kissed her.

We do hope that you have enjoyed reading this large print book.

Did you know that all of our titles are available for purchase?

We publish a wide range of high quality large print books including:
**Romances, Mysteries, Classics
General Fiction
Non Fiction and Westerns**

Special interest titles available in large print are:
**The Little Oxford Dictionary
Music Book
Song Book
Hymn Book
Service Book**

Also available from us courtesy of Oxford University Press:
**Young Readers' Dictionary
(large print edition)
Young Readers' Thesaurus
(large print edition)**

For further information or a free brochure, please contact us at:
**Ulverscroft Large Print Books Ltd.,
The Green, Bradgate Road, Anstey,
Leicester, LE7 7FU, England.
Tel:** (00 44) **0116 236 4325
Fax:** (00 44) **0116 234 0205**

Other titles published by
The House of Ulverscroft:

THE SQUIRE AND THE SCHOOLMISTRESS

Ann Barker

When Flavia Montague arrives to take up employment as a schoolmistress in the village of Brooks, she learns that the school has been closed for some months and that the previous teacher, Miss Price, has been involved in a scandal. Flavia is given welcome assistance in establishing the school by the handsome landowner Paul Wheaton, who seems attracted to her. It becomes clear that one of the pupils, Penelope, has been ill-treated by her guardian, Sir Lewis Glendenning — a name linked with the notorious Miss Price. But is Sir Lewis the brute that he appears to be? And what is the truth about Miss Price?